INVICTUS

by L.L. Holt

Harvard Square Editions
New York
2019

Invictus
by L.L. Holt

ISBN 978-1-941861-64-6
Printed in the United States of America

Published in the United States by
Harvard Square Editions
www.harvardsquareeditions.org

Praise for

Invictus

"This book is spot on to the issues of today's world. A blend of historic fact and fiction, *Invictus* tackles many of the big issues of our time: bigotry, bullying, and prejudice. The Beethoven we thought we knew is a pale shadow of the genius he became. Adversity helped ignite his extraordinary gifts, inspiring each of us to reach beyond obstacles to embrace our dreams. I loved this book and its message for today of courage, determination, perseverance, and hope."

—Don Browne, Executive VP NBC Network News, ret., President of NBC's Telemundo Network, ret.

"L.L. Holt captures an exciting time in history when revolution was in the air, and an intense debate about race and equality raged in universities, salons, and secret societies. Well-written and engaging."

—Lina Genovesi, Ph.D., J.D.

"*Invictus* embodies the spirit of the Age of Revolution in this tale of a young boy breaking free from obstacles of poverty and prejudice."

—Kairy Koshoeva, concert pianist

"An absorbing novel about the young Beethoven and the circumstances that shaped his musical career. Especially interesting because it takes seriously the implications of 18th century racism and rumors about African ancestry in Beethoven's family."

—K.M. Reeds, historian of biology and medicine

"In *Invictus,* Holt makes precise references to Joseph Bologne, aka Le Chevalier de Saint-Georges, whose life as an 18th century Black composer and swordsman in Western Europe is an important reminder that sometimes you have to excel in many different fields in order to survive. And still, the accomplishments can and will speak for themselves decades, centuries after the fact."

—Le Chevalier de Saint Georges
Facebook page administrator

for Sarada

Invictus

by William Ernest Henley

Out of the night that covers me,
Black as the pit from pole to pole,
I thank whatever gods may be
For my unconquerable soul.

In the fell clutch of circumstance
I have not winced nor cried aloud.
Under the bludgeonings of chance
My head is bloody, but unbowed.

Beyond this place of wrath and tears
Looms but the Horror of the shade,
And yet the menace of the years
Finds and shall find me unafraid.

It matters not how strait the gate,
How charged with punishments the scroll,
I am the master of my fate,
I am the captain of my soul.

Prologue

IN THE EARLY HOURS of the Third Sunday of Advent, 1770, staggering footsteps in hard-soled boots ring out from the cobblestone streets of a small German village.

They are not the rhythmic clip-clop of horses' hooves nor the regimented steps of a red coat, nor are they the rough, heavy pace of the baker's wife back from the ovens. Rather, they are the ominous, angry, drawn-out syncopation of the boots of a well-known town drunk, marching home with a headful of notions with no basis in reason or reality.

He is singing to himself, his breath turning to frost in the cool air, and in truth, it would be a pleasing voice if sober, for he is a singer by trade, a servant of the court. But there is nothing pleasing in his manner this dark morning on winter's cusp, and his eyes blaze—hollow, jaundiced, and intense—at some unseen target in the distance.

Not a half mile ahead and to the right lies his destination, yet it is not a scene of death, but of birth. For in these hours before dawn, the son he has craved through years of marriage is being born. The tiny attic room above three squalid floors hard on the edge of the city street glows with candlelight and quakes with the screams of a mother's pain as the midwife eases the bloody child into the cold dark world. A final push, thrusting her feet hard into the straw bedding, and Mary trembles as the child is born. There are some uneasy moments in the silence, for no cry comes. Mary has had a still-born child before, and another who died in early childhood.

"There," says the midwife, a sturdy farm woman with a pleasant face and warm heart, "the wee one has a caul, that's good luck, ma'am," referring to a sack of placenta stuck over the baby's head. She pries it loose and puts it aside on a strip of cloth. "The sailors will pay a good price for that charm," she notes, nodding toward the river at the end of the street. Mary is still panting, her hair matted in sweat, her shaking knees still spread. Then it comes: the cough, the slap, the low cry, the piercing wail of a creature none too pleased to come into a world of darkness and pain. Mary's muscles relax, and she collapses back on the bedding with a slight smile and sigh. "Oh, Henny," she murmurs to her cousin, watching with her this night. "Oh, Henny, that is a beautiful sound."

"A boy, ma'am," says the midwife with a smile, but one that quickly fades. "He is…healthy, yes. Ten fingers, ten toes…" Her voice drifts off. Something is not right.

"Come on, then," Henny cajoles, "dry him off, let us have a look at him!" The midwife looks peculiarly at Mary, then back at the child, who is still screaming his lungs out. At this moment, there is a heavy, uneven pounding on the front door. Henny starts, but Mary puts her hand on her arm to reassure her.

"It's only John," she says, "won't he be proud! Our first son!"

"You better take a look first before your master's here," says the midwife, bundling the child tightly in a cloth and wiping the last traces of placenta from his face. Once swaddled, he begins to calm, and soon is breathing deeply in sleep.

"Mary!" cries a voice three floors below. "Mary, you worthless slut! Come down here and make me dinner!"

"I'll take care of him," whispers Henny, squeezing Mary's hand.

"My own boy," coos Mary, extending her arms. "My own…" Then her voice stops. The midwife backs off in case there is an explosion of emotion, for which she might be blamed.

"What is it, ma'am?" she asks. Mary stops, and cradles the tiny body against her breast. Slowly, she keeps wiping the face, then gently removes each arm from the swaddling and runs her fingers over the child's flesh, up across his chest, shoulders, and neck.

"I do not know," says Mary. "Have you seen anything like this before?"

"Aye, but under very different circumstances, I'm sure," the midwife replies, fumbling over the words. "He is a bit dark, but that could be natural, you know."

"Dark!" Mary laughs, looking away, then her eyes fall back on the sleeping child, and an expression of tenderness sweeps over her face. "Oh, my poor dear boy, you are not dark. Compared with your blond cousins, you are black." She pauses, then slowly her lips lift into a sad smile. "My poor darling. You will be alone in this white world of ours. But it is nothing to me. I love you!" she whispers, placing a kiss on the newborn's wrinkled forehead.

At this moment, heavy, unsteady footsteps trudge up the stairs, in unison with John's booming voice and slurred speech.

"Whasisit…what…the baby, here? The baby? A boy?" John drags himself up the final steps, and throws himself onto the floor. Behind him, Henny pulls on his coat tails to slow his approach, and the midwife throws her formidable weight square between the man who is now father and the woman who is his wife.

"Give me my son!" he cries, losing his balance and grasping onto a post.

"You'd better not hold him, sir, the lad's too young and needs his mother's touch just now," the midwife says firmly, holding out a stout arm. He grumbles to himself, and makes his way to the bed. Mary, already haggard from her ordeal, looks even more distraught, and the midwife—a doughty matron built more like blacksmith than maiden—moves swiftly to the other side of the bed to form a buffer.

The baby settles into a snooze, and the father kneels down unsteadily and turns the child's head his way. There is an uneasy silence. Then it comes.

"What's this!" he erupts, swaying back unsteadily. "This is not my boy, not my boy, woman!" He grabs the corner of a cabinet, the agitated candlelight flushing his features and frame from below, his shadow rising and elongating across the ceiling. He begins to shake, and with him, the cabinet with a wobbly leg, and he trembles uncontrollably, rattling loudly as though in the very throes of death. Rearing back, he lets out a roar that years of vocal training seem to have groomed him for. "Christ Almighty, what does this mean!"

"You bitch!" he shouts. "Who is the black bastard that fathered this child!" He tries to lunge forward, but is too unstable. The midwife blocks his thrusts, her hefty arms held firm and wide.

"Be silent, sir!" she commands. "Y'be in the presence of

God's mystery here, and this woman is worn with bearing!" Mary has folded the blanket around the crying newborn and burrowed with him against the wall, as though she hoped it would open up and take them to a place of sanctuary.

As suddenly as he had erupted, John sinks to the floor, one leg twisted beneath him, coughing and spitting, his head falling down to his chest, his cheeks flushed. The midwife bends forward and grabs his shoulders.

"Listen t'me," she says firmly, "I've delivered many a lad, and this is not so rare as you might think. Blame not your wife, sir. Indeed, look into your own family's past." She knows she is taking a risk saying this, and he hacks violently and stares wildly at her as she speaks, but for now he is paralyzed with drink.

"Who knows what secrets our families hide," she whispers, lowering her voice as she seizes control of the situation. "Your wife, Mary, is a faithful wife and Christian, sir, and practices no dark arts. Be strong and accept this child of your own love, your own flesh. Your only child, sir, the child you have yearned for so many years!"

John rolls listlessly to the side, his hands over his face, then sobbing uncontrollably. Mary turns toward him, the baby now nursing in her arms, and the sounds of infant crying and father roaring are soon replaced by low sobs and less anxious breathing. The midwife pours some water on a rag and gently approaches the father.

"Here, let me wipe your face," she murmurs, and he makes no protest except at the last to push her hand away. Silently, he pulls himself up in the spare, dusty room by grabbing the cabinet handles. He lifts his hat from the floor, and never looking back, feels his way along the rough, splintered wall, out the door, and down the steps to his bed below, tentative footsteps the only sound in the early light.

Mary breathes a deep, dark sigh. "Thank you, Maggie," she says to the midwife, "thank you for everything, and especially, for that."

"Y'both would've been murdered, I swear it," Maggie, turning away, mumbles to herself.

Chapter 1

SNOWFLAKES BEGAN TO FALL from the grey sky. The child's paternal grandfather and a respectable neighbor, Gertrude Baum, arrived at the little house early on Monday morning. The grandfather, who bore the name Louis and lived diagonally across the street from his son's home, was a wise, imposing figure, a man of great sophistication, insight, and depth, and considerable learning. A singer and court musician, it was he who obtained a singing position for John, and it was from the grandmother, now living in a kind of halfway house for drunkards, maintained by a religious order, that John derived his dependence on drink.

Louis had opposed the selection of Mary—a young widow and the daughter of a cook—as the future wife of his only son. Losing his own wife to addiction, seeing the evidence of a similar condition growing in his temperamental son, these were griefs enough for the aging man; but a common wife, with little dowry, no gifts beyond an attractive figure, and no income?

And yet, John eventually got his way, as he always did with great cunning. Now Louis was face to face with the woman whose marriage he tried every possible trick and ploy to prevent. He considered the tired, sunken form under the single blanket, her hair frizzy, dark circles under her eyes: even for a woman recovering from childbirth, her appearance seemed far older than her twenty-four years.

No matter, thought Grandfather, taking the tiny, wrinkled child from his exhausted mother, and it may have been the first time that Mary got a smile from her father-in-law. Unlike the child's father, Louis saw beyond first impression. Holding the baby in the light of the eastern window, catching the first silver glow of morning on this snowy day, the older man beheld his own descendent at last, and a bundle of potential that he would not allow to go astray. Not this time, for certain.

Gertrude was waiting downstairs, having a cup of tea with Henny Marshall, who had plenty of gossip to share, but did not believe any ill of Mary, attributing the child's appearance to some flaw in his paternal line.

In his late 50s, Grandfather descended the stairs slowly, holding onto the railing with one hand, and cradling the swaddled child close to his heart with the other. He smiled again as the babe purred at his breast, like a cat.

Louis was not often seen in such a tender mood. It was not only through excellence and hard work but also clever politicking that he had risen to the highest post in the Elector's chapel: a significant position at a time when court music was an industry much in demand. He earned a reputation for not standing for nonsense, for being tough as well as exacting, and a stickler for detail. The dozens of musicians and singers who performed under him each week viewed him with respect and a little dread.

But then there was today: the baptismal day of his only grandchild. Having long ago given up on his drunken wife and all but given up on his son, destined to go the same route, he stopped at the foot of the stairs and gently rocked the baby, pressing a soft kiss on his dark forehead. Though celebrated professionally, he was a man alone, an immigrant from Holland, still learning and acclimating to the language and customs of this city and state. If only he had been present last year when the first baby was born. Perhaps something could have been done to save that precious child, who died after only a few days. A fair, pink child he was, too. Well, no matter, the grandfather reflected, looking wryly at the boy's complexion. How important could a tint to the skin be?

"You will pass into the light," he whispered. "I will let no harm come to you."

Chapter 2

"DIRECTOR, IS THAT YOU?" Gertrude rustled into the foyer, a well-dressed woman with a perpetually concerned expression, who lived with her sister and niece. "Come on, then, we need to see one of the priests." The two wrapped themselves warmly in scarves and cloaks and hastened onto the cobblestones that led a few blocks to church. It was a slippery path, and Louis had to grip Gertrude's sleeve more than once to stay steady on his feet. The snow abated, as big flakes often do, and soon the street tightly packed with houses was a calm scene of silver grey, backlit by a glow of diffused sunlight. The tall church materialized out of the mist, and the trio entered the large wooden doors.

Shaking the snow from his feet, Louis placed the child gently in Gertrude's arms. "I must speak to the clerk first, around here," he pointed, removing his hat. "Go up to the font, I will join you shortly." He took a final look at the baby, now sleeping peacefully, and tore himself away for a few moments to look for the registry.

As Grandfather disappeared from view, Gertrude carried the child up the nave, sternly decorated with holly and punctuated by snuffed candles. She shivered: the church was cold, as though the ubiquitous grey and beige stones had turned to ice, and an unwavering breeze murmured from some unseen aperture, surrounding her like something holy but slightly perverse.

Gertrude never liked this church, nor the stern Minorite order associated with it, and when she did need religion, went a few additional blocks to a less imposing chapel. As she stood before the font, her eyes rose to a Baroque statue of Mary, her arms outstretched. "Merciful mother of God," she prayed silently, "be with me and protect me, and protect this little child, so in need of your grace!" She looked down at the babe, cherubic in the deep snuggles of slumber. "Well, you don't look half so bad now, do you?" she whispered, adjusting his baptismal cap, then startled as a presence and voice came close behind her.

"Madame, may I help you?" Turning she saw the sour face of a priest. He gazed disdainfully from the woman to the bundle in her arms. "Ah, a baptism. Have you registered? You know it is one of our busiest days."

She nodded. "My neighbor, yes, he is there."

"Hmm. Neighbor. No husband then, correct? You hold your head erect for one in such circumstances. But wise of you to have this creature baptized as soon as possible." Before Gertrude could counter his insinuations, his white smooth-skinned hand flicked back an edge of the bunting so he could see the child. He started, drew back a bit, and scowled. "Very odd, very odd," he mumbled.

He moved forward and this time, pushed the coverlet back a bit further, holding the baby's skull between his pale thumb and forefinger, turning it very slightly in his direction. The baby sighed but did not awaken, probably exhausted from a night of crying. A world of questions and judgments passed through the priest's mind, reflected on his face in the array of candles backlighting the baptismal font.

"It is not my child, Father," Gertrude said, annoyed at his assumptions and implications. "I am but a neighbor…"

"I see, I see. And the man who is at the registry, he would be the father? A blackamoor, I presume?" His lips twitched at the corners. Again, he flicked the blanket over the child's face, as though protecting himself from an ill omen or a devil in the making. "No? Well, we shall see, shall we not? I'll send a lower priest in to assist you. Wait here." As he spoke, Grandfather hustled up the aisle as fast as his arthritic knees would take him, holding his hat over his heart, his white hair fluffed out and bristling, a copy of the certificate in his hand.

"Forgive me, your Reverence," said Louis, nodding to him. "I have here the necessary paperwork, I do hope we are not too late, I had sent a message." As Louis looked up, he locked eyes with the daunting priest. It was an odd moment, one from which Gertrude shrank into the background, as the imposing Director of the Court Choir met the arrogant challenge of the Abbot of the Minorite Order, and the two faced off, immobile for seconds that seemed an eternity, in the flickering light and the wavering cold breeze of the old stone church. Grandfather was unbowed; in fact, rose to the challenge and to his full height, leaning forward into the priest's personal space. "I do hope there is no problem or concern," he said in his most refined manner. "I am the Kapellmeister, Court Choir Director, and this is my grandson."

The priest did not counter parry for parry, but shifted his stance with a bit of shoulder facing his opponent. "Surely, there must be some mistake," he snapped, striding to the candle shelf where a light was burning low. He carried a flame from one of the other candles to the low light, his back to Louis as he continued to speak.

Grandfather felt his blood rising. From behind a column, Gertrude saw her neighbor's face redden, as it seldom did unless he was severely crossed. "Reverend sir," he said after a cold moment's pause, "this is my grandson, I assure you. And made dark by God as he has made you…white," he said slowly, in his deep bass voice.

There was something in his tone that the priest did not care to dispute. He turned, with a swirl of his cloak, looked briefly back at the woman and child, and strode toward the chapter house, his voice rising over his shoulder, "Someone will help you shortly."

The church seemed to grow colder, though Louis's rising blood pressure actually brought beads of sweat to his forehead. Gertrude hurried to his side and put her hand on his arm. "Stay calm, sir, you have the papers, it should not be long, then we may leave this horrible place."

"These damn priests," he uttered, as Gertrude made the sign of the cross in dismay. And in fact, despite what probably was a temptation to let them wait in the frigid chapel, the priest dispatched the lowest priest he had at his disposal to enter the sanctuary and perform the Sacrament. The priest paid no attention to the child, or the sponsors, or anyone, for that matter. As the water was spooned over the wrinkled head, the child awoke abruptly and let out a sudden, shrill cry of protest. Louis exchanged glances with Gertrude, his strained face melting into a half-smile.

"I think he shares our view of organized religion," he whispered to his friend as they walked slowly down the nave back to the entry door.

"Would to God that churches were not this way," replied Gertrude, shaking her head. "Where otherwise do we people go for comfort?"

"Often," said Louis holding the door open with one hand, walking into the glaring grey daylight, "we must go into ourselves and find our solace there. Ultimately, no one can help us but we, ourselves." He unfolded the certificate and looked with pleasure at the date and name of his new grandson:

December 17, 1770. Ludwig van Beethoven.

"Luis," he said, with satisfaction. "Welcome to the world, my boy."

Chapter 3

FOR THE DEVOUT, there is always consolation that this life is a testing ground for eternity. Mary van Beethoven bore her husband's rants, slaps, and tantrums like a saint, and began taking the baby to church with her when the weather permitted. She would sit in the back of one of the smaller chapels in the community. She was becoming used to the stares of passers-by, inured to the gossip and whispers, the muffled snickers and insinuations. When she looked into the deep brown eyes of the mysterious child, she saw only love. The two were closely joined, each unconditionally dependent on the other and bound in a dislike of the one person on whom they depended for their existence.

Around this time, Mary's cousin Henny became a regular visitor to the modest row home, eager for sensational tidbits to take home to other family members and always thrilled with an opportunity to interfere (or "help you out in some way," as she put it). One late summer day, she appeared at the Beethovens' front door with even more eagerness than usual.

"Mary, see what I've got for the baby!" she exclaimed as she entered the house. Henny put her bonnet on the newel post and produced a small jar from her carry bag.

"Oh, what have you got there," said Mary Beethoven, wary but distracted with the darning of socks and kitchen towels.

Henny opened the apothecary's jar and showed Mary a lustrous white powder. "You can't imagine what I went through to get this for you, after I heard what it does. It's such a miracle, Mary! The

Countess herself uses it to keep her complexion flawlessly white."

At the word "complexion," Mary looked up in concern. So that was what this visit was about. And she was fairly certain she knew what the powder contained. "That's not….is it?"

Henny laughed off Mary's look of consternation. "Ha, no, what's in a name, now, isn't that right? I mean, if it were called 'angel tears' instead of, well, of arsenic, what difference would it make?"

Mary snatched the jar out of Henny's hand and threw it into the slops bucket. Henny had never seen this streak of fire in Mary before. "Cousin, never do this again!" she spoke firmly, her voice shaking with rage. "To bring me poison for my only child in the hopes of making him into some pale reflection of himself…and probably killing him in the process!"

She lifted one of the towels to her eyes, and turned away. "Please go, Henny, come again another time, with no such gifts," she said in muffled tones.

Henny surreptitiously pulled the jar from the bucket, wiped it off a bit on her skirt, and left in a huff. "I was just trying to help!" she snarled as she opened the front door, "trying to provide some relief for you, my dear, and that black child who's the cause of all your woes. Don't be blaming me if it turns out he's a devil sent to punish you for some sin!" She slammed the door, and Mary sat down unsteadily. She took a deep breath, and from the next room, a cooing sound rose.

"I'm here, my darling," she said. "No one will harm you, with or without good intentions."

Yet, Mary was not one to shelter Luis from reality. She was determined to take her child out into the world despite the occasional stare or rude remark. But even a simple trip to the greengrocer's could lead to embarrassment and anxiety for mother and child.

Chapter 4

"HELLO, THERE, MRS. BEETHOVEN, got your black boy with you today!" winked Mr. Johnston, the greengrocer, as Mrs. Beethoven led the shy child into the grocery stall. "Don't see him too much, do we now?" Several other patrons turned around to see the child.

"Bring him out where we can see 'em, Missus!" said a blustery but professional-looking man in worn tweeds and a powdered wig, for he was clearly returning from court. "C'mon, lad, let's take a look at you! Don't see your kind oft in town!" There was apparently no other amusement in town this afternoon, so child baiting seemed a natural sport to some.

"Never you mind," rejoined Mrs. Beethoven, "Mr. Johnston, we'll have that fine cabbage…"

"A cabbage!" Everyone laughed, since, in the local dialect, "cabbage" was a slangy term of affection between lovers. Several of the customers in the small, crowded space were smoking pipes with a particularly vile-smelling tobacco. In the warm September air, the smoke hung as acridly as hurtful words.

"Now, Mrs. Beethoven," the store keeper continued with a leer, "I'd say your little pet would like a nice…banana!" The small coterie of customers and staff laughed heartily at this witticism, as the tiny child clung faster to his mother's leg, burrowing his face more deeply into her summer-weight skirts.

"That will be enough!" she said firmly to Mr. Johnston, "I'll just take that slaw, please keep the change, and we'll be off!" She grabbed the produce, put it in her basket, scooped the child up onto her hip, and walked what seemed a very long distance to the front of the stall. Behind her there was laughter, and not of the pleasant sort; a sort to linger in the mind and memory of a small child, even one not yet two years old.

Mary worried how Luis would fare in school in a few years, but dismissed these thoughts from her mind, since there were plenty of challenges to face in the present time without creating concerns for the future. Less daunting were Luis's visits into the world of merchants and shopkeepers with his father, for he had the authority of the court on his side and a formidable relative in his own father, the Chapel choir master. In a word, one did not mess with John Beethoven.

Chapter 5

JOHN DIDN'T ALWAYS SEE IT that way. At times, it seemed as though his important father and pious wife were plotting against him.

"It's more than a conspiracy," John lamented to a colleague, well into his third beer at a popular inn, "more like they're waging war against me." The two sat in a dark corner of the Court & Cloister tap room, greasy lanterns half-illuminating their faces, drawing shadows and lines not commonly seen on faces of men in their 30s.

"You're a good singer, John, you should…well…"

"I should have gone further, is that what you mean?" John started, and slammed his mug on the table. "Yes, those two, holding me back! No self respect, no money…the Chapel Master's only son and poor as a church mouse!"

"The two of them, they're like the name of this pub, eh? Your father the Court, your wife…"

"Damn them!" snarled John, on the brink of his nightly descent into alcohol-enhanced paranoia. He moved into the lantern light, which lit up his sharp, hawkish features, an appearance almost handsome by daylight, a fine head of smooth brown hair, pale taut skin, but a profile drawn like a caricature and as exaggerated as his imagination under the spell of drink and the dark moods of nighttime.

"Well, there's nothing you can do about your father," Gilbert admitted, tilting back his head and gulping down the last drops of his mug. He knew the story well enough, having heard it nearly every time the two got together after supper. But John had been at other pubs lately, and at least it kept the conversation flowing.

"No, no, and he's the one who has made sure I was passed up at every opportunity. But my wife, heh, good thing there's no law against beating the bitch!" he snarled. "She can't do anything right."

"Well, if you mean your children…"

"Leave my children out of it!" shouted John, swaying on his bench.

"Easy, easy man, I'm just saying…"

"No, you're right," John continued, in a mumble, his chin dropping low, "she has some secret life behind my back, but denies it!"

"But naturally!" said Gilbert, excusing himself for a visit to the piss pot. "Stay there, John, I'll have another…"

As Gilbert left, John continued the conversation in his mind, his lips occasionally muttering to no one in particular. "What if it's true, what if I am cuckolded? I am embarrassed by my father's curses at work and at home, I am made the laughing stock as the father of an undesirable with no future. No future! My only child, my only son! I will get the truth out of that bitch…tonight!"

John grabbed the table with both hands, then reached into his purse for a few coins which he tossed on the counter.

"Can you make it home, Brother?" the innkeeper called. "Suppose he can, he always returns!" he whispered to another patron. The two disheveled men laughed quietly at their little joke shared in the dark, smoky tavern room.

John staggered down the cobblestone street, slick with recent rain, his uneven footfall the only sound. It was very dark, and a half-moon was creeping out from behind a storm cloud. How simpler life would have been had he simply fallen asleep at the pub, and dreamed away the perverse imaginings of plots and betrayals.

Instead, the night air refreshed his brain, until it reached a dangerous balance of keen alertness and inebriated disorientation. The delusions were still present in the delirium of alcohol, but there was reason, too, an aggressive, sharp wit ready to slice into an unsuspecting victim.

Chapter 6

MARY WAS A LIGHT SLEEPER, troubled with congestion despite the moist air in their flat only a few blocks from the river, overlooking a dreamy landscape of hills and distant castles. She was a worrier, and with good reason. Their financial situation was not good, and if John's father had not helped them on a regular basis, their finances would have been desperate. John was a gambler, not at cards or lotteries, but in day-to-day small activities. But his hunches seldom paid off. He would take a risk that the butcher was leaving town and would forget about their tab. He would assume that a vacancy in the court choir would result in more pay for him. He would take a chance leaving a student alone so he could meet a friend at the pub, only to have the student run off, and his father cancel their contract.

These spurts of unfounded optimism and wisps of hope inevitably led to more debt and more tossing and turning for Mary. And there were other reasons she could not sleep. One of them was staggering at a faster pace up the cobblestones even now, his eyes burning like a torch, focused at the pleasant-looking house at the end of the lane. Mary heard the steps and recognized the syncopated rhythm. Her instinct was to dash into Luis's room, to shelter him from assault, but she thought better of it. Better he should take his rage out on her than disturb her son.

With each step in the dark, damp air, John's fury deepened. The delusions of betrayal and spite became voices in his head, growing louder and more menacing. "There's something she's not telling you!" "A lover!" "An old family secret. John, you were conned into a marriage with a mixed-race bitch!" "Your father was right: you should never have married this woman." "You have to stop her! Stop her!" the banshees cried. But stop her from what? And whose voices were they? There was no reason and no answer to the questions that rose in his brain as finally he arrived at the house and threw himself against the front door with the power that comes from drink.

"Mary!" he bellowed. "Mary! You bitch, you better be alone!" He opened the door after much fumbling, and lunged into the kitchen, still warm from the evening's meal. After several tries, his hand shaking, he lit a candle from a hearth ember and grabbed the railing to go upstairs. "Bitch, black bastard…" he mumbled as he pulled himself up each creaking step.

In the dark, Mary drew back in their bed, not daring to make a sound. Would it help if she pretended to be asleep? No, it never worked. She had tried every alternative, hiding in other rooms, even in the linen closet, crouching behind the drapery. What was left? Even when drunk, he had a knack for uncovering all her ruses. He was older, he was smarter, he was as sharp at discovering her defenses as he was at avoiding things he did not like. She coughed, and then thought, "I'll pretend I am ill." In fact, she was menstruating, and between that and the perpetual cough, she was hardly the picture of good health.

The bedroom door flew open, and with it an icy draft, causing the lantern left burning in the room to flicker and cast black shadows on the wall. There was silence, then the candlelight rose from the floor. There was no sound except the wheezing and rattled breathing of her husband as he climbed out of the dark, and with a crash of pottery falling from the dresser, grabbed onto the furniture and pulled himself into the room. The mixed lights created the illusion that he was as tall as the room, and as menacing as Satan himself.

"You bitch," he seethed, "you're going to tell me everything!" He stood immobile, almost panting.

"John, John," she murmured, adding a number of shallow coughs, "it's night. Come to bed. You're tired!" She pulled the featherbed around her, as though it could protect her from the looming storm. "John, I'm sick. Don't speak so."

He staggered suddenly across the room, still clutching the lit candle, and fell onto the bed. Mary quickly snatched the candle from the covers and put it onto the floor, exactly at the moment John lifted his arm and thrust it with all his force against her face. She moaned and pulled the bedding closer. "My eyes, stop, stop, John!"

"You deceiver, you trickster!" he swung around over her swaddled body, lost his balance, and fell onto the floor.

The candle flared dramatically, reflecting in the undraped window. Across the street, a servant saw the light and heard the commotion, for there were no other sounds except the occasional riverboat. He rushed to awaken the Grandfather, who himself was sleeping fitfully with breathing difficulties. Both men put on their robes and shoes and hastened into the street.

The front door was open, the servant led the way, while Grandfather shouted, "John! John! Stop it whatever it is!" and followed as well as he could up the staircase. As this occurred, Mary feigned illness, " I'm dying, John, it must be the dropsy that

killed my parents! Go, find a physician. We'll talk more later…"
then she sunk forward with a loud groan.

Jesse, the servant, came to the top of the steps as John
rolled over knocking down the candle which quickly ignited the
edge of the straw mattress. A large burst of flame erupted at the
edge of the bed: Mary screamed, and fell back as John struggled
to find his footing. Jesse ripped the drapery from the side window
and with great difficulty but impressive skill, put out the fire,
throwing his own body onto the cheap fabric. This is the scene
Grandfather saw as his head emerged from the floor-level stairs.

"Oh my God," he whispered, his face drawn and white. "Oh
my God, my Mary. Where is the boy?" He pulled himself up, and
hurried to the next room. There was no sound except the quiet
breathing of the child. "Oh my God, my baby," he whispered.
"My baby." Not wanting to disturb a creature who had slept
through this night of violence, Louis put his hand on his own
chest, as though to calm his heart, and returned to the parents'
room. What a sight, he thought. My worthless son nearly
destroyed everything: his child, his wife, his home…even his
worthless self! Mary! He noticed the young woman with blood
on her face lying motionless on the featherbed.

He all but kicked John aside as he scrambled onto the
mattress, smelling of charred hay, and held her in his arms. In
the lantern light, her face distorted, she groaned a bit, which he
considered a good sign, a sign that at least she was still alive.
He removed a handkerchief from his pocket and wiped her
face. "Don't worry," she muttered, "I tried …to make him
think…I was consumptive…"

"Don't speak, my child," whispered Louis. "Don't say a

word. Jesse?"

"Yes, Lord," the servant replied, rising slowly and double-checking the drapery and mattress for stray sparks, "It is out, I caught it all, Sir." Grandfather nodded. The windows all were now bare, and the last sliver of moonlight had disappeared behind a cloud. Rain was beginning to fall, and it would not be long until dawn, the dark dawn of a rainy day.

Louis cradled Mary in his arms. Before long, John and Mary's servant Bertha arrived, shocked at the scene that greeted her upstairs.

"Don't say a word to anyone," cautioned the Grandfather as he escorted her back to the kitchen below. "A musician is only as good as his reputation. A chapel court musician is only as good as his behavior." Bertha nodded, not sure what he meant, and already dreaming of the lurid tale she was going to tell her friends that afternoon. "Make Mary some soup, would you, child, and be a good girl: when it's light, send for Henny Marshall to help with young Luis today. He must be kept from all knowledge of this incident."

In his own snug bed on the other end of the second floor, the little boy with the luminous deep eyes looked out into the darkness of night. There were tears on his cheeks, and his small hands trembled. He knew it was just a matter of time before he would be the one feeling the slaps and having to hide his bruises from a world already ill-disposed against him.

Chapter 7

As frequently as the nocturnal scenes occurred, so frequently did calm, harmony, and even happiness accompany the daily life of mother and son. There was almost an unwritten pact, an unspoken contract between them in which one did not mention the previous night, as though it were a bad dream destroyed through forgetting. Best, under these circumstances, not to look in the mirror, or dwell on sore muscles and scars. To Mary's simple way of thinking, a man was within his rights, as head of the household, to discipline his family, and, as meek Christians, wife and son should bear their afflictions in silence. Certainly, the priest would agree, especially given the son's distinguishing marks as an outlander. There was something unsettling about the child with the burning eyes who spoke so seldom and was so shy.

That shyness did not exist, however, when alone with his mother, or playing with one of the neighborhood baker's young boys (the baker being an old friend of Grandfather's, whose own father had been a baker in Holland). And mostly, the shyness disappeared when Grandfather was home, for there was no paternal love in the boy's life except the great love of the old man for his only grandchild.

When Luis was nearly three, Grandfather had been fighting some chest congestion that affected his singing voice, and had been ordered to rest at home for a few weeks and recuperate before returning to the chapel choir. He had been chapel master for more than dozen years, and the Elector believed his well-being was worth investing in. As his health improved, Grandfather would occasionally take the boy for an overnight visit. Although the house was only across the street from his own, it seemed like a sabbatical in a foreign resort to the little boy. The elder Beethoven's home was a place of relative splendor compared with his own run-down house, in which every item of value had been hocked or sold to pay debts and what was left supported the father's drinking tab.

The visits were frowned upon by John, who tried to subvert them. But when sober, he would not stand up to what he saw as a domineering father and a conniving wife. Despite this, John did in fact work long hours every day of the week, singing in the choir and local musical theater, giving lessons in voice and piano accompaniment to students in his home. It was not worth worrying about these occasional visits to his father's house. Soon, the boy would have to start learning a trade, and it was to be hoped that the voice so seldom heard now would emerge as a beautiful boy soprano in a few years. Perhaps that would be the result: a graceful swan emerging from a plain cygnet! John and his father could pull enough strings to find a place for him. There could be a future for this child if he played his cards right, John mused.

One late summer afternoon, Mary's eyes danced with happiness as she packed a basket of necessities for Luis to take with him to Grandfather's. The little boy smiled; in fact, he couldn't stop smiling, the thought of getting away to an oasis of peace, beauty, and affection was so overwhelming. His heart beat quickly, and he found himself running around the upstairs rooms and up and down the staircase with uncontainable energy.

"Luis, calm down, you wiggly worm, you will wear yourself out," said his mother, unable to repress a smile herself. How she loved Grandfather, as well, even better than her own father who died when she was barely in her teens and who practically lived at the Archbishop's court as his Head Chef. Yes, the little boy had transformed from an almost morose, taciturn ghost to a bundle of giggles, scrambling up and down the stairs which were really too steep for him, and finally regressing to a crawl back into the kitchen where his mother packed his things.

"Do we have something for Grandfather?" he asked, lying at her feet and flipping onto his back like a dog expecting a belly rub. "Can I give him a present?"

"You are the present," Mother replied, reaching down and gently poking his nose with her finger. So odd, she thought again, possibly for the thousandth time, such an odd nose! Not like anyone's in the family. But adorable, she concluded the thought, just the same.

Luis giggled at the poke, and rolled onto his side in a little ball, sucking his thumb. "Now stop that, do you want buck teeth? That will not do," Mother said, reaching again and removing the stubborn fist. "Look, what I have for Grandfather!"

Luis sat up with interest as Mary removed a bundle from the corner shelf. "Now be nice to Grandfather, you know he hasn't been feeling well. This should help, though." On her skirt she laid out a couple of packages from the bundle: a glass bottle filled with some liquid and a small pillow. Luis drew back at the strong odor. "It's horehound," she said, "right from our garden! The syrup will help cure his congestion, I'm sure of it, and the sachet will ward off evil spirits. What do you think of that?"

Luis looked quizzically at the items, then sneezed. "Well, I don't know if that's the reaction I hoped for!" laughed Mother. "Come on." She helped the child put on a light sweater, picked up the basket including the herbs, and escorted him across the street.

Jesse, a somber-looking soul, slightly bent to one side due to arthritis, melted into a smile when he saw them. "Ah, Mrs. Mary, and little one, welcome, the Lord is expecting you!" Jesse always referred to the imposing Mr. Beethoven as "the Lord" or "my Lord" in deference to his high position, though he was far from royalty as far as the records of peerage go. Luis drew in a deep breath as he passed into the parlor, looking about at the bevy of crystal fixtures, sparkling mirrors with gleaming frames, curtains cut from the finest Belgian lace. Even the furniture was ornate, painted lavishly with depictions of lilies, roses, vines, and ferns. The house had a wonderful scent to it. He closed his eyes and inhaled the fragrance of those same flowers that decorated the tables and cabinets. How different from home. How he wished this could be home.

And then from the next room, the tinkling of piano keys, all five octaves on Grandfather's treasure, a new piano from the south. A tune by Lucchesi, no doubt, spritely, light, and cheering. In fact, Grandfather had sung the bass role in a Lucchesi opera to high acclaim just that past May,

"Do you hear that?" Grandfather's voice called from the adjoining room. "The composer Lucchesi, certain to be regarded as one of the greats! I met him, you know, a few months ago, and he was very kind in praising my interpretation."

The music stopped, and Grandfather appeared in the tall doorway between the two rooms. He was a magnificent looking man, despite his illness, in an oriental style dressing gown, with satin slippers, his wispy hair, flattened by years of wig wearing, still betraying traces of the reddish brown mane of his youth. His eyes were mellow and brown, and there was an aristocratic tilt to his firm dimpled chin and expressive lips. His nose was almost aquiline, giving him the perfect expression for a performer on stage, for he could be viewed as either sharp and commanding, or soft and affectionate. The commanding aspect soon melted into the affectionate as young Luis ran into his outstretched arms.

"My boy, my boy," he soughed, engulfing the happy child in swathes of silken bedclothes. Little Luis wrapped his arms around the old man's knees so hard he nearly toppled him, but Jesse moved quickly to stabilize the pair. Everything about his grandfather gave the child a sense of security, safety, and love.

After a few minutes, Mary called, "Luis! Didn't you forget something?", gently waving the bundle. The little boy peeked from behind the folds of fabric and then hurried to his mother, grabbed the package and brought it back to his grandfather.

"Well, what is this, Luis?" He sat on one of the painted chairs and opened the package. "My, Luis, this is a lovely gift. Is this from your garden?" The child nodded, biting his lower lip, his hands clasped behind his back. "Well thank you, my child, and Mary," Grandfather looked affectionately at his daughter-in-law, "thank you, too, you are so thoughtful."

Mary smiled and nodded, but her heart was heavy. She could see how tired the old man was, how the usually passionate spirit was dim, as though someone had cast a net over the sun; his movements slow and painful, and that wheezing sound when he breathed—something she had experienced herself when ill—

that was of particular concern.

"Are you sure you are all right, sir?" she asked, moving beside him, and putting a small hand on his shoulder.

"Better than in weeks, thanks to this (he pointed to the medicine) and this (pointing to the boy)." Luis threw his arms around his grandfather's neck. Mary was pleased to see the shy, introverted child blossom in the presence of the charismatic old man. The child's dark face glowed. How odd and a bit sad, she thought, that a young boy would blossom here.

"We'll have supper soon, right, Jesse? Then we will have a nice chat, and Luis can look at books and see the new piano," Grandfather said, as he accompanied Mary to the door. It was such a change from the daily routine of strange looks, whispers, and an unstable spouse. She looked around the lovely home, thinking it must be a taste of heaven, gave her son one last loving glance, and stepped into the twilight.

It was a happy, peaceful scene, the old man and grandchild, talking and laughing over the beautifully set table to one side of the parlor, with lace and damask coverings, fine china, and silver gleaming in the soft light of candles. A large blue-and-white tureen sat in the middle of the table, and Jesse carefully spooned a hearty beef stew into the child's plate. He sat on a high, firm pillow placed on the chair, for even for a child he was small of stature. As he greedily dug in to the plate of stew, Grandfather tapped his hand softly. "Not so fast, lad, you must have manners to rise in the world!" It was clear that the old man had big plans for the small boy.

Luis ate more deliberately, at least when his grandfather was watching, and flashed a gravy-rimmed smile from time to time.

The candlelight and crystals reflected in his dark eyes, which seemed large for his face, perhaps because the cheeks had not yet caught up with the rest of him. The Beethovens did not go hungry, but neither did they eat good meat that often, and vegetables were mostly from the backyard when Mary could not face the greengrocer. Luis did not notice that Grandfather mostly had broth, which he sipped intermittently, with a slight frown.

The meal concluded with a special macaroon-type cake of ground almonds and sugar and studded with currants, which Luis spit into his napkin as Grandfather signaled Jesse for a small glass of brandy. "I like the cake," said Luis sincerely.

The elder patted him on his head. "My, your hair has a mind of its own," he said with amusement.

"Momma is forever patting my head," the child replied, "like I was a bouncing ball!"

"I'm sure she does it with affection," said Grandfather, rising from the table and giving the lad, crumbs now covering his chin, another hug. Oh, if his son John had seen them now, who recalled not one embrace from his father in his more than 30 years!

"Come, let's sit down by the piano, I want to show it to you, it's quite new." Grandfather took the boy's hand and led him to the other formal room adjoining the parlor. The room was a bit darker, but sconces illuminated the square piano, a light-brown furnishing under the window.

"That is like Papa's," said Luis, running over to the bench.

"Well, hardly," sniffed Grandfather. "This is new, your father's is old. This is excellent pearwood, I don't know what your father is using these days. It sounds like some cheap composite when I visit, and he is teaching, and it's not even five octaves!" He caught himself, remembering his guest was not yet three. "But no matter...

"So this, dear Luis, is probably the best piano you have ever seen or heard. Music is the industry of our city, as surely as the business of food and wine." The black and white keys glowed in the candlelight. There was no cover to flip back as in later pianos. But in the early 1770s, it was state-of-the-art: a masterpiece of sound and design.

"Luis, there is a clavichord in your room, isn't there? It's small and has a soft sound. Listen to this."

Grandfather sat beside the boy (they both barely fit on the bench) and began playing a spritely minuet, his fingers flying over the keyboard in true showmanship. "Oh, Grandfather!" laughed the boy, "how do you do that!"

"My lad, this piece was written by a boy not much older than you!" The old man looked closely at his grandson. "Doesn't your father play for you or tell you stories about music?" The child shook his head, and suddenly threw both of his hands, fingers spread, hard on the keyboard, releasing a crash of discord.

"I know, I know, I'll talk to him, all right? As soon as this blasted cough is cleared up." Grandfather gently picked up the child's hands and held them in his as he gently went up and down an octave scale. "Do you like that?"

The boy nodded. "I like the way it makes my fingertips tingle!" he said solemnly.

"Well, let's make them really tingle!" exclaimed Grandfather, holding the boy's hands as he punched at keys at a furious pace, tracing the notes of a fast courtly dance. Luis began laughing and couldn't stop, finally developing hiccups. "Jesse, some water for the boy, quick!"

After recovering from the laughter which shook his entire body, the boy snuggled up against his grandfather. "I love to visit you," he said. "You make music fun!"

"Music is fun, and it will be the great passion of your life, just you wait a few years. Why," the elder Louis exclaimed, "you can start even sooner, when you're three. I don't think that is too early, do you?"

And so the pair—ailing old man, now with rosy cheeks and a lively manner, and eager young child, forgetting all about shyness and diffidence—spent a happy evening together, creating memories and a haven from the cares of a rather inhospitable world.

Chapter 8

WINTER CAME EARLY THAT SAME YEAR. The city was cold by nature, in northern Europe and bordered by a great river. It was only December and already tiny icicles, like frigid daggers, clung tightly to the edges of windows and eaves. Luis's third birthday seemed overshadowed by dire activities that drew his mother increasingly across the street, and sent his father into fits of walking about, daydreaming, talking to himself. There seemed to be fewer music lessons being given in the house, and John would disappear and return with some rough-looking friends, carrying pieces of furniture or boxes that appeared to contain crystal, silver, and porcelain. The items did not stay long in the house, though. Luis was small and quiet, but attentive. He noticed the march of familiar items into his house and then out the door again.

At the same time, John was busier than usual with the choir as Advent and Christmas music was being rehearsed and performed. But busier did not mean the household was free of his temper…and intemperance. Luis's sleep was disturbed many times by slamming doors, his father's loud, slurred speech, his mother's pleadings, and sometimes the sound of violence. One night, Luis heard a puzzling discussion through a crack in the wall.

"So, let's see what you have this time, Mary Magdalene, so well named!" John bellowed. "You can't get it right, can you! They're either dead or black, and I don't know which is worse!"

"John, stop it!" cried Mary in a soft, troubled voice. "They were your children, too, as this one will be."

"I'm not so sure!" John hissed, and the sound of a sharp smack reached Luis's ears. "We'll see come spring. I have enough to worry about now. You hypocrite. My own mother is put away, and yet I have to live with you day after day." John collapsed in a corner and began sobbing. Luis covered his ears with the pillows and tried to sleep.

The tension reached its zenith on Christmas Eve. The town was bright with street lamps, and decked with holiday greenery. As John about leave the chapel following a performance of the midnight mass, a messenger ran up to him.

"Sir, are you John Beethoven?"

John was tired from the exertions of two performances on the twenty-fourth, and eager for a drink. "I am," he said, "but follow me to the tavern, you can tell me there."

"Sir," the boy replied, "I musn't. It's very important. It's about your father, sir. The missus said to fetch you no matter what, please go home."

"Merry Christmas," said John sarcastically, slipping a small coin into the boy's cold hand. "I'll go home when I'm good and ready. Tell them, all right?" he boomed, turning abruptly on the child, who nodded and ran off into the night. Merry makers and holiday well-wishers were streaming from the chapel and filling the streets, truly a once-a-year sight in the usually quiet town. Horses and carriages and coaches, people bundled in furs and coats made from blankets, women in crisp bonnets and muffs, distinguished aristocrats mingling with the humble poor. The sound of bells, an occasional whistle, sung carols, laughter, gossip. John walked to the closest pub and bought a refill for his flask. "I'm afraid I can't stay tonight," he told the surprised innkeeper. "Trouble at home, I fear."

It was trouble, but as John mulled what the message meant, he thought it was a mixture of trouble and opportunity. His agile, self-serving intelligence mulled the possibilities as he took a long draught from the flask, a deep breath, and entered his father's house.

Mary rushed up to him. "John, I am so sorry," she said, her face flushed and damp. "Your father…is dead. The priest was just here…"

"Damn the priest," muttered John, and elbowed her to the side as he walked into the dimly lit house, past the new piano, up the stairs. There in the master bedroom lay the body of his late father. The old man, always tall and well built, was now an inert parcel of bones and hide. His skin was pale and drawn, cheeks sunken, a ridiculous stocking cap covering his wispy white hair. The light green satin bedcover had been pulled up under his chin. His right arm had been laid on top of it, and his hand held a rosary.

I bet he died a Protestant, though, thought John. He was clever to hide that, all those years as the choir master. It was as lethal to be Protestant as to be…black, he thought with a grimace. Although there were many Protestants in other parts of Germany, some cities such as Bonn and Cologne remained strictly Catholic in outlook.

Imagine being caught between two generations, one a heretic, the other a misfit. John put his hand over his eyes and shook his head, and those others present mistook this for grief.

Mary tried to comfort her husband, but he brushed her

aside. Her thoughts turned to Luis, now the only Luis Beethoven in the family. (It was common at the time to pronounce or spell a Christian name in other commonly used languages. Luis was sometimes called Lodavico, Ludwig, Louis.) Her thoughts ran in several directions at once, and she sighed heavily, as though the sound would drive them all away.

"Jesse, I have to check on Luis," she whispered, grabbing her cloak. In a short while, she was in the kitchen where Henny was rocking Luis in sleep.

"Does he know?" she asked, yet another wave of worry and concern flooding her careworn face.

Henny raised an eyebrow, like an all-knowing Sibyl. "What do you think, Mary? Of course, he knows something. I believe he knows his grandfather is gone."

Mary collapsed onto a hard chair. It was as though all the effort of keeping up appearances and acting as nurse to her father-in-law, dealing with her husband's indifference to the tragedy unfolding around them, as though all that effort gushed out of her at once and left her hollow, not unlike the remains of the dead.

"My poor Luis," she sighed, leaning back, her head resting on the brick wall. "What will become of us?"

Henny rearranged the sleeping child on her lap. "I am sure John has his eyes on his father's position. He's wanted that for some time," her voice rose with feeling, "and you know as well as I that he believes it is his right!"

It was not unusual at that time for the salaries of deceased choir members and musicians to pass on to heirs who were similarly employed in the court. And family members sometimes inherited superior positions upon the death of a relative.

Mary did not respond, and Henny knew why. There was no way John would inherit his father's position. Leading singers, directors, and composers from throughout Europe, perhaps even the greats Mozart and Lucchesi, would be vying for this position once news of the vacancy spread. John may have seen himself entirely as a pillar of excellence buffeted only by bad luck, but how would the Elector and his agents view a tenor with a spotty attendance record, a pattern of heavy drinking, and a voice that was dimming in quality as time passed? There were other blots on his record, as well, ones that would not make the official dossier. Most prominent among these, a peculiar-looking child was no asset in the world of ecclesiastical politics.

All this was not known specifically to Mary, but she suspected the case was stacked against her husband. Dealing with his delusions in the months to come, and then his ultimate disappointment was a prospect almost too horrifying to imagine. She absently rubbed a large bruise on her thigh the result of one of his nocturnal rages. "Oh my God," she murmured. "My poor babe. And another on the way."

Henny bit her lip so as not to suggest matters would be even worse if another dark-skinned child were in the family. And who would defend these children, now that the socially prominent grandfather, who had amassed a small treasure of wealth for them, was no more present to be their benefactor and defender?

"So much to think about, and I am so tired," said Mary with a cough. "Here, give me the boy." He was passed from one strong-armed woman to the other, and didn't wake. "He must have been up for a good long while," Mary said tenderly. She kissed his forehead gently and smiled. "Ah, he does take the pain away," she nodded.

"If you say so," said Henny in a slightly exasperated tone. "You two go upstairs, I'll stay in the house with John and the others, and try to keep him away from you both. In a few days, you should stay with me for a fortnight, it would do you both good!"

Mary nodded again. "I will miss him so…my father-in-law, that is," she said, looking into Henny's cool blue eyes. "He was a friend and champion, and loved Luis unconditionally."

Henny's wry expression said silently, "For whatever reason, we'll never know!" but she held her tongue.

"I'll go over now," Henny said, grabbing a sewing project and tossing on her shawl. "I had the foresight to take a long nap this afternoon, something you should do yourself more often, especially in your condition." Without ceremony, she left the mother and child on Christmas Eve to reenter the house of death.

Christmas morning dawned darkly. Mary bundled up Luis for one last visit to Grandfather's house. She put new mittens on his hands, and gave him a kiss. "It's time to say goodbye to Grandfather," she whispered. The small Christmas tree downstairs looked forlorn in the austere parlor where John gave music lessons. Luis nodded and followed his mother across the street as he had so many times before, now for the final time.

They entered the once beautiful home, already cold and bare of holiday ornamentation. Luis looked down to avoid the looks of strangers, some of whom stepped away from him as though he were a bad omen. "Come, come, dearest," mother whispered, "we'll say a prayer at his bedside."

The pair climbed the steps to Grandfather's room. Mary

entered the room, lit by candles, but Luis hung back at the door. He looked at the high bed covered with satin, a bed he had seen so many times before. He stared at the white figure sunk beneath the coverlet, and then looked away. It is always a shock, our first glance of death and its ravages, to see the lifeless shell where once a vital, larger-than-life personality dwelled.

He stood there in the doorway some time, until slowly the tears ran from his eyes and his shoulders shook in silent sobbing. Luis finally ran down the steps and into the drawing room, where he threw himself on the piano. "Grandfather, grandfather," he sobbed, collapsing on the keyboard in a crash of clashing notes, as though the old man's soul was in the instrument, not in the pale visage upstairs. His short legs hung from the piano bench, seemingly sapped of life.

"Now, now, Master Luis," said Jesse, who ran into the room and sat beside the boy, putting his arm around the quaking shoulders. "We must all end some day. Your grandfather was a good man, God bless 'im, and had a good life. Lad, he did love you, never forget it!" He gave Luis' unruly head a friendly pat, and the two sat in silence for some time as the overtones lingered and slowly died in the cool air.

"I will never forget you, Grandfather," whispered Luis earnestly to himself. "I will always love you."

Chapter 9

HOW GLOOMY, a winter funeral, just before the New Year, but how short lived is grief. Little by little, Grandfather's house was stripped of its finery, and after he had assisted in the dismantling of property, Jesse too was dismissed. Soon there was nothing left. Henny hectored Mary regarding the placement of crystal, books, musical instruments, fine fabrics, but Mary only shook her head sadly, her hands folded over her growing belly. John had debts to pay, and friends to entertain, and wine to drink. But if it bought peace for her, her son, and her child to be, the wasting of the Grandfather's estate was a small price to pay. He would live in her heart, anyway, not in his property, though she managed to secret away his grand portrait, so Luis would always have a sense of his presence in their lives. And she knew Luis felt much the same, though he had not confided in her. In fact, he had been unusually quiet and subdued since the funeral.

One night, John sat at dinner with his wife and son, a rare enough occurrence. His eyes gleamed in the hearth light and he held his knife and fork so tightly Mary wondered that they didn't snap. "What is it, John?" she asked mildly, fearing some unsettling news.

John smiled slyly. Now that he had sold his father's property, he was ready for change.

"We're moving," he announced. Mary dropped her soup spoon causing Luis to start.

"W-what do you mean?" she asked.

"I thought you'd be pleased, Mary," he said with a smile. "Yes, we are coming up in the world. It won't be long before I'm appointed chapel choir master and our fortunes will rise! Imagine," he gushed, leaning over close to Mary's face, "having your own small carriage, a better servant, more rooms, a nicer neighborhood…"

"But John," cautioned Mary, "I'm happy here. I have you and Luis, and my friends…"

"You have nothing!" he snapped, drawing back suddenly. "Nothing! We're poor, Mary, and getting poorer," he added, gazing at her belly. "We have enough liabilities as it is," he added, glancing at Luis, who sat quietly watching his parents. "I can't advance in the court from this hovel. We need lodgings in keeping with our increased status. Indeed, I need a better address now, if I am to be assured of my promotion." He stabbed at his stew and nudged a potato off the plate. "You don't have to worry about it, Mary," he said in lower tones, between his teeth. "I've taken care of it all, you just have to see to the packing! I've put a deposit on a nice rental at Three Corner Place."

Mary gasped. "John, we can never afford that!"

"That's not for you to determine," he nearly shouted, half rising from his bench. "Start packing tomorrow, and if you are nice," he added sarcastically, "I may even take you for a visit to see our new home!"

Later that night, Luis sat in his little room, already being rearranged to accommodate a new brother or sister. He heard his mother crying, not an unusual circumstance, but went into the master bedroom where she sat on a chair, softly sobbing over some needlework. How haggard she looked in the long shadows of the candlelight.

"Ah, come here, son," she said kindly, wiping her eyes, "you shouldn't see me like this. There is so much going on, I know that you know what is happening." She looked lovingly at her always disheveled little boy, so earnest and serious, and yet capable of great bursts of laughter and good humor.

Luis nodded. "Yes," he said, "a baby soon, and grandfather gone…" He paused. "What did Papa mean, 'we're moving,'?" he asked.

Mary sighed. "We are going to move to a bigger house," she said, trying to make it sound like a good thing. "On the other side of town, not so close to the river. It will be warmer, and very pretty, a bit like Grandfather's, and we may even have a pony!" she added with a smile. But her hopeful words did not convince Luis.

"I don't want to move," he said, stubbornly. "I like it here!"

"Well," said Mary, her eyes wandering off into the night, "it may not be for long. At least we all have each other," she smiled and drew him near. "As long as we are together, everything is fine."

"Everything is not fine," said the little boy. "We are not together. Father is never here, and I don't mind. But Grandfather!" His eyes became watery, and Mary gave him a tighter squeeze.

"It all depends on your father's good luck at court," she said. "We have to trust him, and God will do the rest."

Mary was quite advanced in her pregnancy when moving day arrived, and could not help as much as she would have liked. John begrudgingly had to pay an extra servant to help with the relocation of items. As Mary observed, she noted how few—if any—of her father-in-law's things were among their possessions.

"I am glad I insisted on keeping his portrait," she thought as the simple artifacts of daily life were loaded into a cart and taken away. Anyway, who would have bought a portrait of an old man?

The Beethovens settled into their new home, not so very far from the former home, but far enough so it was a bit out of the way for Henny Marshall and Mary's other friends to visit.

But Henny made sure she was present at the birth of a second son in April. This time, John was at work when the event occurred, and he fairly ran home from the court to see the child with his own eyes. The birth of a child at that time was an uncertain affair, especially for a mother who had lost two already. But of equal concern was the appearance of the next child. Would the babe be light like his parents, or dark like his brother? When the midwife brought the screaming boy into the world, this time there were smiles and even laughter. John ran up the stairs to the bedroom, threw open the door, and was relieved instantly by the sight of beaming faces. In his wife's arms was a pink-and-white squealing creature. It could have been a pig, for all John cared at that moment, as long as it was a rosy one.

"My boy!" he blurted, and fell to his knees by the bed. Mary smiled, too, cuddling the infant. "Ah, Mary, all is forgiven," murmured the still sober husband, nuzzling wife and child, and throwing an arm around both. In another room, listening, sat the older child, and it is fair to say that it was a familiar sensation to feel unwanted.

"Another son!" said John. "This is cause for celebration!" And before he was even properly welcomed to his own home, he was in the street, singing his heart out in the warm spring sunshine. "A fine boy, a fine boy is mine!" he cried, soon embraced by his drinking friends and ready for a long night of revelry.

Things were not so fine with Luis. As Carl survived the first critical weeks of life and began to develop, Luis's moods became more pronounced. His father was home more often than usual, partly because the Easter choral season had ended just days before the baby's birth, but also because he was thrilled to have a healthy son who more closely resembled his family. The birth so closely followed the death of the beloved Grandfather. Mary tried to give Luis the love and attention he was used to, but there was no doubt that a baby made great demands on a woman not in the best of health to begin with.

For John, the future appeared promising at last. Even though his promotion had not yet come through, he was able to pay his debts for the first time in years thanks to the proceeds of his father's estate, and his good fortune to be the only child. As nature emerged from the bitterness of winter, his heart was light as he attended rehearsals and performed with the other seven singers in the Elector's choir. Occasionally, he filled in for one of the violinists, and had several private students—two young ladies and a boy—who brought in some ready cash and could be palmed off on a grateful colleague once his new position was official.

Mary noticed the change in John, and, along with taking care of the new baby, she was in a good frame of mind. Flowering trees were in blossom, and there were few rainy days. The baby had his own small room adjacent to the parents' room in the larger house, and Luis was able to keep the privacy he treasured, divided between the garden and neighborhood, with its rows of lime-green trees and vegetable plots, and his own room, well illuminated with the morning sun. A tree by his window offered bird songs at dawn and dusk, and the amusing scoldings of squirrels.

Best of all, he began to explore the clavichord, a simple precursor of the piano, stashed in his room, across from his small bed. The clavichord made him remember sitting beside Grandfather, and its sounds were so soft, he could pound the keys forcefully without alarming his mother or annoying his father teaching downstairs. He would sit for hours, touching the black keys with his dark hands or pressing the white sharps and flats, not knowing yet those terms, and noting how the colors were the opposite of those on his father's piano. Why was that, he thought: the good instrument has white keys, the lesser one has black. And yet, I like the sense of having secrets and hidden places with this small instrument, he thought. Even when I pound it, it whispers. Sometimes I make my own lullaby.

The spring calm and the world of lullabies was not to last. As late storms gathered in May and soaked the Three Corner Place, revealing leaks and weaknesses in the house structure, so did a storm sweep down from the Electoral Court. For several weeks, John was on edge and refused to tell Mary what was worrying him. She braced herself for some dire event, not knowing for certain what it could be, but suspecting the worst. Then toward the end of May it happened. John did not come home for dinner, in fact, did not return at night. Later the next day, she left Luis and Carl with Henny, and walked into town, asking for him at favorite inns. After several unproductive stops, she came to the Wharfside, which was always open and active.

"John Beethoven?" mumbled the tough innkeeper, who must have had a rugged sailing career in his youth. "And you would be…"

"Mrs. Beethoven," she said, "his wife. Have you seen him? He didn't come…"

"He's here all right, but you might think better of disturbing him, he's just getting his first sleep upstairs. He's had a blow…"

Mary started. "An attack! An accident?"

"Nay, a worse blow than that, don't you know? Women! Always missing out on the important things in life!" He spat over his shoulder. "Look," the innkeeper said, lowering his voice, bending toward her ear, "I'll send him home…."

Mary sank onto a stool beside the counter. "No, no," she shook her head, "he will just go on to another place. I know him. I know what this is about."

The innkeeper stood up and struck his chest, saying, "Well, he didn't lose his job!" Just then, a respectable-looking young man at a side table rose and bowed to Mary. He was wearing a powdered wig and, to judge by his good, though not fine, clothing, had clearly been at court earlier that day.

"M'am, excuse me, I am Joseph Demmer, a colleague of your husband's," he said, taking her by her arm gently and steering her away from the door. "Please sit down, would you like a glass of ale? No? Yes, it is so, I fear you know what has transpired. John had unreasonable hopes, and those hopes have been ended. He will not be the chapel choir master. But, at least he still has…"

"Oh, God, I knew this would happen." said Mary, moving from stool to bench, shading her eyes from Demmer's gaze.

"It is true," said Demmer, the very basso who had assumed Grandfather's singing duties the previous year. "The announcement has been made—I have a copy of it here!" he said producing a document. "Lucchesi, an established composer, has been brought in from the south and will be installed as our leader. It is not surprising, Mrs. Beethoven." She nodded, still avoiding his eyes. "We all knew the Elector wanted a 'name' composer as well as director. Why, every composer worth his salt in Europe covets a chapel choir master position! Even Mozart, I hear. Please do not be too upset."

Mary stifled a sob, and shook her head slowly. "Look," Demmer said, "I will be here for a while. Let me take him home, you need to attend to your family and prepare something nice for him, to make him feel special. This is a terrible blow for him, and one that only he did not see coming! And Mrs. Beethoven," he added hesitantly, as though not sure he should say anything. "Is there anything you can do to help him…well, I am sure you know what I would say…"

Mary nodded again. "Yes, the drinking, his voice is not what it was." She sighed. They were poor enough as it was, and back in debt with this news. What if he were to go the way of his mother and land in a home for unemployable alcoholics. Would they all end in the poorhouse?

Mary thanked Demmer for his kindness, and wrapping her cloak tight, left the drafty inn with its strong smell of brine, and went out into the late spring afternoon. The rain had ceased, but a cool dampness hung in the air. She hurried home out of duty and obligation, for there would be no happiness and only dread, dread and a future filled with misgivings and inevitable despair.

Chapter 10

JOHN WAS A SORRY SIGHT and uncharacteristically glum. The usual sharp temper that arose from too much wine was not in evidence this night. He drifted off early and slept a long, troubled sleep. Mary slept in the spare room they hoped to rent out to visiting musicians or to use as a guest room. Tending to Luis and Carl absorbed her attention. Interesting how motherhood could act as a drug to help one get through life crises.

The next day he ate sparingly, in silence, with no more than a glass of wine imbibed with meals. His silence was deafening and in some ways, for Mary and Luis, as terrifying as a scene, which was expected and would pass quickly. Finally, three days after receiving the news of Lucchesi's appointment, John washed, dressed himself, packed up his sheet music, and spoke to Mary at breakfast.

"I am done with it," he said solemnly. "This is as far as I'm going. We must look to our children if we want to get ahead in the world."

With no other word, he turned his back on her and the boys and walked out the door as he had countless times enroute to his work at court. Mary did not know what to think. It was good to see him stable, sensible, and resigned to being no more than a breadwinner. And realistic, too. Given a choice, wouldn't she in fact prefer poverty to raging ambition and dashed dreams? But where had that ambition gone? It surely had not evaporated during two nights of sobriety. What form would it take next?

Would he be happy to remain a mediocre singer, perhaps picking up more work at the theaters or by adding a few private pupils? What did he mean by "look to our children"? Mary gazed lovingly at Luis, quietly eating his porridge, and Carl on her lap. Whatever did John mean?

The dry spell did not last long. Soon, John was back in his old habits, drinking in his favorite pubs, producing bottles from the dirt cellar where he had hidden some of his father's stock. As spring slipped into summer, there were fewer singing and other performing venues available, though John had been able to engage a few more private students. But finances were tight. As the year slipped by, the couple knew they would have to move back to their old district where rents were more reasonable.

And there was more. The time had come to begin instructing Luis in music. He and—more likely—his brother were now the hope of the family's survival. It would be years before the boys would be working in the court, but one other thought arose in John's active brain, recovering its former nervous vitality and ambition. He first spoke about it to his friend Hoffmann at the Wharfside after a rehearsal.

"John, how is it going with your boy, the dark one?" Hoffmann asked. It was a brisk late autumn evening, and the men were finding more warmth in ale than in their tattered coats.

John put both hands around the stein, as though it contained hot spirits rather than cool. He looked out past the hearth where embers flickered and faded and rose up again in small flames.

"That boy has potential, if only he would obey!" he said. "He has no voice, I've given up on that. Imagine a Beethoven with no voice! He sounds like a grunting boar when he tries to sing!" Both men chuckled at the thought of the peculiar-looking child making the noises of wild animals.

"Well, John, you know there's more money in instrumental music, unless one happens to be a shapely soprano or an Italian castratto."

"Yes, and he already has one strike against him," said John, slamming his stein on the table.

"Not so much for an instrumentalist, my man," countered Hoffmann. "A singer is center stage, a violinist or cellist blends into the shadows. And what if he can compose…"

John laughed. "Ha, you should hear him 'improvising,' not even four, and he thinks he is the cock of the walk! When I have visitors—the parents of pupils or prospects—do you know what he does? He sneaks up to the piano and begins playing sequences of chords with his right hand! Nothing I've taught him, just doggerel of his own! Garbage it is, and supremely annoying. I wouldn't be surprised if I've lost accounts because of his rude behavior, and he's gotten the stick for it, too!"

Hoffmann nodded. "Well, you know having a dark son isn't necessarily a bad thing." John gave him a strange sidelong look. "No, seriously, John, you know about Joe Bologne, right?" John's face was blank. "He calls himself, 'the Chevalier de Saint-Georges,'" Hoffmann added. A look of recognition swept over his friend's face.

"Ah, yes," said John, stroking his chin, "the new conductor of the Concert Spirituel! Violinist, courtier, uh…'friend' of Marie Antoinette…and dark as night! Caribbean, isn't he? Son of a slave?"

"A slave and a French plantation owner. He's made quite a

name for himself as a composer. I've seen a copy of his Six Quartets, they look good enough to me, but listen, John." Hoffmann brought his head closer to John's ear, almost conspiratorially. "The fact that he is black is his advantage. He is an exotic! The court women fawn over him, and who knows for what reason. If you win the hearts of the court women, your career is made."

John took all this in and slowly nodded his head. "Very interesting," he mused distractedly, "but a person would need the marketing skills of a Leopold Mozart to pull that off. Though," turning to Hoffmann, "what about a dark-skinned person who did not have an African pedigree? I don't know."

"What do you have to lose?" Hoffmann hinted. "I'm sure Mozart is no longer the Wunderkind he once was. What do you ever hear of him these days now that he's grown? Soon he'll be forgotten. Well, sure he's still working, but not conspicuous in his success, not, for example, a chapel choir master…oh…sorry, John, didn't mean to say that…" Hoffmann nearly blushed at the faux pas.

"It could work," John thought aloud. "A child to succeed the Mozart legend, and at the same time, an exotic specimen just waiting to be some countess's pet! Well, it's pretty far-fetched," he admitted, shaking his head, "and yet…" looking Hoffmann straight in the eye, "what do I have to lose?"

Chapter 11

UNKNOWN TO HIS FATHER, Luis had been exploring the keyboards in his home since Grandfather passed. With his mother distracted with a new baby, he was not interrupted nor scolded for playing nonsense on the keyboards in the parlor and spare room. The little boy learned quickly how to pull himself up onto the bench and push back the cover on one (the other had no cover), and try to imitate what he recalled of his father's hands on the instrument.

Not long after his father's revelation about the potential inherent in young children, John came home one day to find Luis engaged in one of his battles with the piano. "Luis!" he shouted, and the boy froze on the spot, his deep eyes searching behind him in the shadows for the encroaching figure of his father.

John strode firmly but not hostilely into the parlor. He soon loomed over the small boy, who now looked up at him with a mixture of defiance and trepidation. His hands dropped from the keyboard to his thighs, and he sat very still. John lifted one of the hands and sat down beside him. Carefully, thoughtfully, he examined the child's hand in his own, looking closely in the candlelight.

"Hmm, I see you have been banging the keys for some time now, son," he said. Luis tried to hide his hands.

"Son," he said, in a continuing even tone, "how would you like to learn to play? To play like me? To play like…your grandfather?"

The child continued to sit very still and look straight ahead, beyond the instrument, toward the window, its drapery closed for the evening. Then he began to shiver a little, and he withdrew his hand from his father's very slowly.

"What do you mean?" he asked. "Would you teach me, Father?"

John forced a friendly nod. "Why of course, my boy," he said, "I would teach you, and then, should you do well, as I expect you will with discipline and practice, then other teachers could be brought in to help you develop." The father paused, then said, "My son, you have a responsibility. To support yourself and help support this family through our family profession, which is music."

He put his arm around the child's shoulders and felt the slight tremble. "Are you cold, Luis? Or have you been ill?" The boy shook his head. A mixture of emotions and thoughts arose, uncommon for so young a boy. Images of playing the piano, getting the notes right, making the huge sound that Grandfather had made, and the roar of the organ at church.

But also memories of having disobeyed his father, of not having done something right. Being hit and trying not to cry out, the threats of even worse punishments not yet experienced, like being kept in his room without food or, worse, being banished to the cellar, all these thoughts, feelings, and intimations boiled together in the child's fine nervous system and caused him to shake under the now kind hand of his master.

"I…am fine, Father," the boy said at last.

"And the lessons? What do you think of that, son?" John gave him a vigorous pat on the back and put his own hands on the keyboard. To Luis, it was as magic when his father played chords and melodies, fugues, and fantasies, teasing sounds out of the instrument that he with his small childish hands could not bring forth no matter how hard he pounded.

"You know, Luis," said John, "our family is a musical one. Our stock in trade is singing, but also playing. You've not shown an interest in singing yet, but you are too young for that. We'll wait a few years and see if we can make a boy soprano of you. But in the meantime, let's not waste opportunity. You clearly enjoy these instruments, why not learn the secrets to their mastery?"

There was a pause, then Luis looked up at his father with burning eyes. "I want to play," he said seriously.

"Good!" said John, rising quickly from the bench. "Then it's settled. We'll begin this weekend, and I consider it a great pleasure to introduce you to the keyboard!" He smiled, satisfied that his plan would now be launched, and without the trouble he had expected from his rough, unruly son.

"But, Luis," he added, "leave the piano alone for now, all right? You don't want to get any more bad habits. It is very difficult to unlearn them, difficult and painful. You will have enough working against you. Do not make matters worse!"

John quickly left the room, relieved that the conversation had gone well and the boy offered no resistance to his plan. For his own part, Luis shifted uneasily on the bench. He was not shivering now, but spread the fingers of both hands wide over the keyboard, resting them silently on the keys, relaxing his hands onto the smooth shiny surface. "You will play for me," he whispered, putting his head closer to the ivory. "I will learn what I must, but then you will play for me, not what my father wants, but what my heart speaks." And just as silently, the boy put his cheek down on the cool keyboard between his hands and closed his eyes, and sat some time as the candle burned low.

Chapter 12

AUTUMN SLIPPED INTO WINTER, and Luis was four. The lessons had been progressing along the lines of two steps forward, one step back. To John's mind, the forward steps were when Luis unquestioningly obeyed and mimicked his instruction. The backward steps were when he caught the boy playing things he had heard or making up tunes or, worst of all, playing pranks on the keyboard, especially when there were guests or visitors in the house. To Luis, the two steps forward were when he played with the keyboard as with a childhood friend—uninhibited, imaginative, whimsical—and the steps backward were when the switch fell across his hands, and he was bullied into scales and exercises.

But despite the harsh discipline, John was no fool. With visions of prosperity before him, John did not relent, but, following the pedagogical practices of the day, drove the small child on.

In spite of the strict training, Luis grew steadily. Though small of stature, he was a large-boned, sturdy lad, in good health except for an attack of the pox which swept through the neighborhood one summer, giving his already dark complexion a ruddier hue. He loved the daytime, when he could play in the garden, even in winter, or wander through the neighborhood. He was developing a thick skin about his appearance, and the occasional taunt did not dismay him, though he avoided places where strangers would comment on his appearance. When his father was at the court, or teaching the children of businessmen or low-ranking officials downstairs, he could slip away to play with the baker's son, or the son and daughter of the landlord, though mostly he would roam through the city, not an unusual freedom for a boy so young.

From his mother, he learned to be kind to others, especially those not as strong as he. As his mother increasingly sent him on errands, he became more responsible and, as the year rolled round to another birthday, had developed an independent spirit that reverenced the memory of his grandfather, heeded every kind command from his mother, and bristled at the very sound of his father's voice. Adversity, including the family's worsening financial situation, did not diminish his self-confidence, and in addition to being reliable, he was becoming self-assured and headstrong. Such was the development of the boy as his childhood slipped prematurely behind him.

It was around this time that a shadow fell over John's behavior, and he was less demanding during the music lessons. One day, he stopped and covered the keyboard, and looked sharply at Luis.

"Be up early tomorrow," he said abruptly. "We are taking a little trip. There is someone we must say good-bye to."

Chapter 13

WHILE A TRIP would otherwise have been a treat, Luis saw the look of exasperation and displeasure in his father's eyes. He knew the trip would not be a pleasant experience.

"Where to, Father? For how long? Why?"

"You'll find out soon enough," John said turning his back on the boy. "Mary! Pack a day bag for Luis," he called. "We're going to see Maria." In the other room, Mary dropped the silver she was polishing with a harsh, rattling clang as it bounced off some cooking utensils by her feet. "I must bid her farewell, and Luis must see her before the end."

"Are you sure…"

"Be quiet," snarled John, jogging down the stairs. "Just pack."

Early the next morning, in a light rain, father and son headed north in a coach containing two other male travelers. It was a short, but bumpy and uncomfortable ride, as coaches often were. Luis was apprehensive, his father was moody and silent, looking out the window as the dark sky grew faintly grey in the dismal dawn.

Luis was looking out the window eating a sweet roll as they approached the city, much larger than home, with graceful church spires and buildings that would have been colorful on a sunny day, not uniformly whitewashed like his own neighborhood.

"Come on," John said as they stepped down to the cobblestones, "here, put on your hat."

"I don't like hats!"

"I said put on your hat!" The hat was slapped onto the child's head and pulled down tight. "We have a bit of walking to do, all right?"

Luis wiped his mouth across his sleeve, and followed his father up the winding path into the amazing city, so foreign in every way from his home. They walked a half hour past shops and offices, and soon horses and carriages and vendors on foot were beginning to crowd the streets. At last they made a sharp turn, and John grabbed his son's arm.

"Here, this is where we are going."

"Who is Maria?" asked Luis.

"Just wait," the father replied. They were in a kind of courtyard before a gloomy stone building, a monastery or convent of some type. John rang the large, noisy bell hanging beside a massive wooden door. After some time, a nun answered it, and John said something to her that Luis did not hear. The nun looked down at Luis, and frowned.

"You want to take him there?" she asked, almost in disbelief. John nodded. "Is he a servant's child?"

"No," said John, making no pretense of kinship to the boy, "just take me to the wing, I haven't been here in years."

The nun looked at him with a superior air, as though holding back words of stinging criticism. "All right," she said, "this way."

The three walked into the convent, the visitors scraping their boots before proceeding down the long dark hall. Although it was late summer, the building felt cool, as though its windowless passageways had stored up a hundred winters. The ceilings

were very high and at every turn, a shaft of cold grey light
sliced across their path; Luis paused and looked up toward the
ceiling but could make out no details or ornamentation.

They walked through several hallways and sets of doors
until finally they came to one heavily chained. Here the sister
took a ring of keys from her rope-like belt (which also held a
dark rosary where a large crucifix hung at the end, like a weapon),
and after two unsuccessful tries she was able to unfasten the
lock. John helped lift the latch and opened the door, which
groaned with a low abrasive creak.

"She is still in the same place?" asked John.

"She is," said the nun. "Do not stay long, she is ill. Leave
when you have had enough. I will be outside the door and will
see you out."

The nun disappeared into the darkness, her full grey habit
billowing silently, and John and Luis moved forward into the
dimly lit room. There were cells, as in prison, though a bit larger,
and each cell contained a person, and some of them had beds.
The room was quiet except for some soft moaning and coughing
sounds. Luis looked about and felt a shiver of fear. What was
this place?

John's fingers gripped tighter on the boy's arm, and he
directed him to the back of the room to a cell with a bed, and on
that bed was a figure, sitting up at the edge. As they came closer,
the figure became sharper, and Luis saw it was a shape of an old
woman, with rounded shoulders covered by a nondescript cloth.
She coughed, and coughed again, the rattling, tubercular cough so
common at that time and so fatal. John pulled Luis as he strode
into the room and beside the bed, and with his other hand,

touched the woman's shoulder.

"Hello," he said in a monotonous tone. "Mother?"

Luis now clutched his father's leg, and hid behind his cloak. The woman did not speak. After some time, she looked up, and Luis saw her face: drawn, thin, sallow, with dark circles under the eyes and a trembling lip.

"Do you recognize me?" John said, slowly lowering himself onto one knee. "No, of course not." He looked away.

"Sonny," the woman's lips murmured. "Sonny. What have you got for me, eh? Did you bring me something, Sonny?" Her thin fingers grabbed his collar with surprising strength. "I'm thirsty, Sonny, they don't take care of me here. Who are you? What have you brought?"

Astonishing to Luis, John reached into his pocket, producing a flask. "Ah!" the old woman smiled, coming to life. "I knew God was good!" she crooned as she opened the flask with hands that shook violently, and attempted to drink the alcohol. But it had been too long, and her throat rejected the longed for wine. Coughing, she spit it out, hacking, wheezing, and bending over the faded bed clothes. Luis noticed that she spit out blood, and not a little bit. It was then he became aware of the awful smell of the place, and felt faint.

"Father, Father, I feel sick, let's go, please, please!"

John slowly rose up and eased his mother back into the covers. Her coughing gradually died away, and she rolled with her face to the wall, muttering meaningless sounds to no one in particular.

"Father!"

John turned and grabbed his son's arm again, pulling him back toward the door. "Are you all right?" he asked suddenly, squatting down beside the child. Luis drew back at what may have been his father's first and only expression of concern and kindness to him.

"I want to leave. I want to go home!"

John got up again. "So do I, my son. But take a look around. This is where beggars and drunkards wind up," he said bitterly. "My mother was not a beggar, but a drunkard, and this was the only hospital that would have her. Remember your grandfather if you like, but remember also this woman. Remember and be afraid," he said with greater feeling and urgency, "be afraid of failure. Do not fail, ever, or your own mother or I or even someday you yourself will wind up here!"

With this horrible admonition, John opened the great door and slammed it behind him. His mind reeling with sensations and fears he'd never imagined, Luis was soon in the carriage, and when they arrived home later that day, he ran straight into his mother's arms, hugged her tighter than ever before.

A few weeks later, John received notice that his mother had passed. "There goes the medical stipend," he said bitterly. "It looks as though we will be moving again."

Chapter 14

WHEN LUIS WAS FIVE, several changes occurred in the Beethoven household. Mary once again began complaining of stomach upsets, and by early summer, it was clear that yet another baby was on the way. At the same time, John lost an opportunity to increase his salary, necessitating more teaching of scales and arpeggios to minimally talented locals. With mounting debt, his drinking resumed in earnest, and soon the Beethovens could no longer pay their rent. A move back into their earlier neighborhood, with fewer rooms and closer quarters at a time when the family was expanding, put further strains on a family that was beginning to fray at the edges. Only Mary's resolve to endure the storms of her marriage and the poverty of her home kept the family together, but the price paid was large.

Yet all was not squalor and misery. Around this time, the Elector announced a ball on the occasion of his 25th anniversary as leader of the state. While many of the court musicians were required to play, the Elector had actually convinced his tightfisted minister to splurge for once and engage some additional musicians from outside, enabling the senior musicians at the court to attend the gala as guests. The affable Elector, known for his appreciation of all things soft, aesthetic, and feminine (and in particular the female form), knew the importance of treating his musicians well, even if he was not allowed to be generous with their remuneration. Although his most esteemed musicians were considered servants, there would be a place for them at this elaborate party, and they would not need to "play for their supper."

Like the other musicians' wives, Mary worked feverishly to add bits of inherited lace to the one good dress, a brownish lavender blend of fabrics, which she kept in the back of the bedroom cabinet. Wigs were fluffed and shaped, and fresh powder applied. Pert satin bows updated a familiar pair of shoes, which had stretched over time to accommodate the spreading feet of a hard-working woman. Mary needed no paint or preening for her own face, though. Her eyes sparkled with some of the old fire that first caught John's eye and made him stand up for once against his father's opposition so many years before. On the evening of the gala, her cheeks flushed with excitement, not rouge.

"I hardly know you," admitted Henny matter-of-factly, unwilling to bestow a much deserved compliment and not entirely resigned to her drab role as caregiver. "Well, enjoy yourself, these lads will be fine, just don't tire yourself too much."

John, handsome as could be, wrapped a cloak about Mary. "Wait, wait," she laughed, "I have to say goodnight to the boys." Carl, now two, was on Henny's lap and looked the other way, but Luis sat at the table, an ambiguous expression on his face. "Good night, Luis," said Mary, bestowing a kiss.

"Have a great time mother, and bring me home a piece of cake!" the child said seriously.

"Cake indeed!" interrupted John, bundling Mary toward the door, "you'd better practice, boy. Henny, don't let him off with less than two hours of exercises tonight!" Henny nodded, but her eyes said, "In your dreams, sir!"

The couple left the house and entered a carriage containing two other couples en route to the Palace. As the wheels squeaked and the hooves of the horses pattered into the distance, the boy dashed into the parlor where he could indulge to his heart's content in the forbidden fruit of musical doodling and improvisation. Ignored by the woman and child in the other room, and as his parents rode on to the palace, he immersed himself in the experience of pure happiness.

Mary had been to palace functions earlier in her life as the child of a court chef and later during a brief first marriage which ended with the untimely death of her husband. But it had been many years. Still, when the carriage drew up to the palace door and footmen attended the ladies as they left the coach, she felt fresh and renewed. She was once again in a world without poverty or want, without lewd, drunken advances, and heavy objects thrown at her head; and worst of all, the sounds of slapping, hitting, crying from the nightly piano lesson. All that vanished in the crisp night air as she stepped from the coach as a princess in a fairy tale, her handsome prince—well behaved but with darting, watchful eyes—not far behind her.

The palace was an oblong structure built around a courtyard and formal garden. This night, the central fountain was illuminated by what must have been a thousand lanterns; bare trees hung with crystals tinkled in the night air and glistened as though full of their own fire. Inside the main hall, two large, graceful staircases swept up to a mezzanine. At one end of the vast hall, filled with brightly attired aristocrats and a few fortunate tradesmen and artisans, a small orchestra in splendid military-style regalia played the latest works from Mannheim and Paris, as well as a few airs by the new chapel master. Aromas of roasted meats and highly spiced fruits and punches mixed with aromatic perfumes and pomades, and the nearby swishing sound of ladies' fine gowns nearly overpowered the distant music. A grand bronze clock kept watch over a balustrade; the walls were dazzling yellow as though the Elector had captured the sun and released it for a late-winter surprise. The footmen and waiters were as finely attired as nobility, and Mary forgot she was herself but a servant's wife in an old dress cleverly remastered.

As Mary caught sight of an old friend and hurried to the other side of the room, John fortified himself with yet another draft, and inched more closely to the conversations of minor aristocrats and court officials. Though a servant, John—perhaps because of his experience as an actor and theatrical performer as well as singer and musician, and in part because of his own father's example—could give the impression of being of higher social station. And so, though not physically imposing, he mingled seamlessly with the almost elite.

One conversation he found himself involved with concerned the impending revolution in the American Colonies, but touching also on the neighboring problems in France.

"It's all a powder keg, you'll see," said the wearer of a dapper military uniform in dazzling red, festooned with golden braids. "The life we lead? It will be gone!"

A buzz of coughs and assents rose from the little group, as a man who might have been a viscount added, "No, Wally, I don't see why that has to be. Why, none of these disasters have to happen. It's all a matter of managing the masses…"

Another wave of humphs and hahs arose, as a third man, perhaps a nouveau riche, offered, "Of course, we cherish liberty. But liberty for the ruling class, and most affluent who support their reign. But there must be kindness to the people…"

A roar of protest arose from the circle. "Daniel, don't be ridiculous," barked the uniform, "the people need to be kept under tight reins. Look how effective the Bastille has proven in Paris! Why, a better model for controlling the vicious individuals who instigate riots has never been conceived."

And so it went, John nodding here, nodding there, offering an "Aha!" and "Good point!" Then one gentleman, deeply tanned, with a French accent, turned the conversation a bit further.

"You know," he said, "what this is all about. It is about race! Yes, race, do not pretend you do not hear or understand me!" Several eyebrows shot up. "Race: the white rulers, the thinkers and developers of the world, versus the masses of dark people…Jews, Africans, Indians, who threaten to pull down the pillars of civilization. On my plantations in the Caribbean, do you think there is an iota of disobedience? Do you think there is a place for a black person to worm his way into the hierarchy and make trouble? No! Believe me, unlike you, you who do not know these issues first-hand, I see this every day when I am in my island home. This is what is behind the unrest in the Colonies, and in France, and throughout the civilized world."

The others rubbed chins, nodded again, mumbling uneasy agreement.

"Well," ventured the viscount, "there is a point to what you say. But surely, there are exceptions! Why, we are intelligent men. It's true: we do not have blacks in the German states the way that the French, English, and Spanish do. I can't say I've even seen a true African within our borders in my life! But surely we believe that any dark-skinned person of hard work and obedience to the rules of society can develop into a civilized creature, perhaps even doing good!"

The group was beginning to side with the foreigner, and laughed good-naturedly at the viscount's attempts at reason. "Give me one example!" smirked the uniform.

"Well, let's think for a moment," said the viscount, who was known as an intellectual with a large collection of literature and many subscriptions to current publications. "Our plantation friend here clearly depends upon slave labor…"

"…and appropriately so!" the Frenchman exclaimed, "For none of the sweets and fine woods we enjoy would be ours without this, this natural resource!"

"Perhaps," said the viscount dismissively, tugging at his lace cuffs. "But surely there are some from, say, Africa, who have made their mark…Why I know of someone, and you would too if you would only read your own regional literature! The philosopher of Jena and Halle: Anthony William Amo!"

"Oh, Tony, don't start your intellectual posturing again," said a tall nephew of a duke, leaning lackadaisically against a pilaster. "Tony, no one reads philosophy, and no one will in the future, least of all anything written in Northern Europe!"

"Fine, let's try another field…a military man, Major General Gannibal, you've all heard of him, especially you, Tom, you probably studied his strategy…"

"Oh, that's a freak of nature, Tony, honest to Pete!" squirmed the uniform. "You are hunting for needles in the hay…"

"Next you'll be touting Cleopatra!" exclaimed the nephew, and everyone laughed. "But no artists, I venture, no musicians or composers from that torrid breed?" The viscount frowned, not wanting to spend his evening playing 20 questions with those who outnumbered him. "No, I suppose you are right," he said, "I can think of not one composer…"

"What about the Chevalier de Saint-Georges?" All eyes turned to John, who was not even recognized as part of the clique. John was well into his third or fourth glass of wine, just about the level that assured him of maximum brilliance, at least in his own mind. "Surely you've heard of him. Why, Gentlemen, the Elector's own private quartet played his latest works no later than Advent!"

The viscount nodded. "I do believe you are right, you are…?"

"John. John Beethoven, son of the late chapel choir master as well as a leading educator of court ladies and gentlemen, and a soloist, I may add."

"So, John, yes, the Chevalier, I totally forgot about him! And not only a master composer and conductor is this wonder, Gentlemen, but a championship fencer and equestrian, a linguist, and even….lover of court ladies!" A roar of approval rang up, but quickly died in a word from the military man.

"Such anomalies occur, my good Viscount, and often in France!" Laughter. "But they are nothing more. I will say this with certainty: no man in our great civilized land will arise to prominence for any good thing, be it politics, ideas, or musical performance and composition, if he so much as looks like a black from Africa!"

With these words stinging in his ears, John left the group inconspicuously. He had other contacts to make, and more wine to drink. His resolve, though, was unshaken. Rather than, "They are right: I will give up," what he heard in his head was, "They are not right about me and my plans for the prodigy. I will never surrender my dream!" As he crossed the hall alone, his fist tightly clenched, his teeth set and his eyes staring unwaveringly ahead, another thought propelled him. "And I will do it, if it kills me," he said half aloud.

Mary decided to ride home with a bassist and his wife whom she knew; John would not expect her to stay. She enjoyed society, but concern about home kept her pleasures on a short leash. Bidding goodnight to her companions, she stepped onto the cobblestones and looked up at the clear night sky. The Milky Way stretched across the heavens like delicately spun sugar, and a cool breeze rolled off the nearby river. Soon, she entered the house to find Henny asleep in the spare bed, with Carl dozing in his cot. Luis? She knew where to look. Downstairs in the parlor, wrapped in a table cover, bundled under the piano. She smiled, and reaching down, pulled out the unkempt roll of bed and boy, and he didn't stir except for a heavy sigh as she brought him to his own room to sleep. After laying him in the bed, she watched him for a while in the moonlight, and lightly brushed a stray lock of hair from his forehead.

Mary went to sleep, but it was not to be a peaceful night. John burst into the house after 2, and slammed the door furiously behind him. "Mary! Mary!" he called, "you bitch, get down here!" He staggered past the hearth-side table, his elbow raking across a row of earthen bowls that crashed to the stone floor.

Upstairs, Mary's eyes opened wide, and her heart beat rapidly. It had been a while since he had come home this loud, this drunk. She regretted she had not hidden her son in the same room with Henny and his brother. "Oh," she put her hand to her head, as the pain of unaccustomed drinking seemed to punish her for a few hours of enjoyment.

John appeared in the doorway, a wavering lantern flame illuminating his face from below. "You and that black bastard...you'll tell me! But I know, I know now...he's going to pay me back! He's going to pay me back for all the misery and embarr...arrass...all the shit I have to put up with!" He rocked to one side of the doorway and then the other. Mary knew there was nothing she could do.

John staggered down the hall and pounded on Luis's door. "Why aren't you practicing, you...loafer!" he shouted, reverting to a term of derision similar to one his own father had used against him. In the room, Luis was braced for the worst. He didn't have time to hide, and his father would find him in the small room at any rate, and then be even more furious. Experience had taught him to comply, but only for the moment. His mother had advised him that he would grow up quickly and be earning money soon, and be away from his father. But for now, he needed to weather the storm. It was a terrible lesson for a child to master, a child of only five.

"Come in, Father," he said, his young voice unsteady. "I practiced! I swear I practiced! Ask Miss Henny, she had to hear me, I practiced all night! Everything you taught me, all the exercises! Over and over, all night!"

John slammed the lantern onto a table. "Well, we'll see about that!" he glowered, grabbing the boy by his nightshirt collar and slamming the back of his hand against his head. "Father, no!" the boy cried, "stop! You're hurting me!"

John grabbed the child's arm and pulled him roughly to the small keyboard beside the window. "Here! Show me what you can do! Play the arpeggi…chords…broken…in all the sharp keys, athend…ascend…up and down! Don't confuse me!"

Holding on to the side of his head with his left hand, Luis pulled the small stool up to the keyboard and began to play. "Play while I talk…" John said, dropping onto the bed beside him. "Listen! You are our only hope! You can't sing, you have to play, and you have talent, but you are lazy…lazy! Do what I tell you…" John's head sank back into the pillow, "Lazy black bastard…." and his head turning to one side, and beginning to drool, he fell into the catatonic sleep of the drunkard.

Mary was at the door, ready to spring. At the first snore, she swept over Luis, and bundled him close, taking him into the spare room where Carl slept, but Henny sat upright, a look of stern disapproval and disgust on her face in the light of a single taper.

"Mama, my ears," the boy sobbed.

"Don't worry, we'll make it stop!" she cooed, rocking him gently. "I found a different teacher for you."

"I don't want a teacher! I don't want a father!" he cried, sobbing hard into her shoulder. "I am so tired."

After a while, he was asleep. Mary brought him into her room and bolted the door. John would sleep late again and not remember a thing that had passed.

Chapter 15

As ANOTHER YEAR PASSED, financial difficulties increased, and the Beethoven family once again chauffeured their dwindling possessions to a new location, this time a very unsatisfactory flat that was at least conveniently close to the palace and theaters on one side, and the market square on the other.

Then, as though things could not get worse, one January night Luis woke up coughing. He heard warning bells, and looking out the windows, noticed a red, undulating cast to the sky.

The palace was on fire.

With his house just two blocks away, Luis could clearly see the flames from the back window. "Mother! Carl!" he cried, as the night sky turned into a blaze of gold and crimson fire. Panicking horses neighed, fire crackled, not so distant beams collapsed with a loud roar. Luis could hear floors of nearby buildings crashing down one, two stories, disgorging hundreds of people onto the narrow streets, past those fighting the fire bravely, those fleeing with what possessions they could carry.

Clutching his mother's skirt, as she attempted to carry Carl and the new baby, John, out of the glowering house, Luis looked back at the crimson glow, spreading in horrid waves across the night sky, rolling like a demonic dawn toward the river bank. Stumbling in the night, he felt himself pulled along past others who had poured into the streets.

Men, women, children stared, frozen to the spot, jaws dropped, eyes dazed in disbelief, their faces lurid red; coughing, gagging, retching. Luis's bare feet hurt from the cobblestones as he was dragged through the lunging crowd—sometimes fleeing, other times moving back for a better view of the magnificent Palace that symbolized the entire life of this cultured and prosperous community. Luis let go of his mother's skirt to wipe his face, and Mary spun around in panic at the sensation of a lost child.

"Don't let go!" she screamed, as his body shook at the violence of his mother's voice. Scorching heat, shouts, screams, calls for loved ones filled his ears, as the family of four pushed through the crowd toward the river.

Safe at last on the river bank. Luis started at the clang of fire caisson bells. Warning horns and alarms called volunteers. Mary cradled the baby close and eased herself down the side of a shanty wall, holding Carl tight. Luis ran up the outside stairs of the hut and watched flames shoot up from the huge rectangular building in the centermost part of the city's finest district. "Luis, do not wander off!" his mother called from below, but her voice was weak with exhaustion.

The din and conflagration reached to the other side of town, beyond the Munster. There, John dashed his stein on the stone floor, embraced his friend Grossmann, and asked what else could go wrong.

Grossmann turned his eyes from the fiendish light, and looked with hard, cold eyes at John. "Don't you think you'd better head home?" he said. John nodded, and unsteadily left the inn in no particular rush.

The Palace was the city and the livelihood of its people. The fire raged all night and into the next few days, finally dying off as snow fell and smothered the last embers.

The city mourned as for a monarch. It was more than the economy: the Palace was the mother of an extended family, a seat of beauty, knowledge, and enlightenment. In his dreams, John recalled the swirling staircases, the golden walls, noise of commerce, and chatter of conversation day and night. But of greater note, the grand pipe organ was no more, its great voice crying out, its stops unloosed, as the console collapsed from the high berth into a mound of smoldering rubble, mourning for Counselor von Breuning, one of the Elector's most trusted officers, and the others who perished in the blaze. John buried his face on his folded arm, but nothing would smother the pain.

Chapter 16

ONCE THEY MOVED CLOSER to the Palace, now a charred, foul-smelling ruin, Mary lost touch with her friends, even her cousin Henny, and felt more isolated than ever. It was a mixed blessing when, yet again, the growing family loaded all their possessions into a series of carts and said good-bye to the flat on New Street, moving farther back again into the noisy, foul-smelling River Street home. John kept his position in the part of the Palace that had been salvaged, had a new group of private students, and even a gig with his friend Grossmann, the local theatrical impresario. But the money was not coming in quickly enough. John's solution was to find paid work for the scruffy six-year-old child, he reluctantly acknowledged as his own. The time of the Wunderkind had arrived.

"Hmm," mused Grossmann over a pint of ale in the Beethovens' kitchen, "so this is the child."

"Don't let his appearance mislead you!" John said quickly. "Look! Look at these hands." He nudged his son who splayed his dark, flat fingers before the impresario. "I have trained him myself and can assure you that there is no child keyboardist in the region to match him for speed and discipline!"

Grossmann continued to rub his stubbly chins, to raise one shaggy eyebrow, then the other. "Does he have…southern ancestors?" he asked in an off-hand manner. John frowned a little.

"It's on his mother's side. It has nothing to do with his playing…" then a thought occurred to him, "…except, perhaps, to add some fire and spirit!" John smiled as Grossmann nodded appreciatively.

"Well," he said, "boy, let's hear some of that fire!"

John pushed the child into the next room as Grossmann followed, and lit some candles around the piano. "Luis, play the Haydn, you know the piece, the one with the gypsy air!" Luis thought for a moment, then brightened, as it was one of his favorites. He scrambled onto the bench, and immediately launched into a rousing performance, with a cascade of fortes and pianissimos, and an avalanche of arpeggios at the end. Grossmann's jaw dropped, and he steadied himself against a chair.

"My God!" he exclaimed, as the little boy swung around with a smile of triumph. "Where have you been keeping him, John, he is good! You are good, my boy!" Grossmann bestowed the expected head pat. "How old did you say he was?"

"Uh, five, no, not quite five, you can see…how small he is, very small, more like four, wouldn't you say?" As John studied Grossmann's expression to see which age made the best impression, the boy swung around, brimming with confidence, and started improvising variations on the Haydn theme. It was a few minutes before his playing attracted his father's notice. "Luis, stop that noise! Mr. Grossmann doesn't want to hear it!"

"Indeed, it is most interesting. Boy, continue for a bit, let me hear what's on your mind," Grossmann said mildly, casting John a withering glance. Grossmann moved his considerable bulk between John and his son, and watched as the small dark hands flew over the keyboard.

It was some time later that Grossmann gently stopped the child's excited performance, and John suggested he go upstairs to help his mother. Grossmann was obviously stirred, and put his arm over John's shoulders. "My man, you have a prodigy there, I don't know if you realize it." They walked into the kitchen, and sat at the table. "Now my world is primarily the theater, as you know, but there is some overlap. I can use an oddity…no, excuse me, I should say a 'novelty' act such as this. Can he learn popular songs with the same passion? He is remarkable!" murmured Grossmann, looking back at the vacant space where music had lately rung. "Remarkable."

John brightened at this news, confirmation of his heart-felt dreams, and even forgot to take a drink. "Uncanny, uncanny," Grossmann continued, helping himself to a basket of rolls, "and you say he is not yet five? And exotic, too! You know that performers from the South are drawing the crowds now. But, you've promised his talent to the Church, no doubt! That would be a steady income stream."

"No, no!" insisted John, waving his hands and shaking his head. "No, we are far from that stage. The child has no voice, he has no future in a boy choir, and is so small he would fall into the organ-works and be crushed!" They both chuckled at the image that conjured up.

"Is he obedient?" Grossmann asked suddenly. "Does he take orders, not feign illness…"

"Like a soldier, Friend. He does everything I tell him…and only obeys me!" added John firmly, to ensure his control of the property.

"So…you would need to accompany him? Like Leopold used to do with Mozart?"

John beamed. His hopes were coming to fruition as the

evening transpired.

"And his teachers...there is you, is there another? Someone for composition, improvisation? I know those are not your strong suit."

"Only an old Italian who used to play in the court."

"Oh, we can do better than that," whispered Grossmann in a distracted way, brushing the crumbs from his chest. "I know a fine teacher you can hire. Get rid of that Italian. John, bring the boy around Thursday night. Do you have some popular songs? No? I'll have some for you at the theater tomorrow. He should be able to play a few and add some embellishments without much practice, such a bright boy!"

Grossmann rose and slapped John on the back. "I see some real possibilities," he said as he wrapped his cape over his shoulders and, putting on his broad-brimmed hat, stepped out into the snow.

John eagerly collected the popular scores the next day: dances, marches, minuets, but with an eye for pieces that were fast, racy, and bright. Airs with a Turkish lilt or a gypsy swagger made the final selection to land on the child's keyboard. "Never mind the exercises, master these, today, tomorrow! Practice!" John yelled as he dropped the sheet music with a thud, and raced out late to choir practice.

Later that day, Luis was in unusually high spirits as he sorted through the short scores and tossed them onto the floor after quickly scanning each edition. "Ah, here's one, a Rondo alla Turca, I bet I can wake them up with that!" the boy said to Carl who sensed something exciting was about to occur. Luis smashed the paper against the music stand and pounced on the keys. "Luis! You will break the strings, for sure!" Carl laughed, as his brother feverishly pounded the keyboard in an explosion of sound.

"Hey, how about this," he said, looking over his shoulder at Carl with a grin, letting his hands move so quickly on the keyboard they became a blur. "Hold back, Luis, Father will not like this!" Carl cautioned. But Luis kept playing, adrenaline unchecked.

Later that night, Luis played the lively airs for his father with the restraint and discipline his parent demanded. But Luis thought fondly of Grossmann, clearly a man who appreciated the child's free creative spirit. Well, so Luis thought at the time, with a child's transparent trust of anyone who bestows praise. Compared with the father who sometimes beat him and locked him in the cellar, Grossmann was a savior, a promise of life beyond the small troubled household. But there was more to Grossmann than either father or son surmised.

Late Thursday afternoon, as John completed a lesson with his student Joanne Averdonck, a young singer of promise, Mary bundled up Luis for his visit to town. "Remember," she said, pulling the scarf too tightly under his ears, "stay with your father! You don't know what those theatrical people will be up to! Don't fall for their flattery, for they do not have your best interests at heart, do you hear me?" He nodded as best as he could with the swaddling around his neck. "Remember: you can only trust your mama and father, do you understand? We don't know this man Grossmann, so be on your guard." Then she smiled warmly and gave him a hug. "You will do well, just be yourself, my son," she whispered. Luis smiled, and patted Carl on the head as the child tugged on his pant leg.

John said good day and bowed elegantly to Joanne, then went into the kitchen where Luis was being packed into his traveling clothes. "Mercy, Mary, we're just walking a half mile up the road!" he said, double-checking the portfolio of music the child was holding. "Yes, it's all here, good. Mary, we'll be there a few hours, keep some dinner warm for us," he said as he shepherded the bundled child out of doors.

The theater was not much to look at it. Though in the years ahead, Grossmann was to make a name for himself as an impresario of note, at this point he was making his first inroads into the world of entertainment. He surmised, and rightly so, that a sophisticated city so dependent on the Church for livelihood needed a down-and-dirty theatrical scene where locals could unwind and relax. The first of Grossmann's theaters was about a half mile from the palace, but a world away in terms of character and atmosphere.

John didn't look twice at the seedy façade, set back from a winding dark alley smelling of horse dung and stale beer. The black front of the theater, distinguished only by a sign thrust over the cobblestone pathway, belied the scene lurking behind it, for as they entered the building, a bright array of lanterns illuminated the darkness, and the sounds of people already drinking and carousing greeted their ears. Beyond the drink-dispensing foyer, there was a small theater with a proscenium swagged in cheap purple velvet. A piano sat off to one side, and on the other, a comic actor exchanged rude remarks with a stagehand. Tallow candles lit the stage from below, giving it an otherworldly, but not heavenly, glow.

"Over here, Beethoven!" called Grossmann from the far end of the theater. "No performances tonight, but tomorrow, we'll have a few new acts, and maybe…" he looked down at Luis, "…maybe you!" Father and son made their way to the front of the seating. Grossmann was smoking a cigar, a rather odd thing to be doing at that period of time, and grabbed John's arm to help him onto the stage. John in turn lifted his son to the side of the piano. John walked around to the keyboard and played a few passages. "Not bad," he said. Luis coughed and turned his face from the cloud of smoke attending the impresario.

"Will you have better light?"

"This will have to do," said the director, looking at the child from several angles. "Though we will have special lighting on the boy."

"Special lighting?" asked John. Grossmann led the child to the piano stool and helped him up.

"Here you go, how do you like this?" he asked, pushing back the key cover. Luis looked down at the keys, which were rather dirty. He ran his fingers up and down the octaves.

"Sir," he said, looking up at Grossmann, "there are some broken strings!"

"Oh, no matter, you can play around those, right?" said Grossmann, flicking ashes on the floor. "You can entertain us without those keys, isn't that right?" He smiled and was no longer so attractive to Luis. The floor candles distorted his face, which was also quite yellow in the gaudy light.

John paced a bit as Luis placed some sheet music carefully on the instrument and squinted at the page. "Yes, play something, let's see how you are here, with me as your audience!" said Grossmann smoothly. Luis launched into a country air, followed quickly by a Turkish rondo and a march. He found it easier to play the simple pieces from memory than to try to see the scores in the peculiar yellow light which increasingly became dense with smoke and made his eyes burn.

John and Grossmann were talking about money. As Luis played, he felt less comfortable, with none of the excitement or glee he had experienced when the theatrical manager heard him play at home. Though concentrating on his performance, the child could not help but hear a few words of conversation and saw Grossmann hand John a playbill.

"What do you mean?" asked John, "You plan to advertise him as a mixed race child? A gypsy?"

"Why not?"asked Grossmann, draping his arm over John's shoulder, "you have to make the best of his liabilities! If you have a black child, you have three options: powder him white and pass him off as a European; leave him as is and hope for the best (never a good choice); or accentuate his native features and pass him off as an exotic. Now, I don't know about you, but I would choose the path leading to maximum profit!"

John scowled and stopped pacing. "Beethoven, I know my audiences!" the manager said, sounding less unctuous and more annoyed. "Do you or do you not want to make a dollar with this boy! You'd better decide quickly, chances like this won't come often! He has talent, for sure, but not in the right package. He's a dark, dirty boy, John, and that's not a pretty face. Here, I not only guarantee a silver piece each night he plays, but the crowd, especially at the midnight shows, will throw pennies at him, I'm sure! Imagine…"

Luis stiffened and pounced on the final chords of a pavane, throwing his entire small body into the sound. John turned to Grossmann. Even John—mercenary, bigoted, sometimes violent, self-centered parent though he was—found this too much to bear.

"Come on, son," he said, "you're too young. We'll find some other venue," and without so much as a good-bye to his friend, strode from the theater with the boy in tow.

"You'll be back!" called Grossmann, oozing back into a congenial mood. "You can't turn down a good offer like this!" and then to himself, "...you miserable loser, it's pathetic...take what you can get...."

To his own surprise, John's respect for cash was exceeded by his own self-respect, at least on this occasion. He would be laughed at in choir, patrons would take away his private students, he could not show his face in the streets if he permitted his son to be paraded like a curiosity and be scorned for his appearance. Luis, who had developed a thick skin and knew how to hold back tears, felt his eyes burning more than ever, and thought perhaps, it was the odd combination of candlelight and smoke.

"You're back so soon!" exclaimed Mary when the two arrived.

"We'll try another way," John said. "There are other theaters, and we don't have to be center stage. Perhaps, we should try the church first. You did your best, son," he said. Luis looked up and recognized it was one of the few kind things his father had ever said to him.

Chapter 17

MONTHS PASSED, and John had other things on his mind. Arriving home one evening, he only slapped Luis for carelessness when he saw the child's red hand, the casualty of a schoolyard scuffle. "Idiot," he mumbled. "Those hands are our fortune!"

Luis was surprised he got off easy. Mary observed that John was distracted and uncommunicative, but not violent or grim, and in that mood common among alcoholics when they are lost in silent reveries with great concentration, as though focusing on an external icon no one else can see.

In the days ahead, the reason became clear.

"Do you know Miss Averdonck?" John asked Luis the next morning. The boy nodded. She was a very pretty girl in her teens and hard to ignore. Lately, she had even paused and looked at him kindly, as though she was on the verge of saying something. "She is ready to debut in a public concert," he continued, "and I've arranged for her to sing a series of arias in Cologne this spring."

"What does that have to do with me?" asked Luis.

John tilted his head a bit as though sizing up the boy. "I was going to accompany her," he said, "and will in a couple of selections, but this might be the perfect opportunity for you to step out as well. How would you like to accompany her on the keyboard? It would be your first concert in public!"

Luis thought his heart was going to burst out of his chest. Had he loved his father, he would have rushed to him, crying "Papa, Papa, Papa!" but instead he started laughing and put his face in his hands, his shoulders shaking. John wasn't sure whether this was laughter or tears.

"Yes," the child said, "I can't wait!" It would be a first step away from the provincial, restrictive, prejudiced world of his childhood, a step toward that future his mother had told him to focus on when things seemed unbearable.

John was encouraged when the boy looked up with a smile, and looked like he wanted to run around the room. "Well, don't become too excited," he said, rising to go downstairs. "You'll need to brush up on your violin playing, too, as there may be call for a short piece. Miss Averdonck will be here later this morning. She already has agreed and is thrilled, as well." John didn't really care that the children were excited, only that excitement could lead to better practicing and results. "We'll be looking at repertoire in the next few days. You are a quick study. In the meantime, I'm getting rid of your other teacher. I have a couple of fine organ teachers in mind."

At times, John's shrewdness took on flashes of brilliance, and this was one such occasion. His new plans for Luis, to be undertaken immediately, would immerse him in the two worlds of society at that time: the sacred and the secular. Becoming an official pupil of the Elector's senior organists would secure him a foothold in both the church and the church-run state government which the Elector presided over. Debuting at a public concert in the free city of Cologne, which had a secular government separate from the Archbishopric of Cologne, gave him an "in" with the world of secular performance. There were rumors on the wind that secular performance might catch up to and even overtake the sacred in future years; time would tell. For now, all bases were covered. All the child had to do was perform and obey. What could possibly go wrong?

"I'll have you meet her at her next lesson," said John.

*****

"Hello, little lad!" smiled Joanne Averdonck a bit too gaily. She was dressed in an emerald day gown with ecru lace, ruffles around the throat, and a fine green headdress on her day wig, with a cluster of sausage-shaped curls bunched behind her neck. She was, of course, disappointed that her teacher was not to be her accompanist, but then, he wasn't a very good pianist, and perhaps it was to her advantage to have someone of his selection instead. But a boy of seven or eight? And one who would be advertised as five or six to create the illusion of a Wunderkind? Well, we'll see, she thought. Nothing had better go wrong, or my Papa will set Mr. Beethoven straight!

Luis hadn't minded the traveling around town in recent weeks to audition for the local organists. He was a healthy boy with plenty of energy, and a round of appointments and new places was as good an outlet as any. It also allowed him some time away from school, though problems there had eased as the bullies found other victims, and decided he wasn't worth their efforts. And another plus: with other music teachers, there were fewer physical attacks from his father, and John had even eased off on the drinking that so afflicted him and the family before. At least, this was the case for the time being.

And so the pretty teen watched as Luis settled at the piano and smoothed out the sheet music his father handed him. "I will leave you two alone to become acquainted," he said. "Play the Hasse aria, then something by Handel…here, this one, isn't that the one you like, Miss Averdonck?" She nodded and took her place next to the piano, looking over Luis's shoulder. "I expect some real progress by the time I return," said John. With that, he left the flat, leaving the two musicians alone together, with Mother and the two boys upstairs.

"So, Luis, let's have a little chat," the singer said, sitting down on the bench with a swish of stiff fabrics and crinkly underskirts. "How old are you, really?"

Luis did not look up but continued to play with the score before him. "Oh, I don't know…six, I think," he said.

"You don't look six," she said. "I'd say you were seven, or even eight!"

Luis was uncomfortable. He was not used to girls, let alone those who hoped to become fine ladies, and certainly no females as forward as this creature. "My father says I am six," he said. "Do you want to sing this aria?"

Joanne looked closely at the child, then decided to stand again. He was a scruffy lad, very ill-kempt, and there was a slightly unpleasant odor about him. Joanne had promised to find out all she could about this mysterious child and report back to her best friend, Cecily, sister of Luis's friend Godfrey.

"I do," she said, "but Luis…I hope you don't mind me calling you by your first name…are you not in the habit of dressing for visitors?"

Luis squirmed. It had been all he could do to climb down from the tree behind the house and make it inside in time for the appointment. "I dress for concerts," he said, with an important sound that surprised even him.

"Well, I'd hope so," Joanne said. She rose again and walked around the small, plain room. "Luis, who is this man?" she asked, stopping at the portrait of Louis Beethoven. The child turned and watched her as she stood in front of the picture in a posture of thoughtful observation she no doubt had copied from a popular print.

"That is my grandfather," said Luis.

"Well, he is an important-looking man," she said with satisfaction, swishing back to the piano. "Luis, if you don't mind my asking, whom do you take after in your family?"

Here we go, thought Luis, I really need to think up something to say every time this comes up! "What do you mean?" he asked. Then, "We'd better start practicing. Father will be back soon!"

"Well," she continued, "you don't look like your father or grandfather. And I've seen your mother, and even one of your brothers!" Then she paused and bent over to catch his glance. "Are you...adopted?"

Luis could feel the blood rising in his veins. "Miss Aver*dork*," he said with some malice, "we had better play or my father will be mad!"

Joanne stepped back and raised her chin haughtily. "That wasn't nice, little boy," she said. "Do you want me to complain to your father, or worse, to my father, my father who pays for your house and that fine suit of clothes!" she said with disdain.

Luis bit his lip, and to his credit, tried to apologize, but it was just too much. Everything always came back to race and class. He was the freak, everyone else was the norm. No matter how hard he practiced, how good his playing was, no matter how well behaved and how he swallowed his pride and mastered his temper, it was never good enough.

"Yes," he said, fuming, "yes, I am adopted! I am the lost son of a prince of Africa who was sold into slavery in Spain and won his freedom in a great battle!" He hopped down from the bench and put his hands on his hips, remembering the stories he had heard about the black French composer, Saint-Georges. "And he was a champion fencer, and he met my father when the Archbishop visited, and I was adopted, and that is how I got to look this way!" He ran from the room, outside, and up into his favorite tree.

Joanne's jaw dropped, and she backed into a chair and collapsed with a gush of crinkly sounds. "My word!" she exclaimed. "What a terrible child!"

Luis had left the door open and a rush of cold air came in. It didn't take the young lady long to feel its effects. She thought for a moment, then pulled her cloak from the coat rack, and stormed outside.

"Luis!" she called, "Luis, come down. Don't be this way!" A sudden vision of her failed concert debut rose up before her. She had provoked the boy, that was true. He was obviously headstrong and disagreeable, but she had clearly lit a fuse she did not intend to ignite.

Luis was mad, that was certain. He sat up in the tree, still bare in late winter, his arms folded hard and fast across his chest. "Come down!" she pleaded. And, then, something she had never said before, "Luis, that was my fault. I am sorry." And just as Joanne had not previously apologized for a pert, irritating remark, so Luis had not heard those words--"I'm sorry"—before. He sat, cold, shivering in the bare tree, his body cooling as his temper calmed. Eventually, he climbed down and stood before the girl, looking at the ground.

"OK," he said, "I'm sorry too. It's just…" he looked up, and saw her smile.

"Come on, never mind," she said, taking his scratched hand. "Look at you! Your father will get a start when he comes home and sees you like this!"

The thought actually filled Luis with secret pleasure rather than the fear he would have felt several years ago. The two returned to the parlor, and soon there was singing in the Beethoven household, singing and an almost too energetic accompaniment on the pianoforte.

Chapter 18

ONCE THEY GOT PAST their initial animosity, Joanne and Luis hit it off. There was less than six years difference between their ages, though they didn't know it. Joanne liked Luis's maturity (complemented by the occasional tree-climbing and keyboard antics) and Luis enjoyed the company of a female of a different type than his doting, sedate, and long-suffering mother. Joanne was brimming with energy, and like Luis, she brought this spirit to her performances. Although the combination of spoiled merchant-class adolescent and poor dark-skinned boy would seem odd indeed to most people, it led to an enchanting musical partnership which John picked up on right away.

Before long, it was late March, and representatives of the Averdonck and Beethoven households respectively were shepherding their charges into separate carriages for the ride to Cologne. John had advertised the concert well, expecting a good turnout from subscribers and those who bought their tickets at the last minute.

The carriages rumbled into the large city, a capital for the region, on a sunny afternoon. Luis squirmed to look out the window as the seemingly endless array of buildings unfolded. In the distance cutting a broad swath was the familiar river, and overlooking it in the city square was a magnificent cathedral, catching the bright sunlight in all of its many faceted windows. Two towering spires seemed to pierce heaven itself, and Luis could imagine the clouds parting above, but he couldn't quite envision what they were parting for.

But even more interesting to the child was the parade of people on the boulevard, people such as he had never seen before. People of all ages and types, many very well dressed, some in elaborate ecclesiastical regalia, others in the dark frocks of lawyers, and medical men. He saw workers and women with male companions, and some walking briskly by themselves, perhaps professional models or entertainers. Even more intriguing were the different types of people. At home, everyone looked pretty much the same, or as though most of them belonged to the same family. But here the people were dark as well as fair, some truly black, not the sooty tan color of his own skin, which others referred to as "black." Other passers-by were paler than his mother. Some had light, smooth hair, a few had unruly hair like his own.

"Father, look!" he pointed.

"Hmm, uh huh," mumbled John, still making some pencil notes on a page of music. "You look, I've seen the world," he said distractedly. A group of people in turbans walked across the road, and an elderly woman in a dark green shawl smiled at the young face pressed against the carriage window.

John and his son stayed in a small neat room near the academy hall, not far from the concert site on Star Street. There were many preparations to make and details to arrange, such as contacting the hall management, checking on ticket sales (how much, but also, who was buying), making sure the musical scores were in order. Luis would be required to practice downstairs at the hotel, although he could practice the violin in their room. Yes, the violin: not Luis's favorite instrument, and one on which he was not particularly gifted.

But to make the program more enticing, one of Haydn's G major trios had been added, featuring John, Luis, and a local cellist. Of all the aspects of the concert, this was the only thing that caused John a little uneasiness, but he had buried this piece in the middle of the program so his two students could begin and end the evening's entertainment with works that showcased their talents.

As usual, Luis received some arch stares as he moved around the Rococo hotel with his father. Although it was not an elegant establishment, the footmen wore livery and powdered wigs. It reminded Luis that he, too, would need to don the dreaded wig for the next night's concert.

"Begging your pardon, sir," said the manager to John as the pair approached a piano in the lobby. "Are you staying here with your boy?" He said the word "boy" as though he meant "servant."

"With my son, yes," said John, accustomed to this tone of voice, and feigning dignity. "We are giving a concert tomorrow and need to practice."

The manager continued to smile slightly in a forced and patronizing manner. "Oh, I see. Why don't you go to the servants' quarters in the back of the building. There is an old piano there, it should suffice. We wouldn't want to disturb the guests."

John bowed and complied, but Luis felt a pang of resentment. "Father," he whispered as they walked past and behind the kitchen, "why do we have to do this? I work so hard! Don't people want to hear me play?"

John didn't say anything, but grimaced, and smacked the child sharply against the back of his neck. "Shut up," he grumbled.

"Just as in music, you must play by the rules!" Luis's heart sank; perhaps his father was reverting to his old ways again.

Then there was the matter of the rosin. Focusing more on his piano solos and duets with Joanne, Luis had not practiced the trio as much as he should have. When he opened his violin case in the back room, he looked for the rosin, a small bar of amber resin used to add friction to the bow strings.

John was testing the out-of-tune piano when he looked up and saw Luis searching through the violin case. "What is it?" he asked. "What's wrong?

Luis kept searching, but there weren't many places to look in the small case. "I...I can't find the rosin!" he said, looking up, and knowing his already annoyed father would be pushed even further by this disclosure.

"What? What do you mean?" John said, rising and grabbing the case from his son. "Damn. I don't know why I even try!" he turned away, then back to look harshly at his son. "Well, we don't have time to search for a shop." Nor did John know a local violinist who might be able to spare a piece of rosin for a child in distress. "I'll ask Bernie."

"The cellist!?" exclaimed Luis. "Father, I can't use cello rosin! It's softer, it will make an awful squeaking sound! I'm not good at the violin to begin with!"

"Quiet!" exclaimed his father, grabbing him by both shoulders. "Listen to me! You will perform so well with Joanne and with your solos, no one will notice, I guarantee. That trio is quick, you don't have to play loudly, just go easy on the attack. Stay here. Here, practice the piece by Gossec. I know where I can find Bernie. Here's key. Go to your room when you've played everything at least once!"

With that, John left his son, asking some kitchen staff to keep an eye on Luis. If only his mother had seen him now, left alone in a strange city with only insouciant kitchen maids to watch over him! John was out, and Bernie could be found at the tavern of the inn a block away. It was one hell of a day, and John needed a drink.

The next morning, there were final rehearsals, and, in the case of the trio, the first rehearsal as well, as Bernie Maurer shook the small hand of the young child, and winked at John. "You sounded mighty grown-up in those pieces, Luis," Bernie said. He reminded Luis of Mr. Grossmann, but his amiability seemed more sincere. "Well, let's give this a try, hope the rosin works out for you!"

They ran through the Haydn twice, Luis keeping his tone soft and gentle, looking frequently at his father's face at the keyboard. "God, I hate out-of-tune pianos!" he swore at last, pulling down the key cover with a crash. "Well, we've done as much as we can with this, I think it's a go. Joanne, one more run through with the Cavalli, I'll accompany with this one…" Joanne was with a chaperone, and looked the diva, though she had yet to put on her best dress.

The musicians were satisfied and after a midday meal together, the two parties split, with John, Bernie, and Luis heading over to the theater. In less time than anyone imagined, it was 5 p.m., time for the concert.

John looked out from behind the heavy brocaded curtains at the audience. "A good crowd!" he noted to Bernie, "I think we'll recoup our expenses and then some." He noted the nobles among the attendees, and observed the accoutrements and deportment of those entering the hall. Yes, it was a great place to debut a

Wunderkind! He smiled to himself, and scanned a program to make sure there were no typos or oversights.

The recital went well at the beginning. It was late afternoon, and there was still light from the setting sun complemented by dozens of lanterns and candles throughout the hall, most especially around the stage. The hall had a lovely soft glow to it, a combination of natural outdoors illumination and the artificial light of the theater.

Joanne was exquisite in a flattering dark blue dress, her wig gently sparkling with a dusting of shimmering powder. After a little initial nervousness, she sang two lovely arias with John accompanying her. Her voice warmed as her nervousness abated, and she became one with the music. After polite applause, she smiled and disappeared into the shadows behind the piano. John rose from the keyboard, walked to the front of the stage and, in his rich, well trained voice, introduced his son.

Luis sprang a little too energetically to the footlights. His excitement was so palpable there were a few titters of amusement in the audience. He looked so small on the stage, dressed in his one formal coat and breeches, his wig neatly pinned in place, but looking so foreign on the energetic child. In the odd lighting, his skin took on a golden glow. He bowed quickly and sat down at the piano, first warming up his hands with a few runs and arpeggios, then launching into short works by Gossec, Gluck, and finally a complex set of variations by Handel. The natural hum of the audience began to quiet, and soon there was no sound—not breath, not rattling programs, no coughing—as the boy became a conduit for the effusion of music that poured from the keyboard.

"Not so fast, not so intense!" John whispered from his position next to Joanne, but Luis did not hear. He played and played, or rather the music seemed to play itself, it took off, leaping high into the air, and dancing across the ceiling, like some unchained living being. The music filled every corner and crevice of the room, and penetrated the heart of every listener. By the end of the Handel, there were murmurs of appreciation and even disbelief, as though the boy was performing some conjuring trick. He concluded with a few extra repetitions of the final chords, pouncing on the keys with a power that simply could not come from a small child.

The audience burst into applause, with shouts of approval one did not usually hear in a northern recital hall. Luis bowed several times, a broad smile on his face as he tilted his face up to the highest lights. He was like a turtle on a rock on a hot afternoon, basking in the attention and soaking up the delight. This was good. This was what he wanted to do for the rest of his life.

John was conflicted. Pleased with the attention and praise, but annoyed that the boy had gone off on some sort of musical tangent. Well, no matter, the audience loved him. John approached the front of the stage, put his arm around Luis and the two bowed together, though it took a strong fatherly tug to pull the boy out of the limelight. There was a short intermission, not a common thing for recitals and chamber concerts, but designed to accommodate the children performing, as well as the needs of audience members, for it was not uncommon for men in attendance to have a nip from a flask or take snuff together in the lobby.

"How was it, how was it, Father?" Luis asked behind stage,

dancing around in a little circle as Joanne was greeted in the left wing by doting family members and friends.

"Good, good, but too exciting. Calm down, all right? Here, have some sugar water," he said, also producing a damp towel to wipe the child's face, and then his own. He looked across the room and caught Joanne's eye, giving her a smile and nod of approval, which she accepted with haughty delight as she returned to her admirers.

Luis ran to the back of the curtain, and peeked out at the audience, wishing he could hear their comments. But before long, the bell was rung, and the crowd reassembled. Daylight now was gone, and the hall was illuminated only by candlelight. The scent of perfume, pomades, burnt wicks, wax, alcohol, stale tobacco, and human sweat mingled in a new, exciting odor to the young boy, a kind of pheromone that heightened all his senses.

Joanne had three more songs, this time accompanied by Luis, who added some flourishes which would have upset the singer had she not known and liked the pianist so well. After enthusiastic applause and a few shouts, a flushed Joanne left the stage, rustling her skirts smartly. She, too, had tasted triumph, and now was ready for bigger things.

The final work on the program was the trio, moved from the middle of the program to be the capstone of a captivating evening. Bernie entered the stage with his cello and immediately received some clucks of approval from audience members who knew him, for he was well liked and a popular musical performer in the city.

John and Bernie arranged the chairs and sheet music, Luis opened the violin case and thumbed the strings, holding the instrument up to his ear to make sure it was in tune. They took their seats, and at John's nod from the keyboard, began to play in G major.

It was not a great work of music, and to a certain degree, John, who controlled the performance, made it more boring than it deserved. Perhaps he was trying to neutralize the (to his mind) overly emotional performance his son had given. But dullness was not to be, for shortly into the first movement, the effects of the cello rosin on Luis's bow began to tell. A nerve-wracking screech came from the violin. John was horrified, but kept playing, perhaps a bit louder. Bernie provided a smooth, rich counterpoint, but the damage was done. The next solo violin passage contained a similar squawk like an owl descending on a mouse.

"Softer, softer," whispered John over the keyboard. Luis was persisting, continuing to play, and as he played more softly, the noise diminished. But by now, he was becoming nervous and self-conscious, his little hands cold and damp. The audience was roused, and sat at attention, at first concerned, but then a titter of laughter started in the back.

The second movement was slow and rich with some impressive cello work, and Bernie, seeing the disaster unfold beside him, took charge, and emphasized his own playing in an attempt to minimize the squeakiness of Luis's playing. But even as he played more softly and tried to lessen the sound, the child's weak technique also began to tell, and at one point he lost his place in the score. As they launched into the last movement, the child was blushing visibly, even in the golden light.

Meanwhile, the titter swept forward in the hall, and even some of the more privileged, high-ranking aristocrats in the front row and boxes smiled or whispered in their seats. In the speed of the final moments, the screeching occasionally pierced the sound of the hall. Now there was actual laughter in the audience, and at the peak of his final trill, the high E string on his violin snapped. By this time, the audience was in high spirits, fueled no doubt by some of the alcohol consumed at intermission, and a roar of laughter burst from one section of the hall. John and Bernie managed to recoup and complete the piece with minimal improvisation by Luis on the lower three strings. The child was suffering the tortures of the damned as the work came to a bright conclusion, though not one Haydn would ever have imagined.

The audience was divided, some laughing, some expressing disgust, some whispering. John firmly grabbed Luis by the elbow and forced him to the front of the stage to take a bow. There was even greater laughter, and from the front rows, the child heard, "Did you see him turn red? Like an Indian from the Americas!" the jibes continued.

"Rousseau would love this," the jiber's companion retorted. "What a story to tell our friends! And to think I almost didn't come tonight!"

John was adamant. He would take the jibes, the comments, and he would make his son endure fully the punishment that comes to those who do not practice and do not follow orders. This is what happens when you go your own way. This is what happens when you follow your headstrong impulses and do not heed the advice of your teachers and betters.

The ordeal ended at last, and backstage, Luis got a stern shaking from his father, who would have included blows had Bernie not been there in a conciliatory mood, trying to actually make the boy feel better.

"You did wonderful," the cellist insisted, kneeling down beside him, "I never heard such an ovation for those solo pieces! The violin…it wasn't your fault! I've had strings break, you'll get over this, I promise!"

"You are not helping, Bernie," said the father sternly. "This all comes of his stubbornness!" He tried to level a blow at the boy's head, but Bernie intercepted it.

"Not so rough, John," he said, standing up. "The boy did well on his own instrument, remember that."

"We'll talk about it later," grumbled John beginning to walk away. But as he turned, he came face to face with a tall, well dressed gentleman accompanied by a short, round-faced woman with a fine high wig and an aristocratic air. John stopped, not certain what to do, but thought a bow would be in order. A bow, even though the man had African features and was the color of smoke.

The man nodded, and said, "Mr. Beethoven. My wife and I enjoyed your performance. The young lady's voice was enchanting. But the boy's performance was mesmerizing!"

"I trust you mean on the piano," said John wryly. The stranger looked at Luis, lurking back in the shadows as he might have done several years earlier. "Do you mind if I speak to him?" the tall man asked.

John motioned for Luis to come forward. Bernie smiled to himself, as though knowing who was about to address him.

"Come here, lad, don't be shy," the tall man said. "I am Baron Etufu, from Cambridge and the Gold Coast. My wife, Elsa, and I enjoyed your playing very much and wanted to give you encouragement," he said in his elegant accent. He turned to the father, who was actually speechless. "We were passing through the city and heard of the concert. We are fond of music, and happy to attend."

He turned to the child and held out his hand. "Lad, place your hand in mine, please." Luis shyly placed his small hand in the hand of the tall man. He looked at the two hands together and noted how similar they looked, though the Baron's fingers were long and narrow while Luis's own fingers were short, stubby, and over-developed.

"My boy," he said, squatting down as no local aristocrat would ever have done, "the man who is master of his trade, no matter what trade it may be, is the true aristocrat. You have proven yourself today, so do not despair. You are so young, so small, but you have a wonderful future ahead of you. Do not let the detractors and critics deter you. Do you promise me that?"

Luis nodded, and looked up at the man's kind face. Luis noticed his features, his high cheek bones and broad lips and nose, the clear expanse of his forehead. "We must go now," he said to John as he stood up. "You have done very well teaching your son, sir. He will make you proud. Do not pay attention to this business with the fiddle!" The Baron smiled and nodded toward Bernie, then took his wife's arm and departed briskly.

"Well," said John, looking after the couple, "I never."

Bernie chuckled to himself. "My friend," he said. "It has been quite a day."

Chapter 19

THE REMAINDER OF THE YEAR was a busy one for the Beethovens. Whatever his carefree habits were in youth, John now had few idle moments during the day, though he had returned to carousing after nightfall with a good friend who had returned to the city, Toby Piper.

Toby was no mean musician, and John saw the opportunity to enjoy the company of this engaging scalawag, perhaps profit through his connections, and also gain another good teacher for his precocious son.

Mary rolled her eyes when she heard that Toby was in town, and protested firmly when John told her the affable rascal was moving in with them in the back bedroom. With three young sons already and another child on the way, she told John she did not see how she could keep house for another adult, especially one who would be a bad influence on the children.

John just laughed and put his arm around Mary. "He won't be a problem, I would stake my life on it!" he said in a reassuring tone she had come to distrust. "He is a fine musician now, you'll see, and not only a great teacher for our Luis, but he'll pay his rent and board in lessons, just wait!"

It did not sound like an ideal situation to Mary. She already had so much to deal with, and knew from experience, that Toby would lure John back into his old drinking patterns and the resulting misery it would bring on the family. But there was no arguing with John. She sighed and sent a note to her friend

Henny, indicating she would appreciate any help that stalwart companion could offer in the months ahead.

In the meantime, Luis was learning how to juggle lessons from a growing and ever-changing complement of teachers. His school lessons were irregular, and John would often pull him out of class for days at a time to perform or meet a new teaching specialist.

So the whirlwind of his life continued. With John as his teacher and now his life coach, Luis never knew from one day to the next where he would be studying or what he would be doing next. At day's end, Luis would sit before his bedroom window, gazing out at the Seven Mountains darkening in the distance, listening to the horns of vessels on the river, his brain a-swirl with the busy moments of his life: teachers, instruments, school lessons, his bratty brothers, the new baby on the way, strangers attending impromptu concerts in the music room, Father, loving Mother, now Mr. Piper down the hall. He felt fortunate now to have a small piano in his room. For when allowed to, when all the people and responsibilities were gone for an hour or two, he could play as he wanted and what he wanted, even if it was just the weaving of musical dreams and the spinning of songs that only he could hear.

Late one night as John and his houseguest sat in the kitchen drinking and grousing about perceived injustices, the boy's father heard a movement down the hall, and hushed Piper suddenly. "Luis!" he called. "Is that you? That freaking eavesdropping blackguard…"

John steadied himself and got up and staggered down the hall. Piper heard a scuffle and shouts, then, "Toby! Come here, you have to hear this boy practice the Bach. You may be a wretched creature, boy, but you got the Bach right." It was close to midnight, and the tired child, in his long nightshirt, was dragged into the parlor, wishing all the while he hadn't gone into the hall to listen.

"John, what's the matter?" Mary called downstairs.

"Shut up, we're going to have a little recital here and then a music lesson. We get these lessons from Piper in payment, so let's get our money's worth, right?"

Mary shook her head sadly, but it was a familiar story, one she had hoped would stop as Luis got older. Again, the quiet night was broken by the music of the pianoforte, as the small hands first magically unfolded the preludes, then, tiring, began to make mistakes, and then came the shouting and encouraging and berating. The crying. Finally, after several hours, the men retreated to the kitchen for more refreshments, taking the boy with them, and pouring him an ale. Then back to the piano and an "official lesson" from Piper, as the night continued on. By dawn, the two men were asleep, one on a couch and the other on some curtains pulled into a corner of the floor, while Luis had dragged himself upstairs to bed. His fingertips were sore, and there was no one to comfort him.

Although the pattern of night drinking and late practice had returned, there were also times of refreshment for the boy and his family, prompted by two occasions: the Elector being away and not requiring the choir's services; and the arrival on the Beethoven doorstep of Cousin Frank.

Chapter 20

COUSIN FRANK ARRIVED on one of the rare days in which Luis was at school. Mary opened the door, stared, and then burst into sobs of happiness, hugging the young man gleefully. "Frankie, Frankie, oh, I'm so happy to see you!" The tall young man blushed deeply, embarrassed by such a show of affection, not realizing how long it had been since Mary had expressed so much emotion.

"Aunt Mary, I hope I haven't disturbed you…"

"Frankie, Frankie, come in," she pleaded pulling his arm which was already laden with several pieces of luggage and a violin case. "Oh, Frankie, how many years has it been? I don't think you were more than 15." She ushered him into the kitchen and sat him down by the fire. "What brings you here, sonny?" she said, reaching for an earthenware mug and setting the kettle to boil. "I hope you like peppermint tea."

Frank smiled softly and brushed back his hair. He was a handsome, otherworldly looking young man, spectacles perched on his nose, with a nice mane of hair of which he was obviously proud. He put his baggage on the floor and let out a little sigh of weariness.

"I've been traveling a few days, yes, mint tea would be welcome," he said. Mary looked at the luggage with his name stamped on it: F.G. Rovantini. John would not be pleased to see a relative from the Italian side of her family in the house, even if he were only half Italian and had visited Milan but once.

"Thank you for inviting me in, Aunt Mary," he said, gratefully accepting the tea and taking several of the small cakes she offered. Despite his almost ascetic appearance, he did devour them ravenously, thought Mary. I wonder what story he has to tell, she thought.

It didn't take long for the story to emerge. Frank had been working in the south, but a new bishop had reduced the musical staff by a third. Frank knew of a few freelance openings in the north, near the river, and decided to seek his fortune, being only 20 at the time. But life had not been kind to the mild-mannered musician, whose great talent was eclipsed by his self-effacing and modest nature.

"Frankie, where are you going to stay?" Mary asked after hearing his hard-luck story. With no response, she quickly added, "You must stay here!"

"Oh, I couldn't do that," Frank protested. "Aunt Mary, you are expecting a child. Do you have others?"

"Three boys," she said, smiling, "and a husband, who is more trouble than a child sometimes. Then there are other interlopers who pass through these doors. That scalawag Piper is staying in the end room, but he does pay his rent in terms of lessons for Luis, he's our oldest boy." She looked fondly at Frank. "You know, you could teach him, too, I am certain. He has so many teachers, I can't keep track of them, but my husband thinks he could be some sort of Wunderkind and support us all, but I just want the boy to be happy and have a decent living, that's all. Heaven knows, he has enough strikes against him!"

Frank looked up, and wiped the steam from his glasses. "What do you mean?" he asked. "Has he a handicap of some sort?"

"In a way," Mary said, lowering her voice. "Do you remember Uncle Ebert?" Frank raised an eyebrow.

"Dark, is he?" asked Frank.

"Yes, not just dark, but he has the features, too, and his father insists he has the disposition, but I don't know what he means. The boy is as gentle as a lamb." Mary looked away, grimacing. "We thank the good God for making all mankind, then curse those who are made differently."

Frank nodded. "I know," he said, "just being Italian is bad in the north, unless you happen to have a bishop or Elector who is fond of Italian music!" he noted. "I believe that is the case with your Elector?"

Mary looked at Frank and smiled. "That is true, I am sure you would not be turned away here. And you are half northern, too, so that is an advantage. Well," she said, "my friend Henny is here today, we'll make up the other spare room, it's been used as storage."

"Oh, please, Aunt, do not trouble yourself, wait until I have a living…"

"You have a living here," said Mary, patting his hand. "I'll talk to John, he'll understand. Tell him all about your experience, don't hold anything back! I know you've had an impressive career performing and teaching, and that he would want you to be on his side, not in competition."

Mary's instincts were right, and after quickly making the last spare room inhabitable, she and the wary Henny, not certain whether the young man was sufficiently respectable for the household, helped him move into his new lodgings. Once settled, he went out into town with a list of contacts, and a smile of gratitude.

"You did what? And who did you say this is?" John asked over their evening meal, fish from the river with noodles. He had had a frustrating day of teaching, and the Elector was preparing for a trip to another district, causing a bit of an uproar in the process.

"You remember Frankie," she insisted, "he is a saint that boy, and earned quite a nice living in the south, you know that." John glared at his plate, as though seeing through the fishbones some antagonist invisible to everyone around him. "John, he can teach Luis better than that friend of yours…"

"Piper stays!" said John, punctuating his words with a stab of his knife onto the table.

"Well, see what you think. Frankie can tell you about all the students he had, and how successful they've become! He is quite accomplished for so young a man, and my whole family is proud of him!"

"Your family!" John bleated, but a kinder glow glazed over his eyes as he remembered what he had heard about Rovantini. Those damn Italians, he thought. And yet, that is what the Elector seemed to like. It wouldn't hurt him to align himself, and in particular, the boy, with an experienced musician with an Italian name. And Frank was a polished person with fine manners, good grooming, and a pleasant personality.

"Well," he said, "despite what we both know about your family, he may stay." Mary's face relaxed into a rare smile. "But there are still a few things to straighten out," he said. "I need to talk to him…tomorrow! He needs to find work and pay for that room. I need to determine whether he has anything to teach our boy. And Piper stays!"

It was enough to win one small battle. Mary knew there would be no end to the war.

Chapter 21

ONE BITTER WINTER'S DAY, the cry of a new baby added to the musical cacophony of the River Street house. For the first time, Mary had given birth to a girl, Anna.

"Isn't she sweet," Luis said the next day, racing to the side of his mother. The baby cooed, pale like the other brothers, but flushed. Luis smoothed her baptismal dress and rubbed the top of her little head with his rough hand. Mrs. Beethoven smiled slightly, and rocked the child softly.

Sadly, a few days later, Anna died of a fever. The family was strangely quiet, but the death seemed to affect Luis more deeply than it did his younger brothers. It had been a hard blow for the young boy. He skipped classes at school, and on several occasions, did not sleep at home at night. But he had only slept at the baker Krupp's house, where he was a welcome guest and regular visitor, when time permitted, and always came home with a warm roll or small cake in his pocket. But this was no happy "sleep over" for the child, whose mood grew somber. It was not until spring, and the warm, insistent encouragement of his cousin Frank, that the dark days of winter, the oppressiveness of his spirit, lifted.

One morning, Frank woke the sleeping boy, and led him to the window overlooking a tree just coming into leaf. "Look there," he pointed, with a smile. Luis yawned, but craned his neck, for he knew Frank would not awaken him without good reason.

"Oh, a nest!" he cried at last as his young eyes came into focus.

The two watched as a pair of doves put together a nest of twigs, leaves, and even a bit of string not far from the window ledge.

"It is always a miracle to see," said Frank, kindly. "They have their houses and families, just as we do, and make music, too, perhaps a purer, finer music than man can make. So, Luis, you have company now, and not the noisy kind that steals your pocket money and hides in the hall closet!" he said with a wink. Luis smiled shyly, then propped his chin on folded arms over the window sill. Nature, he learned, could heal all things, even a broken heart.

Nature had, after all, a special meaning for the sensitive young boy. Stopping to sniff a lily, he absorbed the golden color, the brown stamens and pistils, and every speck of pollen dust; he became the lily, golden glow of the lily and how it deepened with the day, and the perfume, undetectable to most, filled his lungs, and spread into his arms and legs and out through the tips of fingers and toes, back into the world.

He became the bee, the hum of the bee, the fur of the bee's coat and the scratch of its claws, invisible to other eyes, but not to his. The green leaves, the earth below, the worms, the little insects all like choristers singing a song that was his own song, for he was the song they sang. And the trees especially, when he ran into the woods, the trees rushed up and grabbed him and wrapped him in their long arms and lifted him up, and he was their sap, and they were his refuge, and they held him up to the sky, the blue, cloud-tossed sky, which had its own perfume which only he could know, a perfume so strong and intoxicating it drenched all the organs of his body, and he himself became the organ of the sky, the vehicle through which it knew itself.

And night, with silver moonlight and millions of shining stars shooting their tiny points of fire, penetrated his innermost being. Every hair on his body stood on end, like little receptors linking outside and in, and his eyes glazed and he could no longer see, and no longer hear, and no longer smell, but only feel, feeling without thought or reference point as though nature and he compressed into one unity of flow. Then the sky reached down to the dark grey Rhine, endlessly rocking to the north, and he would find himself wading in the shallows, with the seabirds who were nothing but projections of himself, and he would spread his broad white wings when morning came, and fly into that rising fire in the East, fall as a ray on a wayside flower and emerge in a shower of light and breathe in all life, all continuity, all cyclicity, over and over again, until something jolted him back into the world of parents and deeds, and he would shake his head, and hurry home.

And as it was with nature, with music it was the same.

That spring was a memorable one for Luis, as his spirits soared after the darkness of the dreadful winter. There were many lovely days made more wonderful by the Elector's trips abroad. This meant more time for leisure activities and outings, and increasingly being treated as a mature person, not a little boy, at least in things musical. John got on well with Frank, after all, and did not seem to hold his southern surname against him. Luis, Frank, and John would sometimes play trios, or invite Piper to sit in with his oboe, an instrument that Luis had no intention of studying. But what Luis loved most, were the trips into the countryside with a basket of cold pork, cabbage, and biscuits, a break from everything and yet an entrée into everything that mattered: the clear blue sky, the humming of bees, the cuckoo, the first warm breezes of spring through the hay and fields of wild blue flowers.

On one such day, John and Frank took Luis to see the orchards and vineyards around the mountains, a good walk from town. The air was clear, the clouds fluffy and abundant, and there were flocks of birds in every direction. The two men let him run himself out while they talked about the latest theatrical news and how they could turn recent events to their own advantage. Frank, though, occasionally looked ahead and smiled softly as he watched the boy romping with a light heart. "Don't let him get too close to the nettles," he cautioned John, who didn't seem to pay attention. "And there are fleas, you know, in those bushes…" Again, no response.

As they approached a large administrative building beside a vineyard, Luis, panting a bit, wound his way back to his parent, and walked between the two men as they approached the office, hoping to gain permission to enter the grounds, where there was also a fine wine-tavern where John knew the May wine would be fresh and clear.

"Good day," said John as a rather gruff wine master stepped out to meet them.

"Good day, sir," he said. The man was large with a broad, barrel-like belly, and a thick brown mustache. A permanent crease between his eyebrows gave some indication of his inflexible personality.

"We'd like to try your new wine," said John. Luis wandered next to Frank, and hung onto his arm, squinting at the man.

"You gentlemen are welcome," he said, "but we don't have none of that!"

John looked puzzled. "What do you mean? Should we leave

our basket outside. That is no problem…"

"Leave your black boy out, too," said the wine master bluntly. John didn't flinch, but Frank gave a small gasp and held Luis's hand more tightly.

"We're not having servants and riffraff here," the man said, wheeling around and starting back in.

John turned bright red. "Begging your pardon, sir," he said between clenched teeth, "I must have missed the guest list! I can assure you that the child will not be drinking…"

The wine master turned again, and folded his large, muscular arms across his chest. "I don't care if he drinks or not; we don't let them kind in here, d'you understand? The owners have a policy: no gypsies and Africans, there been some disturbance in the past, some problem with them being too familiar with the women…"

John put his hands on his hips, looked quickly at Frank and then back to the wine master, with a laugh of disbelief. "Sir, I guarantee this boy…my SON!…will NOT make any passes at your womenfolk!"

The wine master spat on the grass near John's feet and looked contemptuously at Luis, who was shrinking back. "I'll sell you a bottle, take it somewhere else."

Frank pulled on Luis's hand and started to walk away, but John put his hands in his pocket for a moment, and weighed the advantages of tasting some fresh new wine, even if not in the Heuriger. "I'll take two bottles, then," he said, "and not another word about my boy!"

The wine master shoved two bottles across the counter, took John's payment, and walked back into the building. A little distance off, Frank looked back with disgust, that John would do business with such a bigot. "How could you do that?" he gushed as John approached. "How could you give him your money?"

"I stood up for my son," said John, "what more do you want? This creature has caused me no end of grief, at least we will get some good wine out of the experience."

Frank did not say much to John the rest of the day. For his part, John enjoyed the wine, and had very little to bring home when their outing was over. Luis's high spirits were dampened, and he hung gloomily near Frank, kicking stones into the underbrush, as they made their way home.

Chapter 22

ROVANTINI WAS DEEPLY DISTRESSED by what had happened at the vineyard. He remembered once as a small child being tormented by a gang of fair-haired children because he was different. Italians had risen to the highest ranks in business and government, certainly in music. But there were few blacks in this part of the world. Rovantini had had a good education, the finest in his family, and knew what the leading thinkers of the age thought about people of color.

And so Frank tossed and turned that night, burning with the twin afflictions of righteous anger and the frustration of knowing there was no way he could change prevailing cultural views.

As Rovantini wrestled with questions of race and equity, another of Luis's teachers was wrestling with quite a different phenomenon. When not playing in taverns and small theaters, or teaching a few students in the Beethoven parlor, Piper would be at the local brothel or attempting to seduce young women waiting tables and pouring drinks at the many pubs he frequented, often with John. For his part, John would have no part of the womanizing: he was too focused on his schemes and coveted the red lips of a bottle of claret more than any temptress. John enjoyed his friend's company, but was concerned about his moral laxity.

"You'll set a bad example for the boy," he lectured, much too often to Piper's satisfaction, "and besides, you'll get in trouble with the parents of our female students. Music lessons set a moral tone; for some, that tone is the goal of lessons, more important than simply playing the fiddle or piano!" But Piper would simply chuckle, pat John on the back, and continue to search the dark tavern with wandering eyes peering over the edge of his stein.

It was no wonder, then, that Luis preferred the lessons and companionship of his cousin Frank, rather than those of the foul-breathed friend of his father, who was in part responsible for those nightlong practice sessions, sometimes ending at dawn. Regrettably, Piper was an excellent musician and a tolerable teacher, and so John kept him on for reasons beyond friendship.

The earnest cousin, at the opposite end of the moral spectrum, one night decided to write to the brother of an old university friend. The brother, Simon, was now an instructor in philosophy at Halle, an institution known for its progressive and enlightened views. Hadn't the black philosopher Amo studied there, as well as one of the first women medical students to graduate with an M.D., Dorothea Erxleben? Rovantini smiled to himself: the world was going to become a different place. Backward towns such as this one, which persecuted people for their differences, surely would fall to the march of Progress! One day, Jews and Gentiles, Blacks and Whites, Women and Men, would work together without prejudice.

Rovantini stopped and shook his head sadly: his idealism was getting the best of him once again. But certainly he could take small steps on his own to improve the world. He would adopt the cause of his cousin Luis, and to do so, must understand all the current thought both in favor of, and against, people of color in the northern states. His first step was to seek this information through Simon Wert, his friend's brother, and to begin to map a plan of action from that point onward.

Rovantini's inquiries, however, did yield a welcome, if unexpected result. Wert wrote back to him within a few days, intrigued by his letter and equally passionate about the topic of human brotherhood.

Frank eagerly tucked the letter in his breast pocket for later review. As soon as the day's lessons were over, he raced up the stairs to his room, closed the door securely, and sat on the old wooden chair by the window overlooking River Street. There in the bright morning light, he unfolded the correspondence and read the words of a man who was soon to be his friend.

My dear Rovantini, the letter began, yes, I do remember you from Andy's conversation and notes. He spoke highly of you and your interests far beyond those of music and theater. The topic you raised in your letter is of great interest to the leading anthropologists and anatomists of our time, who just happen to be clustered in universities between our two locations.

Frank nodded to himself as he read Simon's recounting of the various ethnic arguments prevalent at that time. Simon then invited Frank to accompany him on a visit to a scientifically supervised experiment not far away, where theories were being tested.

Do see if you can break away from your teaching schedule for a few weeks to go with me. A living laboratory in the wild, not in a university lecture hall. There we may see for ourselves what scholarship is developing and perhaps better arm ourselves to join an academic debate.

Very sincerely yours,

Simon Wert

Professor of Cultural Philosophy

Halle University

Frank read the short letter again, and made careful note of the return address. Yes, this was the sort of inspiration and action he was looking for. Like many young men at the end of the 18th century, he was seized by notions of justice and caught up in ideas about equality and fairness. The spirit of the American Revolution, the growing spirit of rebellion in France fed by the ideas of Rousseau (though he, too, had a some unsettling views of race) and other free thinkers, inspired him as well, though he was only an itinerant musician with a serious academic background and some excellent university connections.

But sadly, he was also aware that popular sentiment, while in support of equal rights for men of European origin, did not look kindly on people from other parts of the world, especially Asia and Africa. Indeed, even to resemble outsiders was a crime to the narrow-minded.

I will do it, he said to himself, firmly folding the letter and returning it to its envelope. I have enough funds to support such an adventure, and there is no better time for it, given the urgency of Wert's request, my own independence, and the age and opportunities of my young cousin. Within a day, Frank had written back to Wert and made arrangements to take a coach to Halle, several days' ride to the east. He quickly informed Mary of his journey, assuring her he would be back in a few weeks.

With Luis, his farewell was longer and more revealing, though the child did not fully understand his intention. "I have an opportunity," he told Luis privately in the parlor, "to help make the world a better place, for all people, not just those with pale eyes and a light complexion."

Luis set his jaw firmly. This was a topic that never went well for him.

"I've never been anywhere where I am the norm," the child said with surprising maturity. "My father will never stop referring to me as a black bastard, and the Church will keep on hiding me behind the organ screen!"

Frank nodded, surprised at how much the child noticed and how deeply prejudice had stung him. "I know, but that will change, I am sure. As you grow older and leave this parochial town, you will assert your individuality with your own bold personality and talent. Believe me, this will be so. Throughout the world, right now, people are taking a stand for the respect of all people. I hope my actions will help open a door to equality for all."

Luis didn't quite understand, but looked approvingly at Rovantini, who had become his favorite teacher in a short time, and as good a friend as an adult could be to a child. At the same time, the notion of getting away took on even greater urgency.

"Before I leave, I've asked Zambona to stop by and continue lessons in my absence," Rovantini said. "He expressed concern that you were not learning Latin, logic, and arithmetic in a systematic way, and he will give you lessons in those subjects, too."

Luis was not as thrilled with the prospect of more lessons as Frank thought he would be, but he nodded his assent. Perhaps more learning would ease his escape in a few years. "So now, dear boy, I am off on a great adventure, and will tell you all about it when I return."

Chapter 23

MARY GAVE BIRTH YET AGAIN that winter, to a healthy boy whom, with John's permission, she named after Cousin Frank. This added to the mood of hope and optimism as Frank bid his farewells to the growing family and embarked on a journey east.

The carriage route from Bonn to Halle was a direct one, occasionally through the hills, but bad weather meant time on the road. Exhausted and a little disarrayed by the trip, Frank felt his heart soar, however, as the university towers came into view. It was not a huge complex, but a welcoming sight as one of the centers of enlightened thinking in this part of the world.

Frank left the carriage with his traveling bag and violin, and got directions to Wert's small study south of the library. There were a few students and some faculty on the campus at this late hour, and Frank hoped he would find the professor without delay. Luck was on his side, and Simon was packing up his books as Frank appeared at the door.

"Professor Wert?" he asked, holding his head a bit sideways to get a better look at the young instructor. Wert was prematurely grey, with a large mop of unruly hair that tapered down into a long but thin white beard at his chin. His pale blue eyes were clouded with study, but regained their youthful spark as he came to realize the identity of his visitor.

"You must be Rovantini!" he said warmly, extending his hand. It was cold in the study, and Wert's hand was cool, though energetic, to the touch. The two men did not immediately say anything, as each was tired from his exertions.

"Well," said Simon, "let us have a late dinner in the dining hall. I've reserved a room for your stay for a week. They have some good red wine and goulash, it's really quite tasty here!"

The two men crossed the darkening campus, as lanterns began to appear in windows, and those outdoors were being lit. Once he had transitioned from silent study to human society, the professor began talking in an affable manner, and was scarcely silent the rest of the evening. They talked over a substantial meal served on a long wooden table that looked as though it had been in use since the founding of the school a hundred years earlier, about the time that the composer Handel was born and lived in the surrounding city.

"You are tired, Rovantini," said Wert, as they finished an excellent strudel and poured another cup of wine. "So tomorrow is fine for us to go over my plans. I hope you do not mind that I have micromanaged everything..." Frank gestured that he did not "...but we haven't much time, and we do need, again I am sorry, to ride west out of town to visit the site of an experiment that purports to be scientific, but which is cruelty and bias incarnate, in my opinion." Frank raised a eyebrow and put down his fork.

"That is why I have come," he said earnestly, "to see if there is any way I can assist you in the study of bias as it affects my student and relative, but on a larger scale, affects all people in our land."

The next day, having rested as best as he could in the austere dormitory room, Frank joined Simon in one of the side rooms in the library. Libraries always filled Frank with awe and wonder; a good education had never been invested more wisely than in this talented musician and lover of justice. The main hall had tall ceilings, with leather-bound books in maroon, brown, and black lined neatly on shelves that reached to the top, with two tiers of walkways and ladders all about.

"You are familiar with my friend, Blumenbach, an acquaintance, really," said Simon. "He is conducting some excellent theoretical research into the different types of human beings, those from Europe, Asia, the Islands, Africa, and so forth." Frank nodded. Simon paused for some time before he continued, as though not quite knowing how to phrase a difficult thought. "Rovantini, you know I am a theoretician. I do not experiment on people, though I have some anatomical specimens of animals in my study, you may have noticed. But I am troubled, I must say, by an experiment now underway in the area of Kassel, halfway between our two cities."

"Who is behind this experiment? Is it a university?" Frank asked.

"It is the duke himself!" said Simon. "He toys with people and has no true interest in knowledge unless it will advance his own status and support his stunted range of ideas."

Simon explained that the duke had just started a colony of Africans on a bluff overlooking the Eder River. The avowed purpose was to study their anatomy, their rituals, beliefs, and community. However, rumor in the academic community was that many of these captured people were dying and their bodies, rather than being surrendered to their families, were being subjected to unholy experiments.

"That can't possibly work," exclaimed Frank. "Does he really think people will replicate their culture on foreign soil?

Do these people agree to the experiment, or are they taken by force, like slaves?"

"Clearly, our duke has ulterior motives," said the professor. "After all, he made a good income renting soldiers to Great Britain to stop American freedom fighters, so you can see where his values lie. Of course, even an amateur scientist such as myself knows that you can't uproot people from their environment, place them in a foreign country, and then expect to learn how they behave. The shock of relocation would completely invalidate the experiment."

Agreeing that the project was worth seeing first-hand, the two men called it a day. Wert had informed a colleague in Kassel that he would be stopping in the area for a few days, so the visit was not unexpected, and Frank would be accepted as a necessary assistant to the professor.

"Remember," Simon told Frank, "we must not interfere in the experiment, simply observe." Rovantini nodded, though in his heart knew he could not remain silent if he encountered cruelty or abuse of any kind. The weather was clear as the pair went by coach to the small riverside city. The inn was just in the shadow of the bluff, which could be reached in an hour of walking. Since the men were granted a visit for less than two days, time was of the essence.

"I can't wait," said Frank, energized by the brisk coach ride and the fresh river air, "why don't we head up the hill today. The sun doesn't set until after 8 this evening."

Wert agreed. "We'll take a look, you can take notes, if you don't mind, to keep the appearance of an objective, scholarly visit by a professor and his assistant."

"I've the notebook right here!" agreed Frank. The men

fortified themselves in the inn's tavern, and began walking up the hill. There were markers along the path, though nothing to indicate that anything other than a local building project was taking shape away from the eyes of the town below.

Chapter 24

THE MEN EASILY CLIMBED to the top of the embankment, walked through a clearing and into the beginning of a forest characterized by new growth. After 10 minutes or so, a crude road appeared to their right, which they followed for a few more minutes until it ended in a kind of hub from which three equally crude roadways emerged. They did not have long to make a decision regarding which to take, for the approaching sound of horses and wheels indicated a large coach, perhaps two, were heading their way. As the two men hid in the bushes, a freight coach rumbled by and headed northeast. It was followed by another…and another. In all, four of the transports rumbled by, leaving a spray of dust and a cloud of small stones and pebbles as they flew through the woods.

Frank and Wert now knew the path to follow, and continued about a mile until they came to another clearing with a large, roughly constructed compound set on higher ground. But on closer look, it was actually a mixture of the rough and the refined, the incomplete and the finished. In fact, it was the most curious sight either man had seen before.

In general, the compound resembled a military fort of the sort constructed quickly in the frontier. The complex rang with the discordant sounds of sawing, hammering, dragging, brick-laying, and now the releasing of tired horses, the settling of wagons, all sounds unpleasing to Frank's sensitive hearing. The exterior stockade was only about seven feet tall, but just behind it were stone walls up to 20 feet high in some areas, which masons at that moment were hastening to complete. In the front, a long hall extended the full width behind a gate. The walls were very thick, like a prison, and Frank shuddered at the thought of being pent up behind those walls with no hope of escape.

But even more curious was the design, for a highly sophisticated, unfamiliar design scheme—left incomplete—was the most striking feature of this odd complex. Frank touched Wert's shoulder to get his attention and said, "Isn't that gate rather peculiar?"

Wert nodded without turning his head or taking his squinting eyes off of the entrance. "Yes, quite," he agreed. "Ming Dynasty, if I am not mistaken."

"Chinese, then?" asked Frank.

Wert turned and faced him, "Yes, I do believe the experiment was intended for Chinese subjects. This gate was designed to make them feel comfortable and at home." Both men then scanned the impregnable penitentiary behind the gates, looked at each other, and raised their eyebrows in near disbelief.

Beyond the imposing gate, the Asian theme continued, pagodas intermingled with frontier-style dormitories. A main hall, presumably for administration and perhaps living quarters for facility management, rose from the center of the community, just behind an open court with the beginnings of gardens and a collection of odd, large rocks. The main hall had been completed early in the project for the convenience of on-site management. Crimson paint extended up to the massive double pagoda roof that provided shade on all sides of the structure.

"I don't know what to say," said Frank.

"It is truly remarkable," noted Wert, jotting notes into his travel journal and sketching everything he could see. "Just when you think you've seen or read about or imagined everything! Well, we are expected, at least for a few hours visit. There shouldn't be a problem. Let's see if van Hook, the complex executive, is able to see us."

The two men emerged from their hiding place and walked over to the gate. "Stop!" shouted a guard, swirling about. He pointed a musket at the two. He was a sandy-haired, muscular yeoman in a hat of the type that is typically worn on safari. "Stand your ground. Who are you, what do you want?"

"May I produce documents testifying to my identity?" Wert asked, not daring to reach into his pocket.

"No false moves," warned the guard. "Slowly."

Wert very slowly removed the papers from his pocket and handed them over. A second guard appeared on the scene and similarly aimed a musket at the men.

"Looks all right, what do you think, Jan?" The two men looked at the paper. "I am surprised they can read," whispered Wert to Frank, out of the corner of his mouth.

"Come in," the first guard called once past the gate. The visitors entered the courtyard. It was a busy scene, with building tradesmen putting the finishing touches on a construction that at once resembled a picture from a Chinese fairy tale and a severe penitentiary on the northern frontier. The four freight coaches were visible through a moon gate on the other side of the compound.

In the middle of the courtyard stood a tall man, obviously a foreman or leader of some sort, in a coarse but well cut linen jacket, trousers, and tall boots, with a wide-brimmed hat set at a jaunty angle. He had long red hair and a beard, and as they drew closer, noticed his youthful face and blue eyes.

"Well, you must be the academic visitors from Halle," he said pleasantly, striding over to his guests. "I am van Hook, pleased to meet you. I understand you want to spend an hour or two looking at our experiment? Very interesting it is, too, I think you'll find it meets the standards for university research!"

Van Hook was the sort of man who becomes too familiar too quickly. He wrapped his arm around Wert's shoulder, and half dragged him to the main building, the one with the double pagoda, chatting all the while.

"Let's go in for a moment, I'll orient you, then you can take a look around, perhaps with my assistant, Barker." Another fair-haired man appeared briefly and went back to his writing. As they walked through the zigzagging hall, Rovantini noticed the other men in the building: secretaries, perhaps an architect, then several large black men in rustic garb, clearly guards of the property.

"Slaves, yes," said van Hook dismissively, noting Frank's uneasy stare, "we have to control the subjects and keep out the idle curious. Word gets out, y'know. I'm sure Dr. Banks has filled you in."

"Not too much, actually," said Wert as the three entered what appeared to be the Dutchman's luxurious office. "I know the project is being well protected from idle curiosity, and we are privileged to have even this small access." Rovantini looked around the room, which was designed in the Oriental style in shades of sage green and rose, with potted plants, a large window and a number of mechanical fans. One wall was covered in books, another in weapons.

"Perhaps you could tell us something that is puzzling," said Wert, scanning the room slowly. "Why is there a Chinese theme to this complex?"

Van Hook laughed, a hard laugh of disdain. "That's a good question. They spent months setting up this façade with the intention of studying Chinese subjects, before even trying to find them! The Chinese wanted no part of it, and not being subject to enslavement, at least not on as grand a scale as the inhabitants of Africa, the Duke's men were unable to persuade them to participate. As a fallback, I was called in with the intent of substituting Africans for the Chinese. Too bad about the architecture, but obviously we weren't about to change it all into a make-believe village for Hottentots!"

Van Hook didn't seem to mind that his visitors did not appreciate his sense of humor.

"I am not an authority on the purpose of this project, just an administrator," said van Hook after a pause, taking off his hat with a flourish and sinking into his chair. An attractive black servant brought in a tray of juice and glasses, with some sweet biscuits. "Good, Ekua," he said, reaching over for a glass, his eyes following the graceful woman's departure. "Have some?" he asked his guests. "There's not much to see, really. The Duke demands knowledge, the resident professors are all too ready to serve. They are setting up a lab here, a lab for experiments, but not with animals, and not with humans either."

"Excuse me, sir, but I believe we did see several coaches approaching as we walked up the hill," added Wert, becoming irritated by his host's flippant manner.

"Well, hardly human," he said. He couldn't help but notice the icy reception his words received. "No matter, we treat them well, whether they be men or baboons."

"What is your own background, Mr. van Hook?" asked Rovantini.

"I've done some time in Africa," he said evasively. "Resource management, working with the plantations in Haiti. Well, I would suggest you may want to look at the construction plans. I'll have them laid out in the conference room and library the next room over. You may take notes, of course, but please do not take any of the items with you." He smiled coldly.

"I presume you would want to see the dwellings tomorrow and talk briefly to one of the professors here," he added, as though concluding the interview.

"Why, yes, that would be fine," said Wert. He and Rovantini exchanged guarded glances. "We will accept your offer and view the material in the next room and then return tomorrow. We appreciate your time and the access."

"Don't thank me," said van Hook, rising, "I am just following orders. Hope you enjoy your stay, stop by tomorrow after lunch," he said, taking the men to the door of his office, and quickly closing it behind them.

Wert and Rovantini were somewhat surprised that an armed Dutchman appeared suddenly and nudged them swiftly toward the main gate, like a herding dog with its flock, not allowing time for them to look about, as they had hoped. The main gate slammed, and they were on the hill once more.

"I don't like it," said Wert, as they edged around the compound.

"Perhaps we had better leave," said Rovantini, noticing an armed lookout in the nearer of the two watchtowers. "They could eliminate us and then say it was an accident, that they thought we were intruders."

Wert nodded and the two returned to the village below. They did not have to say to each other that van Hook was not to be trusted or that there was more going on at the compound than their host revealed.

As the researchers planned their next day's visit, life was taking an unexpected turn back at the Beethoven home 170 miles to the west.

Chapter 25

JOHN BEETHOVEN RAN HIS FINGERS through his thinning hair. He held the quill tightly, perhaps too tightly, and his thin fingers were blanched whiter than usual. Clearly, he had not been sleeping enough, driving his son harder with the soft-hearted Rovantini out of the house. Piper was no longer living with the family, having escaped to a nearby town over some impropriety. Well, good riddance to him, a time-waster and not much help with the bills. Perhaps a new instructor was needed at this time.

Two teachers gone, now Luis had begun studying with a person of true merit: the fairly new court musical director, Chris Neefe (pronounced NAY-fuh), from the eastern states. Seems like a solid musician, strong background in theater, too. Knows his Bach, for sure. Not surprising, since he's a Protestant, wonder how that will work out with the court over time, John mused erratically as his quill flew over the pages. So, less with the monks, more with the court, where the money is. This tour will help, no doubt.

Luis at this very moment was entering the music room where Chris Neefe, in his early 30s, sat at his piano, his back to the door. The tall, thin musician had a deformity to his spine which gave him a crooked appearance overall. His long arms tapered down into thin fingers, some which were twisted like claws, that flew over the keyboard, releasing the fragrance of the Well-Tempered Clavier into the stuffy atmosphere. Luis sneezed, and Neefe stopped, quickly looking over his lower shoulder. It took a few seconds for his spirit to cool, but soon, his expression turned to one of kind concern and tenderness. "Come here, boy," he motioned the child towards him. "Ah, what did you think of that?"

Luis walked confidently to the piano, not paying Neefe the slightest attention. "What was that music, sir?" he asked, placing his hand boldly on the keyboard and replicating a few of the sounds just made, perfectly recalling a complex syncopation; then his eyes drinking in the sheet music before him. Neefe's lips turned up in a half smile; he was at once surprised by the child's audacity, but more so by his keen ear and musical memory. Neefe surveyed the boy, from head to toe, noting the shabby clothes, unwashed and unruly head of hair, and of course, noting the dark tint of his skin, the broad facial features, the burning eyes.

"You come highly recommended, Luis," he said at last, sitting back a bit, beginning to relax.

"As do you, sir," said the boy, looking up into the teacher's pale blue eyes. "I have had quite a few teachers," he chuckled to himself, looking down with a smile, then returning the pianist's kindly gaze. "What is this music?"

Neefe patted the seat beside him, and Luis sat down with a jolt. "The great master, Johann Sebastian Bach, dead some 30 years. Not so well known anymore."

"But why?" the boy demanded.

"His style of music is not in fashion. But it is fierce, and will endure," said Neefe, touching the score warmly. "So tell me, Luis, before we begin today, tell me who you are, what you hope to learn."

This was a new approach for Luis, and it caught him off guard. He had hoped to launch into a bravura showcase of his own talent and then begin the regimen of exercises and drills.

"Who am I?" he repeated, puzzled. He looked down for some moments, studying his hands. Then he looked up at Neefe. "I am this," his hand touched the keyboard, "and this," patting the score.

"And what of this?" asked Neefe, resting his hand on the boy's head. "And this?" touching his own heart.

"To think, to know, and to love," said Neefe. "That is what makes a musician great. And practice, of course, there is no way around that."

"I know, I know!" said Luis, rubbing hands that Neefe now noticed bore the scars of the switch. "But I never heard that what I think or what I love matters. And yet I feel that love so strongly when I play!"

"Love is the seed from which music springs, whether performed or composed originally," the teacher said.

"Love...of what?" the boy asked.

"All forms," Neefe said. "Do you love your parents?"

Luis looked away. "My mother," he said. "I love my mother more than anyone!"

Neefe nodded, starting to get the picture, remembering his own uneasy childhood with a stern, unrelenting father. "And what about your teachers and friends?"

The boy reflected. "I love my cousin Frank!" he said brightly, with a smile. "He is like a big brother to me. And, of course, my own kid brothers, though they can be very annoying."

Neefe smiled. "Yes, I suppose children can get on one's nerves," he said with gentle irony, still assessing the 10-year-old before him.

"And what," asked Neefe, "of God, of your religion?" Luis looked over his shoulder. "God is fine, I do love Him, but..."

"Yes?"

"...I think He is really outside in the woods, not inside the church!"

Neefe stifled a smile. "That is quite fair, Luis, quite fair. Genesis says God created the world, not the church. Yes, you are using your head, good work, boy!" Luis smiled slightly, surprised that he had had the nerve to tell this adult his deepest thoughts on the subject, and amazed that he was encouraged rather than criticized.

"Well," said Neefe, fingering the keys absently as he reflected, "those are the foundations of music. If you love even one person, if you love the spirit that is God, regardless of what you think about religion, you have the soul to play, the soul even to invent the most glorious music. But lacking love, you might as well be a windup music box programmed to create the same dull plodding noise over and over, for all eternity. Here, let me hear you play this from sight..." he spread two pages of a Bach prelude on the music rest..."and then you may play for me what you would typically perform for a new teacher."

Neefe slid off the bench, favoring his left arm, and stood to the side as the child sidled over to the center and leaned forward to scan the music closely. Then he raised his hands and launched into a nearly perfect sight reading, filled with fervor, feeling, and power. Neefe nodded slightly to himself, and tried to temper the upward turn at each edge of his lips. He felt the hair stand up on the back of his neck, and his eyes stung, as though he had gotten too close to a roaring fire. He knew in that moment, in the stuffy room with no windows, with the scruffy child drawing unheard of music out of the piano, that before him lay his life's work and mission, and vowed in that moment to let nothing stand in the way of the child's development as a pianist and as a human being.

Chapter 26

LUIS DID NOT MISS ROVANTINI NOW, for he had someone else in his life: a teacher of great skills and understanding, who clearly appreciated and encouraged him as he had never been encouraged before. This teacher gave him his own personal copy of the Bach Well-Tempered Clavier, full of neatly written glosses and fingering suggestions, even an occasional quote from Scripture. Neefe left no page unmarked in some way, and Luis reverenced those comments no less than the masterwork pages on which they were penned.

"I take it you are hitting it off with Neefe," John said over supper one night. The greasy kitchen where they ate had not been cleaned in some time. The rough wooden table was covered by a much mended linen cloth, spotted beyond the powers of bleach and salt. It was late afternoon in summer, and a single hard beam of sunlight shot into the room, landing on the hearth. Bowls of soup sat before the parents and three older boys, and a basket of hard bread was passed around. John Jr. and Carl kicked each other under the table and giggled, as Mary nursed young Frank George, who was barely six months old.

Luis turned his eyes up to meet his father's as the boy slurped his soup greedily. "Yes," he said, wiping his mouth on sleeve, "he is a good teacher, Father. Strict!" he added, knowing that would please his father more than any recitation of Neefe's virtues. "I practice many exercises with him!"

John snorted, and poured more ale into his cup. "You've had

enough drill, boy, now we need to make a working musician out of you. When I was your age…"

Luis's ears closed to the recitation of what was coming. His face was almost buried in the soup bowl, and he managed to grab another end of bread before the younger boys did. His mind was humming pleasantly, though: the small, intriguing puzzles of the Bach carved fresh impressions on the young brain, and the inventiveness of the boy's original thoughts took cues from the Bach and created new ideas. If he had to work, and it was Neefe he had to work with, the prospect was not so dismal. For the first time, his life was taking a hopeful turn.

The lessons with Neefe continued on a daily basis for a while. John had seen that Luis's public school education was ended that spring, with no enrollment in the Gymnasium, a kind of middle school before young men matriculated at a university. To Luis, it was another familiar slap in the face. "You are not worth it," the action seemed to say. Well, no matter. It was unusual for musicians to pursue higher education beyond the basics of Latin, grammar, and calculation. Which was one of the many things that made Master Chris Neefe so unusual.

Luis noticed that in his little office Neefe had hung a diploma of some sort. On the second or third day of his lessons, very comfortable with his new teacher, Luis asked him what the diploma signified.

Neefe smiled slightly (he was not a man of mirth, and a slight smile for him would signify a roar of hilarity in many others). "Well, I've not much need for that now," he said, somewhat mysteriously. "Are you really interested? Well. It's my law degree."

Luis was not certain what law was, but it sounded equally

important and unpleasant. "Oh, really! You are a lawyer?"

"Yes, though not practicing at the moment, and I'd rather not go into that right now. You see, musicians may be accomplished, and yet do many other things, be many other things. There are clergymen who are also musicians, for example. Didn't you study with a brother recently?" Luis nodded. "That is another example, then, though it's more likely you would hear good organ playing in a church than a courtroom!

"You see," he continued, "I started life quite as you: poor and a bit of a prodigy, but not quite enough to make a name in the world. I even composed as a child. But there was the matter of making a living, and (despite my father's objections) I worked hard, won subsidies, and managed the expense of a university education, so I enrolled in Leipzig." He watched Luis's face but saw no flicker of recognition.

"My, they don't teach geography as they used to! That is a very prestigious university to the southeast. I studied hard, for law is like music in that practice yields superior results. But I decided after a number of incidents in my life to return to my first love. And so, as I am sure you have heard, I composed operas, played in theatrical orchestras, and found myself here, in my early thirties, playing the organ in court and teaching the occasional student of promise."

Luis was rapt. He seldom had been spoken to so directly and on a kind of level playing field with a male adult. Not only that, here was a true master musician and the composer of 10 operas renowned in the German-speaking world. Neefe looked at him with great interest, his clear blue eyes piercing his innermost thoughts, but not in a hostile or threatening way. "So, Luis, I have told you about myself. What about you?"

"There is nothing to tell, sir," he said. "I am just a boy who loves music. Music and nature. I like to play, to eat." Neefe's almost-smile appeared. "I love my mother. Is there anything else?"

Neefe pulled up a rather rickety wooden chair, the only other chair in the room, and crossed one leg over the other. His crooked arm rested on the back of the chair, and he rested his chin on the back of his other hand. "I hope this is not too bold a question," he said. "Is one of your parents or grandparents from the South? Or another continent?"

Luis did not mind the question at all, since it was not tinged with derision or insult, but phrased as a friendly quest for information. Still, he paused a moment before speaking. Indeed, he was not sure how to answer.

"It is true," he said, squirming just a little on the stool where he had been sitting. "I do not look like other boys. I can't tell you exactly why. My father blames my mother, and she protests that it is not of her doing, though she loves me dearly. My three brothers are as fair as you, sir. But it has been the cause of much distress in my life."

Neefe nodded, a furrow deepened between his eyes. "I've heard of such cases," he said. "In fact, there was a legal case I studied at Leipzig when I was young. I will not go into the details, because it was quite a different situation, but it impressed me profoundly, for it involved a young woman who appeared to be black, but records showed that her parents were Dutch. She stood to inherit a vast sum of money, but other relatives claimed she had misrepresented her relationship to her parents. Well, I am rambling on. Suffice it to say, I became passionately interested in perceptions and how they affect the way we are treated. I have seen many people mistreated in my life, Luis, in the theater, in the courtroom, and even on the streets, because of some aspect of them was not like the ruling majority.

"And I know the harsh effects of poverty, not only in terms of hunger and deprivation, but also its ravages on the soul. So I can understand your situation, and assure you, this loft will be not only a temple of music, but also a safe haven from misunderstanding and abuse. Remember: you have no reason to walk with your head down, or sit in the shadows, or try to disguise yourself through sloppiness or dishevelment. You will become the equal of any man, and, as my student, you will hold your head up with pride in who you are. Is that clear?"

Luis did not know what to say. Only his mother had spoken to him so encouragingly, and even she did so only out of mother's love, not understanding, not with the ability to put it in a context he did not know existed. But here was a man, born to poverty, thwarted by a domineering father, crippled with some arthritic disease, a member of a scorned religious minority, who had attained high status as a court music master, composer, and intellectual.

"Never mind," said Neefe, patting the child's hand. "Come, let's see what you've done with the Bach."

Truly, to Luis, Neefe seemed like a visitor from another world. Everything about him was different from the people he knew. His splendid speaking voice, richly nuanced vocabulary, his penetrating questions, and desire to engage in an intelligent dialogue with even a 10-year-old child. Then there was his appearance: tall, fair, aristocratic, yet wounded with disease (which Luis would learn later had been childhood rickets).

Neefe spoke to him with an openness of gesture and movement

that was not off-putting like the bourgeois vendors or minor nobility whose children studied with John Beethoven. Though immaculately dressed in simple but stylish attire, there was nothing pretentious or showy in his manner. His personality came from a deep place, one refined by suffering and honed by uncompromising resolution, a place that Luis knew he could never penetrate.

And one other thing. Neefe was Protestant. What did that mean? There had been rumors about Grandfather, having come from the vicinity of Antwerp. But then the boys at school made fun of Protestants, who were extremely rare in this Catholic city. But Neefe had no horns, no devil's tail. This impressed Luis to a high degree, and he swore to himself to find out more about the different paths of the spirit. And equally wonderful was his musicianship, and his insightful, sensitive teaching style. No lashes on the knuckles from this teacher: he was all about helping the student discover the essence of the music—what the composer was trying to say or express—and to develop an individual interpretive style, provided the student had mastered the mechanics of the trade. For at that time, trade it was, waiting to be elevated by some unnamed master of the future to the realm of celestial art.

Near the end of the first week of Rovantini's absence, Mary received several letters in the morning post. One was a chatty missive from her friend Henny, who was traveling in Belgium to visit relatives, and two were posted from a river town to the northeast. One was addressed to Luis. This would be the first time he ever received a letter, she thought, and smiled as she recognized the handwriting on the envelope as Rovantini's own. Mary tucked the boy's letter into her pocket, and opened Frank's letter to her. It was filled with pleasantries, good wishes, a few Bible citations, and some pressed Edelweiss. Everything about the letter was wonderful; Mary smiled again as she sniffed the flower-scented paper, and held the flower up to the window to better enjoy its freshness and form. What a blessing to have a cousin like Frank, she thought, and placing the flower in a saucer near the window, went on about her chores.

It was only after dinner, cleaning up and looking in her pocket for a cabinet key, that Mary recalled the other letter. She looked at it fondly, then, making certain John was not observing her, carried it into the back room where Luis was working on the 15th prelude from the Well-tempered Clavier.

"Oh such chugging, such drudgery that teacher gives you!" she whispered as she surprised him from behind. Luis paused, and scowled a bit.

"Mother," he said, "this may sound old-fashioned to you, but it is really wonderful music!"

"Well, if you say so!" his mother replied. "Say, I hear you are a popular young man!" Luis, puzzled, turned around on the bench and faced her. "You've received a letter!" she said. Luis was astonished, since this had never happened before, and in truth, it had never crossed his mind that he would ever receive anything in the post.

"Don't let your father see it," she whispered, "you know how he is. He would find something negative to make of a visit by the Pope, I'm sure! Your father's out, why don't you take it to your room. I think I know who it's from," she added with a wink. Luis had not seen his mother is so pleasant a mood in many months. He took the letter and scrambled off, up the stairs, and slammed the door behind him (out of habit, not anger).

Sitting on the edge of his bed, Luis read the following:

"My dear Cousin, I trust this finds you well. Are you enjoying your studies with Master Neefe? I hope you are obeying your parents, but have no reason to doubt that you do. I miss our lessons and talks, and especially the picnics outside of the city.

"My young friend, I think you would be very much interested in the research the Professor and I are engaged in. There is a big world outside the town where you have always lived, and I hope you will get to enjoy much of it.

"Visiting other places helps us understand why the world, why people, are the way they are. Remember our talks after the boys at school called you names? Or the time we heard those jokes at the expense of the black violinist Freidig? Surely, he is one of the great musicians of our age, and an architect and artist as well!

"It appears that truth will overcome bias at last. The Professor and I have much to do, and he will publish his findings to a paper he is writing on the subject of freedom and human dignity. I will tell you all about our adventures and the Professor's good work when I return in a couple of weeks.

"Be sure to say your prayers, and say them from your heart, and especially when you are outside, walking among the trees and flowers and listening to the birds. Loving thoughts and blessings to my best cousin,

"Yours, Rovantini"

Luis read the note again, then folded it intensely, and held it so hard in his strong hands that the paper was crushed, and covered with smudged fingerprints. His first letter. A letter from someone he admired. A letter with important information and the promise of a better future. All these ideas impressed him deeply. He took the letter to the small cabinet in the corner of his room, and placed it under a missal on the bottom shelf. Luis's heart beat hard, and he looked out the window at the beautiful day, for both steadiness and inspiration.

In Kassel, however, the ideal drama, suggested in writing just a few days earlier, was taking a terrible turn.

Chapter 27

A LATE SUMMER STORM had rolled in from the northwest in the village where Wert and Rovantini stayed. After a fitful night, they awoke to dark skies and an impenetrable fog, the sort that hangs over the nearby vineyards in October. The mist seemed to penetrate their room, even their very bones, and Rovantini coughed violently as they prepared to visit the compound, unannounced, before what they thought would be a sanitized tour at the agreed-upon time later in the day.

The two men, armed with some provisions, notebooks, extra quills and ink, and a sketchbook in Wert's pack, since he was a competent draftsman, left the inn early, along with some men who made their living on the river and upstream. Wert carried identification with him, as an ambassador of the university, but Rovantini did not. The men had decided it would be best to veil his identity to a certain degree, something that would turn out to work against them rather than in their favor.

Familiar with the layout of the compound from the previous day's visit, the men climbed up the hill, and circled around the fortress, behind the main pagoda but with the large, flat living quarters—probably more like a jail than a residency—sprawling ahead of them to the left. Their plan was a simple one: to get as close as they could, in silence; to hide in the bushes behind the building, perhaps enter it secretly if they could, to take notes, to listen and transcribe what they heard (mostly Rovantini's task), and to sketch quickly (Wert) what they saw.

But after the sights and sounds of the previous day, their plan took on a new seriousness and urgency. Clearly, there was something wrong, something totally unexpected. Van Hook obviously was a slaver, and the men and women who were subject to this experiment were not voluntary subjects, but captured as slaves. What other information would and could they discover?

There did not appear to be guard dogs in the rear of the compound, but lantern lights revealed where sentinels stood watch. The thick, wild woods behind and close to the compound were almost impenetrable except to someone with a team of machete-wielding foot soldiers, and gave the compound guardians a sense of security regarding that part of the property.

Neither Wert nor Rovantini was especially nimble or strong, and Rovantini (never in the best of health) struggled to suppress the cough that followed the weather's change. Perhaps had they known what would await them, they could have enlisted the assistance of another man. It would have been fruitless and no doubt dangerous to alert the authorities, since the Duke himself was the final authority in this province. However, it was too late now. The men lowered themselves against the damp earth, and crouched as they approached the rear of the residential building.

Inside, lanterns were being lit, and the interpreter, Tembi, was walking down the aisle of a dormitory-like room. The room had a capacity of about 30, but there were far more, perhaps 75 or 80, crowded into the space. There were no covers, and many people, including children, were lying on the floor. Some were moaning, and a white guard, accompanying the wary Tembi, would smack them across the back or even the face with a short braided whip. "No," said Tembi gently, turning to the guard, "no, no reason for that. They are scared, that is all."

Scared and hungry, thought Rovantini, whose heart sank, and whose own discomfort vanished in the presence of real suffering and need.

"They haven't eaten since early yesterday, surely…" Tembi started.

"Shut up!" spat the guard. "We'll feed 'em after the horses. If you keep taking their side, you know what the master will do!" Tembi was silent. As he walked by, he put his hand comfortingly on the heads of some of the men and women getting up from the floor.

The two observers were invisible on this side of the building, peering through a corner of the window, and a crack in the wall. They could not understand what Tembi was saying when he spoke to the people softly in their language. There was coughing, gagging, and the sound of chains. It was then that Rovantini started, noticing the glisten of chains in the lantern-light, the glow of metal around the legs of the dark people rising from the shadows. The room slowly came to light, a disorienting collage of light reflected from instruments of cruelty, incapacitation, and oppression.

Rovantini sank down behind the window and stifled a violent cough. He shuddered and leaned against the wall. Wert was busy sketching images of shadowy figures in torment. "Frank, write what you hear!" he whispered frantically. "Don't miss a word. I'll have such a cache of evidence to present when we return!"

Inside the building, the guard spewed racial epithets at the uncomprehending prisoners. Each minute revealed another horror: a dying man, an injured child, a bleeding woman, people kicked aside by the guard, even stepped on, as though they were bags of sand. As the people stirred, their voices became stronger, and there were sounds of sickness that made Rovantini retch.

"Are you writing?" urged Wert, not taking his eyes off of the scene, going through small sheets of paper at a desperate pace. "Damn, I wish we had back-up." At last the guard and Tembi had completed their walk-through. It was obvious they were assessing the group for relocation.

"They are planning to stash them somewhere, mark my word!" whispered Wert. "Our visit later today was expected to be a pretty site: all cleaned up and neat and tidy! I feel like rushing in there and saying, 'Stop! Don't torment these people any further on my behalf!'"

But, of course, Wert did not, not only out of a sense of personal survival, but also because it would make matters worse for everyone involved. The weapons worn by the guard were not imitations, and he looked not only able, but willing, to use them.

"You watch it, Tembi," sneered the guard as he produced a large ring of keys and proceeded to lock the awakened cluster of prisoners behind. "You're no better than them, save you speak a few languages." He nudged the translator with his pistol. "Mark my word, I'd enjoy splitting you open, you black scum!" Tembi bowed silently and walked on a pace, wondering how he would get water and food to these people. Water and food. And keys to their chains. And weapons. But he sighed. Then what. Escaped for a day in a foreign land. Where would they go, what would they do? They would be shot like dogs by the locals. Already they were dying of disease. He closed his burning eyes tight, then opened them, and looked ahead as they moved outside, through the lifting fog and fractured sunlight struggling to free itself from night.

Rovantini had not been of much help. He was feeling ill. "We'd better leave," said Wert, "I have enough information, we can reconstruct this later." It was then he noticed the state of his colleague. "You aren't well, my friend," he said with sudden concern.

"One minute," said Frank, reaching into his provision pack. "Let's leave our food and drink for these people, it's the least we can do." Wert nodded. The crack between boards where he had watched the proceedings gave easily, and he was able to push through some rolls, meat and cheese, and two flasks of water. At first the people near the wall were startled, then realized they were receiving a gift. In a manner that would have shamed so-called "civilized" Europeans, the people calmly received and divided up the food, sharing it with the sick and children. A woman by the window lifted her hand, caught Frank's eye, and almost smiled.

"Here," said Wert to his partner, "you have room in your sack now. Keep these sketches and notes safe," he continued as he carefully placed the paper and notebook in Rovantini's backpack. The two men waved in reply to the grateful people huddling near the window, and disappeared as they crouched back into the rear of the compound.

But word was already out, and despite the early hour, the sound of heavy running feet was heard in their direction. "Let's split, meet you back at the inn," whispered Wert rapidly, taking a turn to the right as Rovantini nodded and ran, low to the ground, straight into a hedgerow leading directly into the thick woods. As he ran, Frank heard the first volleys of gunfire, and his heart sank, but adrenaline carried him on his way, under cloak of underbrush and the strong shadows of the forest.

Another round of gunfire and a cry. Frank did not stop, but ran on, perspiring heavily from illness and fear. The sound of fierce dogs snapping and yelping, and the deep, rough voices of hardened slave guards were well behind him as he furiously made an uneasy pathway down the forest slope to the hidden trail Wert had so cleverly discovered. Frank's hands bled as he used them as a kind of blunt machete to push limbs and branches out of his way. The sun was rising, soon he would lose the umbrage of early day, but before long, he was running on the open trail, down the back of the slope and toward the inn.

Behind and unknown to him, beyond all help and succor, Wert lay dying, face-down in the dirt, as two guards rummaged through his clothes looking for identification and finding no evidence of espionage. "Must have been alone," said one, looking sharply around, his musket ready at his side. "What a fool."

Frank had barely gathered his and Wert's belongings from the inn when the westbound coach appeared. Providentially, there was room for one more passenger and baggage, and soon he was on his way to his cousins' house. It was only then that he began to cough, and the other passengers stared at him with disgust, revulsion, and resentment. Unheard by anyone in the valley, a single shot fired on top of the bluff finished off a man's life and the dream of freedom of those imprisoned people.

Chapter 28

IT HAD ONLY BEEN A DAY since Luis had received the letter from his cousin. He was still excited, and asked his kind master if he could leave a little early to do an errand for his mother. Neefe looked over his spectacles warily, suspicious of such a request on a fine day from a boy in unusually high spirits. Well, no matter, thought the teacher. He deserves a run, certainly he never gets permission at home.

"Yes," said Neefe, opening the Bach to the A major prelude. "I have a meeting this afternoon." As he said this, Luis noticed that Neefe absent-mindedly twisted the gold ring on the middle finger of his left hand. Luis had noticed the ring, unlike any he had seen before. It was large, engraved (with what, he could not tell unless he had grabbed the master's hand and studied it up close), and seemed to have two flanks that bulged on either side. It must have been uncomfortable to wear, and yet, it was a majestic-looking piece, something a chancellor might have worn. Neefe continued to twist the ring unconsciously for a minute as he looked out over Luis's head, distracted with some thought.

"Well," he said at last, coming back to earth, "on with the lesson." Luis smoothed the pages before him, and launched into a performance that brought his distracted teacher firmly back into the world of reality and music.

About an hour later, there was a rap on the door, and Neefe looked up with interest, since he was expecting no visitor. "Who is there?" he asked, rising from the bench and approaching the door with what Luis thought was extreme and unwarranted caution.

There was no sound. Then another tap at the door, and a man's voice, in a loud whisper, hissed, "Glaucus! Glaucus!"

Neefe stiffened and held on to a bar on the side of the loft. Luis turned around fully to see what the problem was. Glaucus. He recalled the name Glaucus in something about the siege of Troy studied in his last days of school, but how could a reference to ancient Greek poetry disturb a teacher as well-tempered as Bach's preludes? If only he had paid more attention in that class!

"Glaucus!" the voice whispered urgently. Neefe recovered, turned to Luis, and said, "Say nothing of this to anyone. Give me your most solemn promise." Luis nodded vigorously. "Stay here, I'll just be a moment. Go over all the chord progressions on page 32, and pencil them in. I'll expect to see it completed when I come back in a few minutes."

Neefe opened the door only far enough to squeeze through, and pulled it firmly behind him. Luis grabbed his pencil and pretended to write, but an intractable curiosity pulled him off the bench and lured him to the rough oak door. What was going on? What were they talking about in low tones in the middle of the morning?

It took a while for the boy's ears to adjust to the muffled tone of the men's voice, but soon he was able to pick out words, even sentences. "I told you not to come here." "…a report…it could upset…" "…afternoon…discuss…" "Your Highness…." Luis scowled. Your Highness? Was the visitor calling his humble teacher by this name? "…assess…assessin…assassin…strike…" The words made no sense.

When certain that Neefe was trying to send the man away,

Luis scrambled back to his bench, picked up the pencil and quickly began making notes about modulations as the heavy door swung open, and a highly flustered, slightly more disheveled Chris Neefe returned to the room with a crease between his eyebrows and a tense set to his jaw. Luis kept his head close to the score, furtively glancing up at his teacher from time to time.

"Yes," said Neefe at last, smoothing his hair and adjusting his collar. "That was nothing, continue." He glanced at the boy's markings. "Not your usual work, Luis. I suppose you have that 'errand' on your mind." Luis felt a flush of embarrassment. "Well, continue now, while I do some writing." The teacher sat down at his small desk, illuminated by a window facing east, and unlocked a storage place hidden below and behind the main drawer. He pulled out a green leather-covered notebook, and dipping his quill into ink, began to write, tilting his shoulder so Luis had no chance of seeing his work. Luis corrected his own mistakes on the score and continued to plod along, intrigued by the mysterious activities of his otherwise dull but considerate instructor.

Neefe sighed and paused. "Luis," he said, "you may leave. I regret I have much on my mind today. Do come again tomorrow at the same time, and I will ask you to play the next fugue, all right? Practice well after your 'errand'!" He smiled for the first time that morning, and Luis was happy to escape into the fresh air but also unsatisfied to leave a mystery unresolved.

Chapter 29

CHRIS NEEFE HASTENED ALONG the street leading from the east wing of the court chapel, into the main part of town where a number of churches and official buildings stood. He paused before one, looked about and then entered the alley beside it. He let himself in the back door and was greeted by a secretary at a desk.

"Director, it is good to see you," the grey-beard offered, rising and bowing. "The board is not here yet, but Mr. Dashell has arrived, he seems most anxious to see you privately."

Neefe nodded, picked up a package of papers and lingered over a letter in the mail with an imposing seal and wax stamp on it. He opened a large, heavy door and entered a lavishly decorated hall, with hanging lamps and decorations in the modern, Turkish style. Pillars carved in the pattern of swirling vines shot up to the ceiling. There were rows of cushioned chairs on either side of the hall, a marble floor, and a dazzling stained glass window behind a kind of raised altar. But there were no religious symbols. A servant greeted Neefe, escorted him to a changing room, and helped him put on a robe and headdress that made the humble musician look like a wizard from the Near East, but there was no apron nor were there symbols of Masonry. Neefe was ready to greet his guests.

Neefe sat alone on the ceremonial chair for some time, absently looking at the rug laid down before him, a stretch of some 10 feet in length separating him from his soon-to-arrive visitors. He withdrew the list of names from his pocket including the local factotum, Dashell. The others were major secret-society leaders from the eastern states: Soemmerring the anatomist, Forster the explorer, and from the south, the emissary known only as Xeno, an assistant sent to represent the Illuminati overlord, Zwack. Both Soemmerring and Forster were from Kassel. Who knows what activities were taking place there? Xeno would provide a measure of corporate perspective, since it was from the south that the Illuminati emerged in the year of the American Revolution, to encourage the cultivation of Reason, the perpetuation of the Enlightenment, and the freedom and dignity of all men (perhaps women, too, but that would have to wait).

"Show them in," Neefe said to his secretary, who bowed, lit several candles on tall pilasters, and walked to the entrance, opening the heavy door with some difficulty. There in the mid-day light, diffused from stained glass windows, stood four men.

"Your highness, exalted Master," said Xeno, stopping at the far edge of the carpet, and bowing low, "we appreciate your willingness to meet with us, at such an inopportune time during the week. But we felt our concern to be of the highest importance."

Neefe gestured for him to continue, as well as for the others to draw nearer. "I appreciate your dedication and concern," he said.

"As you know," continued Xeno, "our society has been fractured of late…" Neefe nodded his acknowledgment of this information, "…but our ideals remain unassailable. Those ideals include the development of Reason and enlightened research and thinking to lift mankind to a higher state of perfection."

The other men murmured their agreement. "Our states have taken steps to ensure equality among men, in which pursuit we hope to surpass the American model," he continued. "Slavery is almost unheard of among our people…" the men expressed agreement with this principle, "…but unenlightened attitudes still prevail, even in regions where our members are most active."

Xeno glanced over his shoulder at the two men from Kassel. "We seek your advice about a situation which some of us (another glance at Soemmerring) know about first-hand."

As Xeno stepped back, Soemmerring looked knowingly at Forster and stepped forward to the edge of the rug. "Your Excellency," he said, with a polite bow, "I do bring some disturbing news from Kassel." He then spoke of what he knew of the racial experiment at Kassel and his role as a leading anatomist.

"Come," said Neefe, "let us not stand on ceremony." He motioned to a sidetable with five chairs positioned under a mullioned window.

Soemmerring cast a quick sidelong glance at Forster, and the men relocated to the mahogany table. Neefe removed his headdress and allowed his assistant to relieve him of his cloak. The light was subdued, and a gentle rainbow of colors streaked across the table surface under the window's stained glass.

"I have been asked to participate in what may be a study of many years, a study of living specimens of different racial groups," Soemmerring said uneasily. "It offers the perfect opportunity for the modern scientist of anatomy, a situation and circumstance not found naturally in the world."

"A study of volunteers, surely" said Neefe.

"These were my thoughts as well," the anatomist said. "I agreed to participate for five years, under a pledge of confidentiality that I would tell no one about the experiment. As you can tell, I am conflicted about sharing this information. And yet, things have gotten out of hand."

"You have done the correct thing in coming here," said Neefe with a note of consolation. Neefe felt a gentle emotional empathy with the speaker, and, though a lawyer by training, could not judge his ethical quandary in a cold or clinical manner.

Forster leaned forward to speak. "Glaucus, this is all true as far as it goes, but the real truth, what is taking place, remains a mystery. Our question to you is a timely one: how should we proceed? Clearly, we are men of science and learning, not of cunning or force."

Neefe rubbed his chin and stared at the colorful shadows on the tabletop before him. Though he had been a member of the brotherhood for only two years, he knew there were still factions at war within their own house. A storm of thoughts and apprehensions flooded his mind. The principles of the order were one thing; the actions and ideas of individual members—often more assertive and aggressive than his own or those of his colleagues—were something else entirely. There was the racist Illuminati member, Meiners, with his developing notions of Germanic superiority, for example, and who could tell where that would lead?

Also, it was impossible to take action without implicating Soemmerring in a breach of confidentiality with the Landgrave, an offense which would mean immediate dismissal and possibly something worse. No, on all scores, his hands were tied.

"Soemmerring, Forster, what do you need? What action do you propose?" he said at last.

"There have been rumors just this past week of a pair of objective investigators visiting the compound," said Soemmerring. "I have tried to find out as much as I can, even attempting to pay mercenaries to carry out the legwork, but without success."

"There was a scuffle, sir, a few days past, of that I am certain," said Forster. "There are reports of gunshots and an altercation of some sort. Rumors are that there was violence…"

"Rumors! And are you men of science!" Neefe's voice rose.

The voices were silenced. "We are men of reason," said Neefe. "But we are not warriors. I enjoin you to do this: to observe closely what occurs at Kassel, to keep careful records, to inform me regularly by post using our agreed-upon code. The experiment you describe has the potential to counteract all our good work."

Neefe leaned back in his chair for a moment, and thought about Luis. Already things were changing. In Vienna, hadn't a black educator and court favorite, Angelo Soliman, recently been inducted into the Freemasons, the first of his race to be so honored?

And yet, even here within the Illuminati, there were factions warring against one another. One side for equality and recognition of the rights of all men, the other indulging in racial stereotypes.

"I have a student," he ventured, before the other men left. "He is the best and brightest of my students, a remarkable boy, but bound to feel the sting of prejudice. If he succeeds in our cruel, unequal world, it will be as much by the force of his personality and determination as from his talent. Let us remember, gentlemen, to keep cases like this in mind—the personal, human embodiment of the principles we elevate in theory—as we live our lives, do our work, seek justice and understanding for all."

With that comment, the men bowed and dispersed. Neefe remained at the table in reflection for a few moments before he went back to work where news of a shocking nature would change his life forever.

Chapter 30

LUIS WAS GOOFING OFF. He had a couple of free hours and a few coins in his pocket. He felt almost smug.

It was late summer, he was nearly 11, no school, and the tutor he saw occasionally wasn't half bad. He looked up at the clouds in the blue sky, closed his eyes for a moment, and smiled. What should he do with this precious time, all to himself? He took a circuitous route in the general direction of home that allowed him to lollygag and still arrive in time for supper.

His friends, the baker's sons, would be working, so it was time alone, time to let his overtaxed brain and fingers relax: no one to be accountable to, or take direction from. He felt keenly, too, the sense that the coins in his pocket were his ticket to freedom, even if only for a few hours.

He sauntered toward the river and found himself testing various ways of walking: a few skips, a leisurely pace, a cocky strut. Well, there was a different bakery, and it was time to eat. He went inside and asked boldly for two rolls, placing a coin on the counter. The baker's wife, with her hard, suspicious face, gave him an odd look. For once, he thought it was because he was an idle boy, possibly a bad boy, at liberty at such an hour, rather than his rough appearance. She snatched the coin quickly and pushed two rolls across the counter. How adult he felt, paying for his own dinner with money of his own earning. He wrapped his purchase in a dirty handkerchief and proceeded to the riverbank, his adult swagger quickly turning into the skip of a child.

Luis found a place to sit near a fountain, with a good view of the boats and sea birds. How refreshing the cool breeze off the water felt against his face. He settled in, and began to eat his rolls. Surely they were the most delicious rolls ever baked! He wolfed down the first roll, then paced himself to enjoy every last crumb of the second. The sea birds above and before him cried in vain: no morsel would they gain from this repast. Luis got up and had a drink at the fountain, then returned to his spot and yawned. The shade had fallen where he sat, and soon, as he watched the occasional ship glide down the river, his eyelids grew heavy and he drifted into sleep.

A few hours later, he awoke suddenly at the sound of sailors working in a nearby barge. Confused, with no idea of where he was, for a moment Luis's heart pounded frantically. Then he recalled his outing, and realized he must hurry home. His panic soon subsided and as he made his way back through the narrow streets, his high spirits returned, refreshed by food and slumber. To judge by the position of the sun, he would be home in good time; in fact, he anticipated a happy welcome from his mother.

But Luis was not to be welcomed, happily or otherwise. As he neared the front door, he saw the doctor approaching the house, as a concerned-looking Henny waved him in with agitated movements. Luis ran quickly to the house and almost knocked over the doctor at the entrance. "Is Mother all right?" he asked.

"Yes, yes, now where were you, boy?" snapped Henny. "We sent for you at your lesson, and neither your teacher nor yourself was there! You were needed at home!"

"What is wrong? What happened?" he persisted, as Henny showed the doctor to the rarely used back room on the first floor.

As they approached it, Luis heard soft crying and sobs. It was his mother. He pushed the doctor aside and ran in. "Mother, what…"

It was then that he saw the body on the bed beside her. A living body, still, but probably not long for this world. Mary sat beside him, pressing a cool, damp cloth against the man's forehead, stroking his arm with her other hand. Luis stopped dead in his tracks. "Cousin!" he said and rushed forward.

Mary shook her head, and said to Henny, "Take him out! This might be contagious!" The strong woman grabbed Luis by both shoulders and pushed him from the room, slamming the door behind her.

Luis was agitated and upset. "That's Cousin Frank, what's wrong, what happened!"

Henny sat the boy down in the kitchen by the window, filled with small pots of cooking herbs. "Yes, he's sick, must have caught something on that mysterious trip he took, who knows where or why," she said. "Now, where were you, we looked all over for you!"

Luis drew into himself and would not speak at first. Finally, after being shaken a few times too many by the well-meaning woman, he told her that the master had been called away, and he, Luis, had some sheet music to deliver. He did not want to lie, but neither did he want to share his moments of happiness with anyone, especially when a tragedy had been occurring at home at the same time. Had he been more conventionally religious, he might have thought he was being punished for having a good time; but that thought did not cross his mind.

"So, a delivery boy are you, eh?" Henny gave him another shake, then relented, seeing how miserable he had grown. "Oh, I know, Frank is your best friend, isn't he," she said, drawing him close in a welcome hug. "Things are not good for our friend. Luis, you must be prepared for bad news, and you must comfort and help your mother, who loves Frank dearly."

Luis nodded, and gently released himself from her embrace. He wiped his eyes against his shirt sleeve. "I will do that, Mrs. Marshall," he said solemnly. "I will do whatever needs to be done."

It was a long, trying day for the household, and Mary did not leave the bedside of her afflicted cousin. He had literally fallen off the coach when he arrived at noon; fortunately, Mary had been at the front window making soup, and saw him immediately. She had rushed out, and called for Henny's assistance. The driver also helped drag the near-lifeless body into the home, back to the spare room, and place him in the bed. The two young Beethoven boys hovered at the back room door with curiosity and discomfort; baby Frank cooed contentedly in his crib.

After thanking the driver, the two women assessed Rovantini's condition and looked at each other in a state of shared misery. For a moment, Mary sat back and sobbed softly, unable to restrain the tears. But it was but a brief interlude. She wiped her face with her apron, and she began to loosen Frank's clothing as Henny went for water, towels, and herbs. The young man was sweating profusely, but as she unfastened the left side of his shirt, Mary noticed the wound. He had been grazed by something, most likely a small musket shot. The wound was dangerously close to his heart, and Frank winced as Mary removed some fabric soaked in blood. But the fever was something quite unrelated. Frank was conscious, and at times opened his eyes, and said, "Mary...I'm sorry..." at one point.

Henny returned with a basin and joined Mary in cleaning the body and dressing the wound. "Lord, I've never seen a body sweat like this!" she exclaimed. It was true: it was as though his life force was flooding out of every pore in his body.

By evening, Henny was more concerned about Mary than about Frank, who was as comfortable as could be under the circumstances.

"Take a rest, Mary, just for five minutes, you won't have the strength to keep this up," she said, wrapping her cloak around her friend and forcibly raising her and walking her into the kitchen. Mary nodded and complied, though she barely touched the soup she had made earlier, in a happier time. This respite was all the time Luis needed. He had been waiting for Frank to be left alone, and quietly slipped into the back room, closing the door gently behind him.

"Frank," he whispered. "Frank, you are ill!" The body did not stir. "Frank, you have to get better! I'm here, Frank!" The boy cautiously walked to the bed, as though disease were an evil beast that could rise up at any moment and devour him.

Frank's eyelids fluttered, and he smiled. "Luis," he murmured. "My boy." Luis's heart beat faster, and he fell on Frank's chest, but recoiled at the soaking towel lying on top of his cousin. Frank groaned, and Luis backed off in fear. "It is all right," whispered Frank in barely audible tones. "Where…is my…bag?"

Luis looked about and saw a rucksack tossed in the corner. He picked it up and brought it over to the bed. "Is this what you mean?" he asked.

Frank nodded slightly. "Keep that, Luis…" he started, in great pain, "do not give it to your father. There is… secret… people…

need help…people…like…"

Luis heard footsteps in the hall, kissed his cousin on his cheek, and said, "I love you, Frank," his black eyes filled with tears. Luis took the bag, opened the window and leaped into the garden below, then ran around to the front of the house to reenter.

The two women entered the room. "Something's odd," said Henny, looking about. "That window! Mary, was it open before?" She closed it with a thud. "Drafts are the last thing this man needs." She turned to see Mary sobbing hard, stretched over the bed. Frank's eyes were cloudy, unfocused, staring into space. There was nothing further either woman could do for him.

Chapter 31

LUIS TIPTOED INTO THE KITCHEN, put the bag on the floor, and poured water and soap onto a towel. Although hand-washing had not yet been established as a principle of medicine, he knew it had something to do with disease prevention. He dried his hands, face, and hair quickly, and as quietly as he could, ran up the stairs, not noticing the muffled sobs and cries coming from the room below.

The bag grew in heaviness with each ascending step, and Luis was aware of its considerable weight as he slung it onto his bed. The boy did not hesitate, but began unstrapping it with feverish energy, stopping only at the sight of a large, dried bloodstain where it had lain against Frank's heart. His cousin's words returned to him, though, and he proceeded to unbuckle the last strap and shake out the contents onto his blanket. Such a large number of things for such a small bag. He sat back and took it all in before he touched a single piece.

Although Luis was an untidy boy, he had a very tidy mind, almost preternaturally tidy and well organized. He knew he should make a list of the contents of the bag, so he opened one of the two notebooks, ripped out a blank sheet of paper from the back, and grabbed a pencil that was rolling away. Carefully, he sat on the edge of the bed and wrote down what he saw:

Three cloths of varying size

Three pencils (plus the one he held)

Two thick notebooks, one with a dark grey cover, one in brown

A large portfolio and sketchbook

A knife

A slice of dried meat, and a hard roll wrapped in a piece of music paper

Crumbs

A pair of socks (made by Mother)

A compass

A canteen, with some water

A recorder (musical: alto)

A small sack of herbs, possibly prepared by Henny Marshall

A page of newspaper with a recent date.

Luis took a deep breath, sat back against the headboard and looked at the list, then at the contents, then back at the list again. The exercise had calmed his mind, and he felt he was doing something for his dear friend, someone who was more than a brother to him. He rubbed his head with both hands, scratching his scalp as though to try and wake up his brain.

"What does it mean?" he thought. He reached over to the small table beside his bed and pulled out the letter he had only recently received from Rovantini. Was there some clue there?

The boy shook the missal his mother kept at his bedside and out fluttered the letter and separately the envelope, since Luis was too excited when he first received it to neatly reinsert the folded paper. He read the letter over several times, his throat aching as he focused on Frank's kind, reassuring words. But what had he been up to?

Luis bit his lip and gazed absently out the window. How could a child find the answers he sought? Surely, his father must not know of his thoughts or findings. On general principle, he would give him a whipping and confiscate all the objects and documents, including the precious letter. Perhaps it was best to be quiet for now, to tell not even his mother what he knew.

In other parts of the flat, prolonged grief was a luxury that could not be afforded. The funeral would have to be within the week. In addition to all the work involved, there would be considerable expense. Mary had another concern: she knew of Rovantini's sister, Anna Maria, his only other relative, who was working as a governess in Rotterdam. That very night she wrote Anna Maria a letter notifying her of the bad news. She invited the sister to see them when convenient so they could visit the rented grave together.

In their own community, the word had gone out through the neighborhood "tree": four neighbors were told of the death, and each told four additional neighbors, and so forth. In this way, a large number of people would be certain to pay their final respects and perhaps accompany the remains to the church and on to the burying place. If only John were home, thought Mary, worried, distraught, with a growing sense of responsibility and debt for the coming days.

John did come home, shortly before midnight. "Why is everyone up?" he observed with a slight frown. "We can't waste tallow, now, can we, Mary?"

"John," she said. "Frank is dead. His body is in the backroom."

The news astonished John, but he didn't seem particularly grieved by it. "Dead! What happened? An accident?"

"Perhaps," Mary demurred. "He had a horrid fever when he arrived at noon." She decided not to mention the wound on his chest, and knew he would be too squeamish to examine or even touch the body. "The undertaker will be here tomorrow." She looked down at her lap, eyes unfocused, but there were no more tears to fall.

"My God," murmured John, "I'll have a look."

"Wait," said Mary, rising quickly, "I'll go with you. Henny is watching, I'll watch a few hours as well, you may want to take a turn before dawn." He nodded, and the couple went into the backroom. Henny looked tired in the light of a dozen candles burning around the bed.

John walked over to Frank's side and looked sadly on the young face, like a church angel in the golden light. He made the sign of the cross, pulled up the sheet and stood silent for a moment. "Yes," he said, turning to Mary, "wake me when it's time.

"A sad world, Mary, and we all wrapped up in our cares," he said. For a moment, John seemed almost compassionate. "But we don't need all these candles," he added, blowing out every other one before leaving the room. Black soot lingered in the air.

During the next few days, the women made the necessary preparations for the funeral activities. Anna Maria replied in a letter that she was heartbroken that she could not attend, but accepted Mary's invitation to visit at a later date. She included a small monetary contribution to the expenses, which was gratefully received. All the slender resources that the family could spare were diverted to the expenses of church and burial. John sent for Frank's things from the Kassel inn, but when they arrived, he sniffed that they were hardly worth the cost of sending for them. But for Mary and Luis, any relics of their beloved cousin were precious.

The day of the funeral, Luis approached his father as he was dressing. "Will there be music at the church?" he asked, "Why were we not asked to sing or play?"

"Hmph," half-laughed his father. "Music is expensive, musicians are poor. Rare is the musician who goes to this grave to the sound of music he may have played or even written. Remember," he continued, "the world scorns musicians. We work our fingers to the bone, give them the music they can't live without, and then we don't rate even a raspy pub tenor to sing our dirge. That is why you must study and work hard, Luis!" he added slapping the boy on his back. Luis did not move, and his father looked curiously at him for a moment, as he had not for some time. "You are growing strong, boy. You will soon be an adult. I am surprised," he said, his voice dropping into a mumble, as though he were talking to himself. "I am surprised how quickly time has passed."

Mary leaned on Henny rather than on her husband's shoulder as they left the graveyard. Luis put his strong hand behind her elbow, escorting her on the other side. John drifted off with his friends, with a sound excuse for drinking early. Halfway home, the two women and boy had to rest for Mary's sake, on a bench near the dry goods shop. Luis looked at his mother, and, perhaps influenced by his father's quizzical glance earlier in the day, regarded her with fresh eyes: a haggard, exhausted woman in poor health. He did not notice the shabby dress and old shoes, for these were not the sorts of things he was brought up to see; what he ignored in himself, he did not notice in others. He patted her hand, and she looked at him with her tired eyes, and smiled. Luis smiled, too, and the familiar wave of affection and hope swept over him once again. Such is a mother's love.

And yet, beyond maternal affection and the reassuring cadences of the priest, Luis craved answers that would satisfy a searching mind and suspicious disposition. He would find the key to those answers in a surprisingly familiar person.

Chapter 32

"I HAVE MISSED YOU," said Neefe, in a clipped fashion, not looking up from the notebook in which he was assiduously writing a list of his recent ailments for his doctor. For in addition to being an accomplished organist and teacher, and Grand Master of a secret society, Neefe was also a world-class hypochondriac. He was the sort who would not complain to others, while hoping they would notice his deplorable condition even as he protested he was perfectly fine. But to the hapless physician who attended him, Neefe's life was a labyrinth of sorrows and sufferings, most of which seemed centered in his active imagination.

"Yes, sir," said Luis, still subdued from the recent events. "You know about my cousin."

Neefe looked up over his wire-frame glasses, a pose which emphasized his long, thin nose and somewhat receding chin. He put his quill down, and folded his hands on the small table top before him.

"I do," he said simply, "and truly, I am most sorry. This cousin was close to you?"

"The closest," said Luis, catching the light in his teacher's blue eyes. The boy needed to say something, and the urge became overwhelming. "Master Neefe, may I talk to you in confidence?"

The teacher was surprised, but not antagonistic. He was, after all, a humanist, and this was his best young student. It wouldn't hurt to hear what he had to say. Neefe closed his notebook, and motioned to a chair. "Tell me, then we can start the lesson without worries nibbling away at your mind," he said.

"My cousin, Frank, was a great musician," said Luis earnestly. "But he cared about people...all people," the boy continued. "People...like me...different-looking people, poor people..."

Neefe's smile disappeared. "Ah," he said, trying not to seem too attentive. "Tell me more about this."

Luis paused, avoiding further eye contact.

"I don't know exactly why, but he and a professor friend had a project they were going to inspect in the northeast," said Luis. "They were going to observe something. My cousin said he hoped his studies and activities would benefit people like me. He saw how I had been treated, by...various people." Luis looked down. Neefe wasn't sure what to make of this, but it was clear that Luis was acutely aware of his appearance and had been often abused because of it.

Then the words "northeast," "project," and "inspect" all came together in Neefe's mind. "Where did they go?" he asked, trying to disguise growing interest.

Luis reached into his bag and produced Rovantini's letter, stuffed into the original envelope. He handed it to Neefe and said, "Sir, please just read this once and then give it back to me. It is my most treasured possession." Luis was keenly aware he had never trusted an adult before in this way.

Neefe took the envelope and looked at the return address. His already pale appearance grew paler. "Do you know anything of this place? How far away? How long were your cousin and his friend there? Have you heard from the friend, and who is he?"

Luis was surprised by the response and drew back a bit. "No, sir, I know nothing except for this letter and what my cousin told me."

"Your cousin," said Neefe, "did he die a natural death?"

"What is a natural death?" asked Luis. "He had a terrible fever." He paused, looked a bit sideways at Neefe, and decided to take a chance. "He may have been wounded."

"Wounded! What do you mean?"

"I heard the doctor speaking with my mother. It may have been a wound from a musket near his heart. There was a lot of blood lost."

Neefe took a sharp breath, and felt his blood pressure rise.

"May I?" he asked, beginning to open the envelope. Luis nodded. Neefe pulled out the small sheet of paper, which had been awkwardly folded and stuffed into the envelope. He smoothed the page on the desktop before him, and carefully read the letter twice, striving to show no emotion. There was little information in the note, and yet it contained so many tantalizing glimpses of what might have been. Who was this professor, and how much had he written? Was he still alive, or did he suffer a similar fate to that of Cousin Frank? Was it a coincidence that the inn listed in the return address was so very close to the Kassel site that Soemmerring had mentioned? Was there any connection at all? Or was the hypochondria that he knew he suffered from spreading to his powers of imagination as well?

Luis watched closely, with some apprehension, as Neefe read the deeply personal letter. The boy had grown to trust few people, his caution protecting him from many hurts and injuries. So far, though, he was experiencing no pain, no fear, no threat. With the surrender of the letter to his teacher, he had allowed Neefe to become the first person to step into the inner circle of his private life.

"I don't know what to say," said Neefe, somewhat bewildered but animated with great curiosity. He folded the letter neatly with his precise fingers and slid it silently into the envelope, handing it back to Luis.

"Do you have any idea who this professor is?"

Luis took the letter and put it back in his pocket. "No, he never mentioned him. Though Cousin Frank also wrote to my mother," he recalled, brightening, but then a shadow fell over his face. "She never mentioned him, though, and would have, what with the funeral."

"I see," said Neefe. "And what about the place he visited, did he tell you about it at all?"

Luis shook his head. "But why are you so interested?" he asked with a new, suspicious tone to his voice.

Neefe sat back in his chair and looked at some invisible object past Luis's head. The pedagogue sat in this philosophical pose for some time, while the boy never took his eyes off of his teacher's face.

"Luis, in some ways, you are very mature for your age," he said at last. "In addition to music, Luis, would you like to learn more about the world?" The child nodded.

"Would you be interested to know about science, history, why people discriminate against those who are not like them?" Luis blushed and looked down at his hands, the strong dark fingers spread over the patched knees of his trousers. "I do," he said, without looking up, "but I am not sure what those words mean."

"Which words?" asked Neefe, puzzled.

"Science. History," said Luis. Neefe took a deep breath. This was going to be more difficult than he expected.

"Let me tell you briefly," he said. "We will forget today's music lesson, all right? And I will tell you about science and history, even the rights of man." Luis nodded, and sat back further into the chair. Then, without ado, the lessons began.

After several hours of teaching and informally quizzing the boy, Neefe was exhausted and reached for one of his pills and a drink of water. "Luis, go get some air, but be back here in exactly 10 minutes," he said, rising himself and stretching, amazed at the lecture of practically all he knew that had come tumbling from his lips.

Luis ran out into the fresh air, starting to turn crisp at autumn's approach. While Neefe, still by his desk, did some of the stretches one of his doctors had prescribed, the boy ran down the street to the far side of the courthouse and threw himself onto the grass, looking up at the tree tops and clouds beyond. So much information boiled in his brain, for once, there was no room for music or ideas of his own. He listened to Neefe's voice in his memory, astonished and grateful, but a bit dazed. He turned and buried his face in the cool, sweet-smelling earth, then abruptly leaped up and ran all the way back to the chapel. He rubbed his face vigorously on his sleeve, and reentered the practice room.

Recovered sufficiently to resume writing his health history, Neefe looked up as Luis burst through the door. "Ooh!" the boy cried, "that was something! Thank you, Teacher, I had no idea there was so much to know!"

Neefe half-smiled and put down his quill. "I am afraid that is just the basic outline," he said. "The most frustrating thing is that knowledge is ever changing, and so, we must stay in touch with the latest developments in every field so we are not left behind. For example, did you know that a scientist discovered a new planet earlier this year? It's called Uranus. Fascinating!"

The teacher continued in this vein for a while longer. When it appeared Luis's attention was beginning to wander, Neefe stopped, and reached into his satchel where his wife had packed his lunch. He pulled out a small cake and handed it to Luis, who sprang to attention again. "Oh, thank you, sir!" he said, grabbing the cake, taking a couple of huge bites. Neefe inched the water pitcher nearer to the boy, and continued in a different vein.

"And now," said the enthused educator, "on to…" It was all too much for Luis. Too much information, too much running, too much sugar, too little music.

"Ah," he sighed, dropping his head onto his arms, folded on top of the writing table. "I am sorry, sir," he mumbled. "It is a lot to take in."

"Luis, we all have much to learn. Life is a journey of learning and becoming. You will be studying with me for years to come. I have already decided to hire you as my assistant in another six months or so, despite your age!" Luis could scarcely believe his ears. "I haven't discussed this with your father yet, but will, and anticipate a positive response. Your duties may also include helping me with my work in the Illuminati, but more of that later.

"So take these thoughts home with you today, boy, along with your Bach and von Dittersdorf. God be with you, Luis, and I will see you for your usual lesson tomorrow."

Chapter 33

AFTER DEMONSTRATING TO HIS FATHER the musical skills he was learning from Neefe, Luis hurriedly ate a dinner of potatoes and trout, and darted for his room. There would be good light for another two hours, and he now wanted to examine the contents of Frank's bag more carefully. He pulled a chair over behind the door, which did not lock, and twisted a dirty curtain on the west-facing window to gain maximum light.

The boy dragged the bag out from under his bed, a dusty nest where human eyes had seldom pried. As he had done less than a week earlier, he emptied the contents on his bed, but this time pushed the clothes and toiletries aside, drawing the notebooks closer. The first notebook actually had Frank's name on the front in small neat writing. The notebook had a brown cloth cover, and contained about 50 sheets of standard writing paper.

The first few pages were notes about travel, expenses, some quotations copied from books, some Bible passages, memos to write to others, memoranda about students, various doodles of no consequence. This went on for about eight or nine pages. Each page was crammed with Frank's small handwriting, which ran up the margins and across the top and bottom of every sheet. Then began a diary commenced on the day of leaving the Beethoven home. Luis was a good reader and familiar with his cousin's script, so he began to read with some interest, then stopped abruptly, and thought he would check out the other book.

He pulled the heavier, grey notebook across the bed into the sunlight. This was the Professor's book. And there on the inside front page, at the bottom, was his name: Dr. Simon Wert, University of Halle. Luis lifted the notebook and felt its weight, noticing that the stitching of a section of the 200 or so pages was loose, and the pages were about to fall out. In addition, there were loose sheets of paper which had been carelessly stuffed into the book as though it were a portfolio.

Despite his curiosity, Luis held and examined the notebook carefully and slowly, as though he were borrowing someone's valuable violin. He began to push the loose sheets back into the book, but noticed they contained pictures, scribbles. He took them out again, and saw some drawings that were very rough, but also very accurate; quickly and emotionally executed, but unsparing in the story they attempted to tell. It was a horrid tale of enslavement and suffering.

Luis felt sick to his stomach, but quickly glanced at the first three pictures, then thumbed through the other four, and dropped them onto the notebook, as though afraid his hands would scorch. They were all depictions of the mistreatment of dark-skinned people. He had heard the word "slave" before, but never imagined that enslavement brought with it such terrors as these. The last few drawings looked as though they were very quickly sketched, with emotional distortions, and incomplete, crumbled before being smoothed out and inserted into the portfolio.

Taking a breath, he stuffed them back into the notebook, and tentatively looked at the rest of the notebook. There was much writing, but of a type hard to understand, both in terms of penmanship and content, and he did not try very hard to read the script. Instead, he took both books and returned them to the pack, stuffing the clothes and other content on top of them.

Luis lay down on his small bed, watching the fingers of sunlight grow shorter across his blanket as day passed. He thought about the images, the notebooks. Who would he tell, what would he do?. If Luis were to confide in anyone regarding the materials stored beneath his bed, was there a better confidante than his teacher?

A cane from downstairs banged against the floor. "Practice!" he heard his father's muffled voice. Luis quietly moved the chair, and ran down the stairs to the better piano. "More Bach, then," his father called from the kitchen, "and something modern, some Haydn, if that's all right with your teacher," he said with some sarcasm, since he was keenly aware he was losing control of this unruly boy day by day.

The small dark hands touched the keys, and Luis thought no more of problems, misery, or intrigue.

Chapter 34

"OH, CHRIS, you are such a worry wart," cooed Susanna, Neefe's wife, placing a kiss on the top of his head as he finished a slice of pie. "Here, give me that diary right now. I promise not to read it, I just don't want you reporting on your digestion when you are supposed to be enjoying a delicious pie!" But Neefe drew the diary close to his chest, and slipped it under his vest.

"My dear, you are certainly right, as always," he said primly, "and I will not write any more right now. You and Greta are both excellent cooks, and I will indeed savor every morsel of this delicious dish!" He smiled slightly, but pressed the diary closer to his chest, covering it up like a precious child being put to bed.

Susanna sighed. She took some of the empty dinner dishes over to the pump and left them there for Greta, who helped with running the house. The Neefes had two young children, a boy and a girl, but they were in their tiny rooms, working on their lessons.

"I don't like it when the days are short again," she said. "Soon you will be as busy as can be, what with the church calendar, local theater, and your men's club." Neefe pretended not to notice, and made a sound of satisfaction as he finished dessert.

"Yes, that was excellent, my dear, I don't know how you find the time to be so accomplished and keep me so entirely happy," he hummed, and he was sincere, on one level, in that he did indeed love his smart and pretty wife. As for sweets, he was not a hedonist, and his seriousness would have dampened the spirit of any woman lacking Susanna's sparkle, intelligence, and perspective.

He stood behind her, wrapped his arms around her waist, and gently nuzzled her blonde upswept hair as she blushed becomingly. "You are a good wife, Susanna, and all the sweetness a man could crave. But now…" he patted the hidden diary and released his helpmate, "I must study while there's still light."

Susanna raised an eyebrow, and gave him a kiss on the cheek. "You do that, Chrissie, I promise to stand watch and protect your privacy!" she said, half teasing. "Go on."

The Neefes were not quite middle class, but had a comfortable small home thanks in part to the teacher's own relentless enterprise and frugality, and his wife's modest but useful inheritance. Through careful planning, both were able to raise their children respectably, and dress becoming to a high servant of the court and his lady. But Susanna wondered whether Neefe wasn't pushing himself too hard, and getting too involved in extraneous activities. Well, they had a good life, she thought, and were more fortunate than many, such as the family of the talented, dark child her husband had told her about.

"You will have to bring him home some time," she told Neefe then. "The world is a cold, unforgiving place, but here he will be welcome." Susanna said such things because she believed them in her heart and had reasoned them with her fine mind. And in fact, she had a third perspective: that of connection maker and intermediary, since she or her relatives had contacts in a number of excellent upper middle class homes throughout the city and just beyond. It was in part because of these connections that her husband was so quickly insinuated into the Illuminati and rose within months to leadership.

The next morning, Neefe kissed Susanna and was off to the

court, with a early detour to check on any messages at the lodge. He had one pupil before Luis, and looked at his watch, surprised that his future assistant was running late. It was close to midday when Luis appeared with two large packages wrapped in old newspaper under his arms, and his music book rolled into his pocket.

"I had quite a time putting these together and getting them out of the house without being seen," the boy said, dropping one with a thud on the guest chair, then the other on top of it.

"And what would these parcels be?" Neefe reached for a knife to cut the string awkwardly tied and knotted in a dozen places. "Some of your own works, Master Beethoven? Of course, I'm curious…"

"Sir!" said Luis, annoyed at his teacher's short memory. "These are Frank's things! And his friend's!" Neefe's light mood vanished, and he frowned.

"You…didn't tell me you had his things," Neefe said as he recovered. "I presume these are documents…"

"They are," said Luis, fetching the knife and cutting the string on the top package. He pushed back the paper, revealing the brown notebook. Neefe's heart beat faster,.

"May I?" he lifted the brown notebook onto his desk and opened it cautiously, as though a snake or something more startling—like Truth—would leap out at him.

Neefe slowly skimmed each page, pausing occasionally to squint, and at one point, to gasp slightly, until he had looked at every page. He then put his hand on his chest, leaned back in the chair, his head tilted back, his eyes closed.

After a while, Luis, who had been standing right beside him, touched his arm and asked if he was all right. Neefe opened his eyes, and resumed his position of authority. "Yes, yes, of course, why wouldn't I be. Luis," he said, "I can barely read your cousin's script, after the first 10 pages, it is nothing like the letter you showed me yesterday."

"I have not read it, I wanted to see what you thought," said Luis.

"But you may be able to help me read his script?" asked Neefe. The child nodded. "And what of that other package?"

Luis took the knife and hacked his way through the newsprint. He then handed his teacher the grey notebook. "Be careful, sir," he said, "there are some drawings, some horrible pictures, but you will need to see them."

His hands shaking a bit, Neefe accepted the heavier notebook and inched the brown one to the side. When he opened the cover, the drawings were the first thing he saw. "Oh my God!" he said, slowly leafing through the seven sheets. Neefe was not good at hiding his emotions, since he had had few external shocks in life, the worst being the death of a young son. But sensitive person that he was, the teacher was gravely affected by what he saw. He quickly gathered the pages, reinserted them in the book, and put his hands on top, as though pressing them into oblivion.

"Have you told anyone else about this?" he asked Luis without making eye contact.

"No, sir," the child replied. "Sir. They are too dreadful."

Neefe looked up, removed his glasses and stared into Luis's deep-set dark eyes. "Luis, your cousin was a saint. These documents provide evidence—I don't yet know how much, but it will be significant—of some horrible crime. You must speak about these to no one, and leave them here with me for safe keeping. Moreover," he added, "I will need your help, as my assistant, in transcribing these writings, can I count on you for that?"

Luis was not thrilled at the prospect, and squirmed. He had enough to do with his music, not only the lessons he was learning, the strides he was making as musician, but also the music that rang and sometimes raged within his head.

The teacher was recovered from the shock of the two notebooks, and said, "No, no. I must not take advantage of you. You are a good student and have far to go. We will keep your activities exclusively to music, though I do plan to bring you to the lodge, which is not unlike a church, from time to time, perhaps to play for our members during functions. Music. Only music can save our minds and souls from the terror of man's cruelty to his own kind."

Chapter 35

FORSTER WAS STILL IN TOWN, of that Neefe was certain. He sent him a note, and was pleased to have him at his door in the court chapel within two days. Neefe left one of his other students to practice, while he and Forster met in the little office, where Neefe had secured the notebooks in an alcove behind some scores.

Neefe took a good look at Forster as he sat in the same chair Luis had occupied when bringing the notebooks. Forster was in his late 20s, a gentleman, but also a man of the physical world, tan and rough around the edges. He carried himself with dignity but seemed uninterested in appearances. His chestnut hair was pulled back in a peruke, and some fell over his left eye, giving him a romantic appearance.

"My gifted student brought these to me," he said. "They are the work, perhaps, of a colleague of yours? My student's cousin may have died preserving them."

Forster's rough hands moved gingerly through the wrappings and lifted the notebooks to the table. He opened them and scowled as he attempted to read Rovantini's script. He flipped through the first book, then opened the second, where the drawings caused his eyes to open wide. "Remarkable!" was all he could say. Neefe watched closely as his guest cautiously moved from page to page.

"Can you have these copied?" asked Neefe?

"Yes, right away, I have a good confidential copyist here, and I can make fair sketches from the drawings," replied Forster.

The men did not have to say more, for each knew what was on the other's mind.

"Be extremely careful with these," said Neefe, wrapping them in muslin. "I know I don't have to tell you that, but the words must be said."

Forster nodded. "I'll do this promptly, then return your originals and ride back to the college," he said, leaving the room. Neefe composed himself, still not certain if he had done the right thing, then returned to his student.

In the afternoon, Luis appeared, and Neefe decided it was best to deflect the conversation from the notebooks.

"Come, Luis, let's work on the new Haydn, all right? I have a copyist making a fair copy of the notebooks, your originals will be returned soon. You have nothing to worry about: they are safe, and things are under control." He smiled and shepherded the lad to the chapel organ loft. "First, show me what you remember about the stops from our last lesson."

He watched as the boy, growing lean and taller than when he first met him, swung himself up onto the organ bench, his feet still barely touching the pedals. While his hands were not large, the spread of his fingers was unusually wide, probably from years of training since a small child. Although it was difficult, he was able to reach the top keyboard by adjusting his body to lengthen the stretch of his arms. He looked rather odd, in fact, like a spider stretching out his legs to the maximum extent in all directions.

After the organ lesson, Neefe sent the boy out for some fresh air, and took a deep breath himself. He put thoughts of his own health aside for the moment, after taking a lozenge and writing several sentences in his book, and considered his own life:

full-time organist with the court, part-time musician nights with the theater, a respected composer of instrumental music and operas throughout the German states, director of the local Illuminati lodge and confidant of great thinkers of the Enlightenment, teacher of several students, one of whom displayed remarkable promise and required careful tending and cultivation, husband and father, and now a sort of humanist-detective, trying to make the world less intolerant and more charitable to people of all races. It was a lot.

Sitting before his small desk, he rested his forehead on his folded hands and prayed, "Heavenly Father, give me strength and health that I may be up to all these responsibilities, and lead me according to Your Will. Help me succeed most in what is of greatest importance to You. For I can do nothing without Your guidance and help."

Outside, Luis had wandered down the full length of the restored palace, a long, three-story building with pleasant walkways and park-like grounds. In some ways, it looked like an attractive dormitory, with its unwavering message of conformity and neatness; but it also resembled a jail. Was there such a thing as being imprisoned by pleasantness?

Luis returned from his stroll, refreshed. Neefe wondered at how quickly the young developed, grew, and changed. He was not the same boy who had come to see him six months before. But Neefe did not have time for daydreams: here was his work.

Chapter 36

WHILE THE ORIGINAL NOTEBOOKS and sketches were returned by messenger at a later date, there was no further word from Forster. Soon the obligations and practical necessities of the court and theater seasons overtook more idealistic pursuits. Even the secret society for which Neefe served as director was turning into a place of skirmishes and petty disputes, much as the larger organization had become torn by dissent and riddled with vituperation. Whenever men assembled, for whatever good reason, ripples of turmoil, egotism, and distress were certain to follow.

Under Neefe's guidance, Luis not only mastered the difficult art of organ playing—so very different from the technique and sensitivity required for the piano—but also became the master's student in composition. Neefe marveled at the boy's inventiveness, wealth of ideas, indefatigable energy. One night, he brought home a bundle of the lad's compositions to share with Susanna, who was a fine pianist in her own right.

"Oh, let me see," she said warmly, accepting the sheets and walking to the piano. Neefe lit the candelabra and sat down beside her on the bench. Still young, her bright eyes had no difficulty reading the works, which had been professionally copied.

"Oh, Chris, these variations, they are so imaginative!" she said, halfway into playing. "But why so sad? It sounds in places like a funeral march!"

Neefe nodded. "Yes, the boy lost his closest friend last year," he murmured, "I think this must be a tribute. Well, here, try this Rondo!" Susanna was a fine sight-reader and soon the air was ringing with lively, crisp, and well commanded chords.

"Chris! This is great, and how old did you say he is? These syncopations, I've never seen anything quite like them. This is fine work indeed!" Chris smiled, pleased that his wife appreciated and understood the value of the boy's work.

"He will have a hard time of it, Susanna, we must give him every advantage. His family is poor, his father is given to drink, and may not last long at this rate. I hear that drinking is a problem for that family." He took back the scores, looked briefly at them one more time, and put them safely aside. "But of all the disadvantages he faces, there is one which may be insurmountable." Susanna shared an understanding look with her husband, and reached out for his hand.

"My dear Christian," she said, "we are all God's children, surely genius, if that is what it proves to be, will triumph over prejudice. Otherwise, what kind of people can we call ourselves?"

Neefe sighed and patted her hand in return. "I know, I know," he said, "that is why my work with the lodge is so important, though it brings us no income. It is an instrument much larger than we are to bring the ideals of civilized behavior and thinking to the leaders of our world. I haven't had time to think about it lately—so busy…"

"Oh, and your health, my poor dear," Susanna interjected sincerely.

"Yes, that, too. Well, I hear from my learned colleagues that science may yet prove to the biased that there is no basis for intolerance. We can only hope, and do everything in our power to create a world in which there is no discrimination based on a person's color or religion or heritage…"

"…or gender!" added Susanna.

 "So true, thank you," he added with a smile. "I am so thankful to have your support and understanding, my dearest," he said warmly. "You are the reason I am able to accomplish so much with the small gifts God has given me." Susanna kissed him, and the young couple, one plain, one lovely, sat a while in the silence of the flickering flames.

On the other side of the city in a shabbier flat, a much different scene was taking place. Poverty, illness, alcoholism, depression, and poor nutrition were taking their toll on the Beethoven family. As always, the house rang with music, but music neither festive nor profound. Scales, drills, exercises, in counterpoint against the restless cries of the three younger Beethoven boys. Mary sat by herself, coughing now and then, as she mended and applied patches to well-worn clothing, squinting in the scarce light. Mrs. Fischer, dropping off some leftover rolls one evening, swore that the child playing the piano would surely go blind. The comment touched Mary's heart, which had been desiccated by care.

"Boys, sit here in the front," she called. She put down her work and put out some of the baker's rolls, broken into bits, leaving them for the children, with small cups of warm beer. She then lit a candle, and made her way upstairs where Luis was practicing on the smaller piano beside his bed.

She did not know what it was he was playing. Any more, music all sounded pretty much the same to her, but she could tell her son was putting his heart into it, and lately seemed more confident, if not exactly cheerful. It must have been the doing of that new teacher, she mused. The result was good, better than she expected, especially since she heard he was Protestant. Luis worked so hard, some day he would become a successful court musician like Grandfather, marry and have a family of his own, not a distressed family like this, but a prosperous happy family, in which all members were respected and honored.

She coughed, and Luis looked over his shoulder.

"Mother! What are you doing here!" he said, wiping his forehead, for he had been concentrating so hard beads of sweat had formed on his brow. "Here, sit down," he said helping his mother to the plain chair in the corner. It was a clear night, and a spot of moonlight lengthened on the floor. "There," he said, blowing out his candle, "we can save a bit on that."

"My fine son," said Mary, "I have neglected you. Mrs. Fischer said you were hurting your eyes playing in this dim light…"

"Oh, no, I work mostly from memory when it is dark," the boy said.

"Come closer," said Mary, "I hardly look at you these days. You have grown so, and you're not so pudgy, are you?" Luis held his mother's hand, and looked down bashfully.

"My son, I don't know how long I can stay up here with you, your brothers need watching, and who knows when your father will return. Sit for a moment beside me." Luis sat on the floor and rested his head against her skirt. "You have been such a good son, and what pleases me most is your sense of responsibility and duty, and your obedience to God's law," she said. "We have had some difficult times, and I fear they will get worse before they get better."

Luis wasn't entirely comfortable with these kind words, since his mother had no idea how many scuffles, fistfights, and episodes of hooky had riddled his checkered childhood.

"Mother, I will be working and earning a wage soon! I already am Master Neefe's assistant, and he promises me I shall have a salary for my work. I will give it all to you, Mother. Providing," he hesitated, "you can keep it from Father."

Mary shook her head. "I cannot do that, Luis, and you should not suggest it. It is God's will that the father is head of the family. This life is not meant to be easy. Suffering prepares us for future glory. Luis, you were made as you were for a reason. Life will be more difficult for you than for most."

"I do not mind," said Luis firmly, "I do not care what people think."

"You do not care what they think, but you must treat everyone with respect," his mother persisted. She did not often contradict him, but her words seemed to have a stronger weight this night, as though she needed to give him the final words he would need in life even if she were no longer present.

"Luis, you must promise me that you will live a moral life, respecting all people, even those who would treat you roughly because your appearance is different than theirs. And, Luis," she paused, "you will be a man in just a few years, and will find yourself attracted to women."

The thought made Luis laugh, though he stifled the impulse. "Mother, honestly, what a ridiculous idea! I can never love anyone but you!"

"Hush," she whispered, secretly pleased. "Yes, you will want to court many young ladies, but son, always treat women in particular with respect…" From downstairs came the sound of young Frank crying, and some ruckus. "Ah, I must go downstairs."

Luis felt a warm glow after she left. It had been a while since his mother had spoken to him with her simple wisdom in this way, and he did love her so. Perhaps things were looking up for him. A loving mother, a supportive teacher, even his father had been leaving him alone. He pulled the curtain to hide the too-bright moonlight and soon went to bed and to sleep.

But it was not to be a long or restful sleep. At some point in the night, he dreamed of loud voices and screams, a horrific nightmare. He sat up in terror, then calmed as he slowly slipped back into reality. But the sounds of a violent row continued. He drew back the curtain for light; the moon was high in the sky and moving toward the west. Suddenly, the reality of what was happening jolted him into action, and he rushed to his parents' room and opened the door. There his father, visibly drunk in the flickering lantern light, was shaking Mary despite her protests.

"Stop that!" cried Luis, running toward his father, who lifted a walking stick, lunged toward the child, and shouted at him in his loudest theatrical voice, "You stop, you savage, you…"

Luis pushed his father so hard, the man fell back against the wardrobe with a horrible crash, upsetting a table, and causing the lantern to send jets of scarlet light up and down the walls. Luis took the walking stick and threw it across the room, then grabbed his father's arm with a strength he did not know he possessed. Looking down at his abject father, quaking before him in a mixture of alcoholic delirium and astonishment, he shook him by the shoulder, then let go in disgust.

"Don't you ever lay a finger on my mother again," he fumed

between clenched teeth. "Don't you ever touch her!"

Mary sobbed, "No, Luis, stop."

"He'll stop, he'll stop now," seethed the boy, easing back to protect his mother. "Get out!" he shouted, and to Mary's surprise, her husband crawled to the door, pulled himself up, muttering, and uneasily lumbered down the stairs.

Luis stood there for a moment, too stunned by his own action even to tremble. Mary looked at her son, first with fear, then with gratitude, and finally with pride. She wiped the tears from her eyes and smoothed back her hair. Her head ached where the stick had fallen, but it was par for the course, living with a man who seemed to have two personalities, to be two utterly different men wrapped in the flesh of one.

"He's…not a bad man, your father," she said weakly.

Luis turned and leaned against the wardrobe, cradling his face on the crook of his arm, his back to his mother. "Luis," his mother said, as she pulled herself up from the floor, and moved slowly to the wardrobe, where she stood just behind him. "Thank you."

He turned and wrapped his arms around her thin form. "I will never let anyone harm you ever again," he whispered.

Mary did not know whether this was the end of an era of pain and uncertainty, or the beginning of something much worse. "Don't think of it, my child. Here, wash your face. Are you calm? Can you go to sleep? Put the chair behind your door tonight. Just in case." He nodded, and kissed her cheek.

Back in his room, there was little sleep for Luis. The moon was invisible now, behind a growing bank of clouds, and the room was dark. As he lay on his back, Luis's body and mind tingled with the aftermath of violent emotions he had never experienced before. He was partly horrified at the unexpected explosion of his own sense of power, of his own capacity for violence. But as the night wore on, he felt something else, something much stronger: that he was glad he had stopped his father. He was not yet 12, and yet at this age, in this time, boys were becoming men. And so it was with Luis. This night was the turning point. It was the dawn of the vision of the man he was soon to be.

Chapter 37

NEEFE HAD PLENTY ON HIS MIND. He had not forgotten the mission that Forster was so eager to fulfill, and in addition to his own performance schedule and musical compositions, he had found a publisher for Luis's variations. There was a market for lively music; every middle-class family seemed to have a keyboard instrument of some sort in the home, and players were clamoring for anything fresh and new. It was the Enlightenment, after all, and enlightened views about music were no exception.

But despite the horror of the notebooks' record and the evidence that two murders may have been committed, Neefe did not hear back from Forster, who became subsumed in his livelihood and work with Soemmerring at Kassel. No doubt the young naturalist had turned over the copies of the notebooks and sketches to his colleague, who must have found them helpful as his work turned increasingly to chronicling the secret doings at the compound.

"Secret, secret, everything is secret, no one dare say anything, even in front of a trusted friend!" Neefe thought to himself one afternoon reading the newspaper. So secret were the doings of his own society, that one branch did not know the doings of a branch in the next town or city. In part because of this secrecy, rumor had it that the Church was about to crack down on the Illuminati as it had already done with the Freemasons, in fact, with any group that threatened its monopoly on ritual and control over people's minds. Neefe wondered whether his being Protestant in this largely Catholic state was a good thing or not. It certainly freed him from fear of the Church and allowed him to act more independently; on the other hand, he could not understand and empathize with other members of the brotherhood whose livelihood and very lives were threatened by the specter of Church discipline.

Working with Luis, however, reminded him that prejudice was very much alive in everyday experience. Once, in the winter when Luis was just 12, Neefe and the boy were scrutinizing a page of difficult fingerwork in a Missa Brevis by Mozart. Luis was completely absorbed in the written notes. "This Mozart, I have heard about him all my life," said Luis, not taking his eyes off the page, "but this music, this is what makes him so real to me."

"There's no doubt, he's the great composer of our age," agreed Neefe. "Master both Bach and Mozart, my lad, and there will be nothing to stop you!" There was an unexpected pounding at the door, so Neefe left the instrument and went to open it. It was one of the Elector's henchman, a particularly odious individual puffed up with the importance of his position and his coziness with people in high places.

"What is it?" asked Neefe, somewhat haughtily. "Can't you see I'm in the middle of a lesson?"

The messenger smirked and pushed his way into the loft. "I've a message for you from the Elector," he said, "isn't that reason enough to interrupt?" He walked over to Luis, who had turned around on the bench, facing the visitor.

"So what do you call this?" the messenger said, casting a condescending eye on the child. He tapped Luis a little too hard on the side of his head, and grabbed his chin, lifting it up to him.

"And who would you be, boy, sitting at the organ?" Luis recoiled, and looked down, not speaking.

"Give me that," said Neefe, holding in a monsoon of emotion, his ears turning bright red as they did when he was furious. "Get out!" He was tempted to say more, but swallowed the words that could lead to disaster for him and for his students. Like other courts, the Elector's entourage was fraught with troublemakers, spies, and sadists, hangers-on jealous of those with real talent and ability. A Protestant appointee was always in peril of immediate dismissal, no questions asked.

"Heh, indeed," said the creature, eluding the musician's grasp. "You'd better clean up your quarter and keep the scullery staff in the basement where they belong! " He left with a loud slam of the door. Neefe exhaled suddenly and loudly, and gave the door a good kick with his boot.

"Damn the man!" he fumed, sitting down and putting his forehead in his hand. "Ah, Luis," he breathed deeply again, and turned to his student. "Pay him no heed." Luis still did not look up, and slumped as he turned back to the keyboard and music.

"Wait," Neefe said. He ran his thin, long fingers through his own hair, for he was not wearing a wig during lesson this day. "Come here." Luis obeyed, and followed the teacher into the anteroom where Neefe kept his journals and writing supplies. "Sit down." The boy did.

Neefe sat facing Luis, the small desk between them. Neefe tossed the message from the Elector to a plate of unopened mail and pulled a magazine from under the table and put it on the desk, to the side. "Look at me, Luis. No, Luis, listen. Look at me. Look into my eyes." The boy was extremely sullen and his usual buoyant mood crushed. If only he were outwardly angry, instead of imploding, the teacher thought restlessly.

"Something happened today, Luis," said Neefe, "that will never happen again. It will never happen in my presence, nor in my lifetime, nor in your own lifetime if you live to be the age of Methuselah." The boy listened, but did not show emotion.

"Do you know what that something was?" Luis said nothing, just stared gloomily at his teacher. "That something was you putting up with some insult or sign of disrespect from any person on earth, do you hear what I'm saying?

"Luis, do you understand? You are no longer a child, and you are my assistant organist. Soon you will be earning a salary and helping support your family. You are a student, but you are more than a student, do you hear that, do you know that?" There was a long pause, during which Luis looked down again, and mumbled something that sounded like "yes."

Neefe's feelings flooded through him, and he leaned forward across the desk. "Luis, listen to me, and look up at me again, show me your eyes. Luis, you will never be cowed by a creature like that again, do you hear me? Never! The most important lesson I can give you, more important than Bach or Mozart or guiding your compositions, the most important lesson is this: you will respect yourself and take insults from no man! Are you listening to me?" Neefe made a fist and pounded on the table, causing the boy to twitch, perhaps it was a reaction to similar fists directed to his head by his father in years past.

But the shocking noise, so close to him, had a different effect. It was as though the recent incident in which he had protected his mother from abuse had returned to his memory, to his consciousness, but this time, the effect was deflected to himself. His father and the messenger were people of a type, people who preyed on those whom they thought were without power, because they were young, subservient, different.

Neefe waited for it to sink in. And sink in it did. The color returned to Luis's cheeks, and his eyes opened wide and glistened, and he sat a little taller in the chair, and frowned, but it was a good frown, a frown of action, not passivity. "Do you mean," the boy said, "that I may resist? How can a child resist the authority of adults?"

"You are not a child when you are with me," said Neefe. "You are my assistant and my student and by God and by all the forces of Nature and Man, I will never allow anyone to abuse or belittle or despise you in my presence. And when I am not there to defend you, Luis, my boy, you are on…your…own, and if you don't stand up for yourself, and speak for yourself, and in so doing, speak for all those who have been slapped down because they are different or small or not of a certain social type, then you might as well forget being a great artist, and just stay a drudge forever!"

The two looked deeply into each other's eyes, and Luis nodded warmly, and reached over and touched his teacher's hand. There was a reason Neefe had been elected the Director of the city's Illuminati, and knew the greatest intellectuals and freedom fighters of his age. It was perhaps Divine Providence at work that this leader and this troubled boy should meet over the common ground of Music, and the elder should pass on the tradition of self-respect, independence, and the inviolable brotherhood of Man to his disciple.

The two sat still for a few moments, then Neefe took another deep breath, patted his heart to make sure it was still beating, and wiped his brow with his handkerchief. "That is not all," he said, more calmly. "I wanted to share with you an article I published in this prestigious music magazine." He opened a copy of *Cramer's*, and taking a pencil circled a statement halfway down the page. "I want you to read this," he said, turning the publication around and pushing it toward Luis.

Luis picked it up and read his name, followed by these words:

"…a boy of eleven years and of most promising talent. He plays the clavier very skillfully and with power, reads at sight very well, and—to put it in a nutshell—he plays chiefly The Well-Tempered Clavier of Sebastian Bach, which Herr Neefe put into his hands. Herr Neefe is now training him in composition and for his encouragement has had nine variations for the pianoforte written by him on a march. This youthful genius is deserving of help to enable him to travel. "

Luis was so astonished, he couldn't believe what he was reading. While Neefe had been encouraging, he never lavished much praise on Luis, in keeping with the pedagogical practice of the day. The prevailing philosophy was that nothing harmed a young person more than praise. But praise could also lead to self-confidence, and Neefe knew that at this moment, there was nothing his student needed more.

"Sir," the young man said at last, tugging at his cuffs and collar distractedly, "I don't know what to say! I had no idea…"

"Of course you didn't, of course not. And that was by design. I don't want you preening your feathers. Now," said Neefe lightly, "back to Mozart, all right? I'll stay here a bit."

The teacher chuckled lightly, then picked up the message from the mail tray. It was good news. The Elector was pleased with the progress of Neefe's protégée. The journal had been brought to his attention (Neefe wasn't above a little self promotion), and the Elector also enjoyed Mssr. Beethoven's recent performance of the double-fugue. "We approve," the Elector wrote. "Do keep us informed of any developments or needs."

Chapter 38

WHILE IT WAS A TIME OF HOPE and optimism professionally, Luis's life at home was still fraught with heartache. In the summer, his youngest brother, Frank, came down with an infection that no care or remedy would allay. After a particularly sultry night, Luis awoke early, as though jolted out of his sleep. The house was unnaturally quiet, even for the early hour, though outside the merchants were beginning to make their rounds while it was still dark.

Luis went to his parents' room, but it was empty. Fearing the worst, he went to the boys' room, and there sat Mary in a chair, as John sat on the edge of the bed, and Mary was rocking young Frank, holding him tight to her chest. Little Carl had fallen back to sleep, but John Jr. was sitting next to his father, rubbing his eyes. "It is over," the father said somberly, as Luis came into the room. "Frank is gone." Mary had no more tears left in her, but kept quietly rocking. Luis went quietly to his mother and sat at her feet, and put his head against her knee. It was a sad family silhouetted against the rising sun.

The death of Frank took the greatest toll on Mary, but life went on for the other members of the household. The necessities of industry and earning a living were an antidote for grief. It was a busy time for Luis, who was also taking violin lessons from Mr. Ries in the court orchestra. In addition to his organ studies and regular performances with Neefe, Luis directed his new-found confidence to musical composition: a song, and then three piano sonatas of formidable size and scope. His father had pretty much given up, and faded into the background of his life. There was still the question of travel, but despite his maturity on many levels, it was decided he was too young and too valuable to tour alone or with a court-appointed chaperone.

A different kind of trip came later in the year, as the young musician accompanied his mother to Holland, where he played several recitals. However, his hopes of income from these performances were quickly dashed. On Sunday, he appeared at the organ loft to the relief and pleasure of his teacher, who couldn't repress a smile of welcome.

"Well, young man, you'll have to regale me with tales of your concert-hall conquests later this week, we have a busy schedule today. Here." he thrust a new score into the boy's hands and stepped aside, to see what he would make of sight-reading under pressure. As it turned out, it was just the sort of challenge Luis needed to make him forget his unrewarding visit to a foreign land. The virtuoso's fingers and feet swept rapidly over keys and pedals as heavenly music rose like incense in the chapel hall.

At the next regular lesson, Neefe pressed Luis further as to the outcome of his first tour. "I did very well," the boy affirmed seriously, and with no false modesty, "but the Dutch, ha! Never again, sir, never again. Penny-pinchers, every one of them!" Neefe smiled behind his hand.

"Now, now," he admonished, "all men are brothers. You'll see one day." Luis said nothing, but thought to himself, "Unlikely!"

Neefe put down his notebook, which by now was full of daily health concerns. Interesting how they multiplied during the months of his best student's leave.

"Luis," said Neefe, after the lesson ended and the keys were covered, "my wife and I would like you to visit with us tonight for dinner. I have another guest you will like to meet." Luis had had his fill of new experiences, but at least he would be assured of a good meal. "I'll send a note on to your mother, I'm sure she won't mind."

Luis accompanied Neefe nearly a mile to the teacher's flat. "That," Neefe said, pointing to a patch of snow and ice in the front, "will be my garden. Did you ever garden, Luis? No? There is no pleasure quite like it, raising your own vegetables from seed, and beautiful flowers. Well," he rubbed his hands together, "it is bitter cold now, but here we are, Mrs. Neefe will be pleased to see you!"

The two wiped their feet on a mat and entered the little home. Everything was bright and cheerful, not at all like Luis's house, nor was it over-the-top like the homes of the Dutch merchants. Susanna came to the door, glowing and beautiful, for not only was she a fine pianist, but often worked as a singer and actress in the more respectable houses of theater. She wore her hair in a fashionable upsweep, foregoing a wig altogether, and her deep rose dress and sparkling white apron gave a gleam to her fair complexion. Luis felt his heart flutter, and colored a bit himself.

"This must be the famous Luis!" she exclaimed, embracing the boy and taking a close look at his face as Neefe put his hand lightly on her back and kissed her cheek. The room smelled incredible: a wild bird of some sort was roasting in the hearth with potatoes and other vegetables. It wasn't like the rich cuisine of his tour, all sauces and cover-ups, but real food, and more important, real warmth and affection, which seemed to charge the little room with its own appetizing delight.

"Daddy, Daddy!" squealed a little girl, running into the room. In the entrance to the kitchen, Luis noticed a servant holding a younger child. Then in walked a handsome young man, well dressed, tall and poised, but with a friendly, open countenance.

"Luis," said Neefe, "this is my friend's son, Wegeler. Wegeler, meet Luis," he said, as the young man extended his hand. Luis shook it, looked him in the eye, and was certain this person was "safe," a rarity in his own realm of acquaintances.

"Wegeler is studying to become a physician, just what we all could use from time to time, some of us more than others!" Neefe added with a self-deprecating laugh.

"I am so happy to meet you, Luis," said Wegeler, "I've heard you play, you know, and you are absolutely brilliant!"

Luis hardly knew what to say, so he remained silent, soaking up the praise like a thirsty sponge. Wegeler's enthusiasm and energy, the affection and good humor of the Neefes, even the vivacity of the little girl, soon had Luis forgetting his cares and resentments, and he found himself telling tales as well as they, stories about his adventures in Holland, and joining them in hearty laughter as they sat around the small table, enjoying a dumpling soup, wine, and what was to the younger guest a repast he would never forget.

After a rich apple cake, Wegeler and Luis sat together in the next room, and talked for more than hour, Luis's sometimes reticent powers of speech unloosed in the presence of a new friend just a few years older than he. Each young man had something to contribute to the other, and was bright-eyed and eager to take on the world. Years later, Luis would always look back on this occasion with joy and gratitude.

But winter was taking its toll and Nature, not always a benign and loving force in the lives of men, had an unwelcome surprise in store for the residents of this small riverside city. A few nights after the visit with the Neefes, the weather warmed dramatically. Luis was awakened from sleep by a loud moan, a horrible squeaking, creaking sound, then more moaning, as though the heavens were crying out over the cityscape. The house shook, and rain pelted the windows, driven and wild. "Mother!" cried Luis, "are you all right, what's going on!"

All he heard was "Oh my God!" screamed and shouted from below. "Luis, grab your brother Johnny, I have Carl!"

"What is that noise?" Luis called as he ran down the stairs to the boys' room, and woke a disoriented little boy from his slumber. "Here, we have to go somewhere, be good…"

It was then that the front door flew open, and water rushed into the downstairs. "Oh my God!" shouted Mary, "Luis, boys, everyone upstairs, take essentials only, quick!" The family, minus the father, who had not come home, climbed to the attic. Mary unlocked the latch and the door to the roof swung open violently, as large, fast-falling sheets of rain pelted the four, stinging like crazed hornets.

"Up! Up and out, follow me!" cried Mary over the deafening roar, scrambling in her nightclothes onto the roof. Luis was beginning to understand and took over, carrying one child, and pulling along the other to free his mother to better navigate the rooftops. The boys' hair was flying almost off their heads, Mary's bonnet was pulling against the tight sashes. "Follow me!" she called, "I know the way to safety."

The boys followed Mary, who haltingly tottered down the

phalanges of the roof, onto a short walkway that connected with other houses in the row. Slowly, the wind and rain, freezing cold, whipping their bodies and clothes, Luis again noticed the moaning and creaking, like the loudest thunder he had ever heard only it was behind and even below him. He couldn't stand the suspense any longer and, tightening his grasp on his brothers, stopped in mid-walk to turn his head toward the river.

There he saw it. The giant sheets of ice that had covered the stream all season had cracked and were rising like a flotilla of Spanish man-o-wars, bobbing and shifting and heaving into the air. Luis was speechless, it was unimaginable. The sky was light green with ominous shadows undulating overhead. Behind the bridge, there was nothing, but in front of the bridge, all the ice had mounted up like a separate city, and as he watched, it heaved against and broke down the city walls.

"Come on, don't stare! We have a ways to go!" Mary screamed and forged ahead, the trio trailing behind her. But they were not the only residents affected, for when it was all over a week later, 200 people had perished, and nothing was left of hundreds of additional homes and businesses. Everything they owned was lost, and the charity they had so long resisted was forced on them at last.

Once a temporary home could be set up with other musicians across town, it was some time before a normal routine could be established. Luis's distinctive appearance did not cause a stir among the friends and acquaintances of the Beethoven family, which proved to be more numerous than he expected, although a few eyebrows were raised among the volunteers from the far reaches of the city, and Luis felt some inhospitable stares and muffled comments across the room.

The turn of events had wreaked havoc on many aspects of their lives, including mail delivery and messaging. As a result, it was weeks after the Elector approved Luis's petition that the certifying letter found its rightful place in the young man's hands. It was with great relief that he learned of the small income that would be needed now more than ever.

After the worst of the damage was repaired, the family was able to reclaim some items from the home. Many of the upstairs furnishings, a few instruments, and the portrait of Grandfather had been spared, but loose sheets of paper were ruined by the wind and rain. Those sheets included all the unpublished compositions of the young composer.

The Neefes assisted in the relief effort, in consonance with their religious beliefs and commitment to social good, and Luis saw his friend Wegeler several times as the future doctor assisted with the medical needs of the community.

The river receded to its normal level in time, and soon it was spring. And yet Nature would level another blow to those who had endured so much: in April, the Elector, the supporter of the court's large music program, died suddenly. With that death, all the hopes and guarantees of an income and a future seemed to come crashing to a halt. What would happen now?

The timing could not have been worse for Neefe, either. There was tumult among the power bases of Europe, and the Church had come down hard on secret societies such as the Illuminati. Neefe's position as organist was no longer safe, and though his home eluded devastation in the recent flood, his own contract was up for renewal. As a Protestant, he knew he might easily be the first to be let go.

Then, another blow struck: the new Elector shut down all the state opera and theatrical houses in a cost-cutting measure. This resulted in the Director of Theaters Grossmann leaving town in search of other venues, and signified a loss of income for both Neefe and his wife.

Little of this, however, reached Luis's ears or captured his attention. While everyone was on edge, something new and wonderful did happen to him that spring. As Luis and Wegeler walked along the river bank one Sunday afternoon, Luis's companion said, "Say, I have some friends you should meet. No, really, you'll like them. They already asked me about you." Luis wasn't too sure, though he trusted Wegeler about as much as he was capable of trusting anyone.

"Who are they? What do they want?" the younger boy asked suspiciously.

"Hey, don't worry! You'll like my friend's brother, Stephen, he's around your age, a little younger. And, his family has 'connections,'" Wegeler continued as they stopped beside a pile of river rocks and clamored up the side to get the best seats. Luis spit out the alfalfa stalk he'd been chewing on, and looked far upstream.

"Come on, what do you say? They have a killer piano, I know that will interest you!" Wegeler lowered his voice, "and the prettiest daughter, she'll grow up to be someone special!" he added with a wink. "I hear they are looking for a piano teacher for the family."

Luis threw a stone far into the river. "Sure," he said noncommittally. "It can't hurt. And if they are friends of yours," he looked back at his companion, "they can't be all bad…or good!" he added raffishly, causing Wegeler to punch him good-naturedly in the arm and chase him back toward town.

Through Wegeler's introduction, Luis came to know Stephen, his sister Eleanor, and two other brothers, but most impressive, and influential, was the materfamilias, Helene. She was the widow of the Court Counselor, who died while trying to save others in the palace fire Luis had witnessed some seven years earlier. It was in this way that the young musician became acquainted with the von Breunings.

Chapter 39

IT WAS RAINING HARD, a strong, pelting rain, when Wegeler, in his spruce overcoat and hat, and Luis, in his usual street clothes, arrived at the massive iron gate before the house. Wegeler, opened the gate, and they both ran through the half-circle carriage-way up to the front door where Wegeler lifted the clapper of the lion's head knocker and pounded loudly. After a short pause, the butler appeared in full uniform, with an impeccable powdered wig on his head. His posture relaxed somewhat when he saw Wegeler, a familiar sight at the house.

"Master Wegeler, welcome, come in out of the…" At this moment, his eye caught sight of Luis, not hiding in the shadows, but stepping forward and looking up, directly into his eye. A ragged, dirty, insolent-looking, rain-soaked, frizzy-haired street urchin, those were some of the repeatable words that flooded simultaneously into the pale butler's mind. Wegeler was quick on his feet though, and in the seconds that ticked by between sight and opinion, Wegeler had pushed Luis into the foyer, and soon the butler was forgotten in the squeals of welcome as a favored guest was greeted by the children of the house.

"So, Breuning," said the affable student to his friend Chris, "I've brought the friend I was telling you about, but I'm afraid neither of us is fit to walk on your carpets with these boots."

"Oh, just kick them off, Larkins will take care of them, won't you, Larkins? So, young man, welcome. Luis, isn't it?" Luis was still feeling insulted, and not very demonstrative in terms of his greeting.

"Hi, Luis," said Stephen, coming right up to him and extending his hand.

"Luis, we can't wait to hear you play, but do you like almond cake?" said Eleanor, a serious girl with merry eyes, grabbing his arm.

Soon, everyone (except Larkins) was kicking off their shoes and socks and leaving them in the corner (and Luis squirmed out of his wet jacket as well, tossing that onto the pile) as the younger siblings shepherded Luis into the music room, followed by Wegeler and Chris in friendly conversation.

The house was palatial, with great tall windows and crystal chandeliers, but didn't warrant a glance from Luis, who was used to fancy houses. Wasn't the court chapel just one fancy rich man's house? Larry, the youngest child, held, then looked at Luis's hand.

"You are so dark!" he exclaimed with childish wonder.

"Larry, hey, no…" Stephen started to interrupt.

"Dark? You want to hear dark?" said Luis with a wink to the younger boy, unusually at ease. Barefoot and coatless, he sat down at the large, showy piano conspicuously displayed in the rear third of the room. With that, he launched into a roaring improvisation in C minor, sweeping up and down the keyboard as though drawing and extending shadows of doom and foreboding. The Breunings and Wegeler stood transfixed, and soon every servant on the floor had scrambled to the music room to see the source of this unheard-of fantasy. "And what an instrument," thought Luis as his hands and arms flew. "I could live here forever!"

At the height of the performance, Mrs. Breuning herself appeared at the door, a tall, slim, aristocratic woman with a kind, intelligent face. But the expression on her face this day was one of wonder and astonishment, as though she had come upon a miracle in her own parlor, which, indeed, she had. As Luis finished up with a sad, plaintive melody, interspersed with bursts of fury and passion, and wound up with a series of crashing chords, the children, then the servants, and finally Mrs. Breuning herself burst into shouts of "Bravo!" and rounds of applause.

Rather than be exhausted by the demonstration of his powers, Luis glowed, and looked as though he might keep on going for a few more hours.

"Luis, that was...I can't even say!" said Chris. "A wonder! Mother! Come in, meet our new friend, thanks to Wegeler here." Wegeler bowed to Mrs. Breuning, a little embarrassed that his companion should have made such a stir, which perhaps wasn't all that welcome.

"My dear child," said Mrs. Breuning, hurrying over to the piano and, sitting beside Luis, threw her arms around his not-entirely-clean and certainly disheveled person, "do you know how good you are?"

Even Luis knew he could not answer that question affirmatively in a social setting. He just smiled, and enjoyed the sense of a kind woman's warm embrace, sweet fragrance, and sincere affection. His mother was right: women could be angels.

Mrs. Breuning released her grip on the young musician, and leaned back, examining him carefully, as he mopped his forehead with a soiled handkerchief. She noticed the unwashed neck and ankles, the matted hair, but mostly the glowing expression, of one possessed, but in the best possible sense.

"My dear boy," she said, "my dear young man. Are you free to spend some time with us?"

"Oh yes," squealed Eleanor and Larry together, while Stephen smiled broadly, "Oh, Mother make him stay!"

"Well," said Mrs. B, "I am sure he has a mother of his own!"

"And a fine one, I assure you, Mrs. Breuning," contributed Wegeler, concerned that Luis's mother would be blamed for his unkempt appearance.

"I see, I see," said the widow, "yes, and let me see your hands." These were hands that had known only work and a hard life, she could tell immediately. "My dear boy, are you available to teach piano to my three youngest children? I will pay you the going wage, nothing less!" Luis nodded gladly. "But I would like you to be more than a tutor. I would like you to spend more time with us, learning about literature and books, history, the classics, learning social skills that will be so important as you go out into the world that appreciates your music, would that be agreeable to you?"

Once again, Luis agreed, exchanging happy glances with Eleanor and the others. "Then, it is done!" said Mrs. B. "Now, go check with your mother and father, I'm sure they won't object, and also with your teacher…"

"That would be Neefe, the court organist," said Wegeler.

"Oh yes, I am familiar with him, a good man, and a composer, too. Well, I'll leave you to get to know each other for a while, but Luis, before you leave today, see me again. I have a nice clean suit of clothing you can wear home tonight, and Peterson (nodding toward a stout, but beaming female servant) will clean you up so your mother won't even recognize you!" Mrs. B. smiled and patted his hand. "Luis, you are going to be a permanent part of our home. Nothing will change that."

After Mrs. B and the staff adjourned, the young people laughed and talked, and there was a bit more music-making, though Luis did not want to wear out his welcome "showing off." Still, he felt incredible. The music had poured out of him, and what an impression he had made! And just as wonderful, here was a group of people who liked and welcomed him, and promised to help him succeed. In the midst of a gloomy year, marked by the flood, prejudice, lost manuscripts, uncertain employment, Luis had found an island and oasis, not one to hide in and forget the world, but a place of nourishment and support, a point of departure for someone ready to spread his wings and soar.

Chapter 40

MRS. B HAD PLANS FOR LUIS, and they were not all musical.

Could she make him into a gentleman, much as Pygmalion transformed a statue of Galatea into a living human being? That was probably impossible, but daunting tasks were Mrs. B's cup of tea. At least he would learn the fundamentals of grooming, posture, etiquette, deportment. He would learn how to pay attention to his clothing, and he would receive gently used clothing from her eldest son and other friends and relations. Hygiene! That certainly would come before all the others, but table manners and such would be close behind.

At his first dinner with the Breunings, Luis displayed all the characteristics that would need to be kindly, almost invisibly corrected: the spilling of water, knocking over a wine glass, reaching across others, standing and leaning into the table to grab a biscuit from a bowl; belching, scratching his head, and picking his protruding teeth with a fork. No, no. This would never do. Mrs. B made certain at this dinner—a happy, cheerful group of laughing children, herself, and a close friend—that Luis sat beside her. With her unmatched finesse and delicacy, she guided the young man so he did not even realize he was guided, but continued to converse and joke with the others, his behavior corrected and improved.

"Luis," she said to him one evening, when they had a moment alone after a fine meal, "you are a wonderful musician and will go far in life. But do not disdain the seemingly unimportant details by which civilized people judge their peers."

While Luis was expanding his horizons at the Breunings that spring and summer, Neefe was experiencing some trying times at the court chapel. Luis continued to play, unpaid, as second organist on Sunday services, but how long would they continue? What if the new Elector, Maximilian Franz, were to eliminate their positions altogether? As a Protestant, Neefe was keenly aware he was skating on thin ice.

One day when Luis was not present, a message was delivered to Neefe's little office. It bore the official seal of the Elector. Neefe held it sometime before opening the letter, his hand shaking ever so slightly. He put it down, took a sip of water, and picked it up again. He placed his wire-rim glasses on his long, thin nose, and carefully unfolded the correspondence.

Reading the short message, Neefe sighed and sank back in his chair. The letter fluttered from his hand, and he cast his eyes upward. "Thank God," he said to no one in particular, "we are safe." The new Elector was keeping on Neefe as well as the younger organist, though there would be an initial decrease in Neefe's salary. Neefe would have to pay the young man out of his own pocket. The teacher knew there was no shortage of music students in the community to amplify his income as a teacher, and though the theaters were closed as part of the government's austerity program, it would not be long before the human hunger for cultural stimulation would force a renaissance of dramatic art.

Luis burst into the room at this moment. "My lad, sit down!" he said, as Luis barged into the loft, then stopped and turned around with a quizzical look. Neefe lifted the letter and held it high, saying, "We are both safe: full-time positions, pay for us both."

Luis burst into a great smile and would have given Neefe a hug had the teacher been more huggable. "That is excellent news, sir!"

Neefe closed his eyes, squinted, and then opened them again, and looked closely at his assistant. "Luis, you are looking good lately, what's going on in your life?" Luis briefly mentioned the Breuning family, and Neefe nodded approvingly. Just the final touches he needed, the teacher thought. What a relief, though, to know the Neefe and the Beethoven families would not be destitute.

While the rushing sound of musical exploration and improvisation rang throughout the otherwise empty chapel court, other developments impacting both men were unfolding throughout the north. Many months had passed since Forster had ridden on horseback to Kassel with copies of the Rovantini and Wert notebooks, and not a word had been communicated back to the local Illuminati director.

That was about to change. Soemmerring had written a book referring to the Kassel experiment, and published it. At the same time, many leaders of the Germanic states as well as Church officials were beginning to crack down on the very existence of the Illuminati as division and dissension tore apart its structure and ability to function cohesively. In some ways, the tolerant intellectual policies of the Enlightenment were backfiring, as the racist viewpoints of a small number of members began to take root and strangle the majority viewpoint that the human community is one. Neefe would soon find himself in the middle of these turbulent, world-shaping events.

Chapter 41

LEADERS OF THE ENLIGHTENMENT were "science mad." Royal and commoner, man and woman, poet and mechanic, they could not get enough data and factual information about the world around them. Amateur experiments abounded, often with dire results to flora and fauna. The search for knowledge knew few if any boundaries as Northern Europe hung precariously between the influence of two revolutions, one an accomplished fact and one a work in progress, not unlike a volatile magnet pulled by positive and negative poles.

This and other topics relating to world affairs came up at a dinner party at the Breunings. A new guest was at the table this night, a Professor Louis Jacob. The von Breunings had been friends with the Jacob family, as with so many others. The professor occasionally looked at the far end of the table and squinted, then would resume speaking with Mrs. B, another guest, Karmela, an artist, as well as Wegeler, about Jacob's own hopes to become an assistant professor at Halle.

"Halle, sir?" asked Luis, hearing this name for the first time in many months. "Do you know Professor Forster?" Jacob's eyes opened with surprise, and he looked over his glasses at the young man.

"Perhaps, which Professor Forster do you mean?" Luis left his seat (to the consternation of the servants and a few giggles from his friends) and hurried to the professor's side.

"I am not sure," he said, "but I know that my teacher, who is director of a reading society here in the city, said last year that Professor Forster was taking some documents to that part of the world. I was never given all the details."

"And what is your particular interest in this?" asked the philosopher.

"My cousin died suddenly last year, possibly after meeting someone in Halle," Luis continued, an earnest, somewhat worried expression on his face. Jacob looked at the boy and wondered how such a dark, rough guest found his way to the inner circle of this refined family.

"Well, yes, there was a professor who disappeared, without a trace," Jacob murmured. "His rooms were searched for clues, but none were found. I'll tell you what I'll do, though. When I return next week, I'll mention your cousin to Professor Forster. His son is somehow wrapped up in an investigation, also involving a man named Soemmerring."

"Yes, that is the group!" said Luis eagerly, "I know there must be some connection. My teacher is Neefe, I'll ask him to contact you, if I may (Luis remembered to add a polite phrase at this point), since he has lost touch with the younger Forster."

"Luis, sit down!" said Wegeler with a wink "you're going to spoil the professor's soup!" The group resumed a lighter tone as Luis hurried back to his seat, but seemed to daydream with a slight scowl on his face throughout the remainder of dinner.

The next day, he arrived earlier than usual at the court chapel, scrambled up the stairs to the organ loft, and was quick to tell his teacher what had transpired. Neefe put down his journal, and listened carefully. "What do you mean?" he asked. "What is the connection between your cousin and Halle? It appeared that all the activity surrounding those notebooks occurred in Kassel which is halfway between Halle and our city."

"Look into it, sir," urged Luis, "you deserve to hear from them, and they have your copies, remember?" That was true, mused Neefe, and once someone possessed copies, who knows how that link would be traced back to him and his young assistant. Here they had narrowly secured employment, and should not be doing anything to draw attention to themselves or jeopardize their positions. After all, they were at risk enough.

"I'll attend to it," said Neefe, calmly as though it were his idea. "Now, show me that sketch for a piano sonata."

The boy was progressing at a rate that astonished even his teacher, and now was a professional with a salary employed by the court. Thoughts of finance were never far from the heads of Neefe, Luis, and other musicians in the day, and directed most of their actions. Here it was, however, that the humanism of the Illuminati provided a larger context than income for musicians and other artists flourishing in the final decades of the 18th century. Through the influence of Neefe and his idealistic brothers, Luis's personal worldview, performance practice, and musical ideas were bathed in the light of a larger vision that embraced all of humankind and all of time.

But it was not to be for long. A small-scale, but dangerous dissent was weakening the egalitarian framework of the Illuminati. At the same time, the pressure exerted by the Church, specifically Jesuit critics, was crushing the organization from without. The overall leadership of the organization split, then fragmented as one leader had to flee for his life, another lost control of the remaining branches.

While the Illuminati throughout its brief radiance shed light over a dark world, the leaders of this movement themselves were tragic characters lost in a tangled web of organizational struggle, intrigue, and decay. The brightest days of the Illuminati were soon to end.

Sensing the time had come to pull back from his leadership role, Neefe wrote to Soemmerring, asking for information relating to the documents Forster had conveyed more than a year earlier. But there was no reply. The scientists had gone on to other subjects. The notebook copies had vanished. No one, least of all an impoverished, overworked music teacher in a distant state, was in a position to follow through and hound the sources like a detective chief inspector. The name of Wert was soon forgotten, the ruins at the Kassel bluff crumbled and were leveled by snow, wind, and rain. Soemmerring went on to become one of Europe's leading medical scientists. The name of Rovantini remained only in the hearts of family members far away, and in the mind of a teacher who had never known him.

Chapter 42

LUIS WAS NOW 14 and fast becoming the breadwinner for his parents, two brothers and himself. He performed as court organist, often playing alone during Neefe's absences, in the loft overlooking the chapel congregation with the Elector and his entourage to his left and the chorus and other musicians to his right. He also worked regularly in the Elector's orchestra, either as the official harpsichordist or in the back row occasionally playing the viola.

Despite the upturn in his fortunes, Luis had been stung by a negative review by a leading music critic the previous year, calling his first published efforts, "the work of a rank beginner." The world of music was rife with spite and sniping outside of the Elector's nest. Neefe encouraged his efforts despite this would-be assassin's single bullet, but there was much work to be done.

"Focus only on the music, what you think, above all what you feel," Neefe urged him warmly, noting how hard Luis had been hit by this salvo. "Life is often a battle, and we are battle-scarred but stronger for surviving an attack."

Luis did not reply at first. But one winter's day, arriving for his lesson, he said, "Sir, I am done with composition. Let's just focus on technique." Neefe did not know what to say, but was stressing over financial and personal concerns of his own.

"Well, we'll see," he said at last. "It can't hurt to take a break," thinking that both their fortunes did in fact ride on the success of his protégée as a church organist and keyboard artist rather than for compositional forays. "You will change your tune, young man," Neefe added.

As he shook off this dark mood over time, Luis continued to enjoy his role as piano tutor at the von Breunings', basking in the maternal affection and attention showered on him by the dignified lady of the house, her soft brown eyes following him smartly. And he continued to make friends outside of the family circle. One such friend was Tony Reicha, a personable teen with curly brown hair and an honest brow, who had just joined the orchestra as flutist. While responsibilities and lessons gave them little free time, the two young men, roughly the same age, enjoyed hanging out, sharing a sometimes boisterous sense of humor, and making music in the von Breuning parlor, which was supplanting home as a base of operations.

Egged on by Tony, Luis decided to see how far he could go in baiting the somewhat self-important tenor, Heller, during Passion Week in March. During the days before Easter, organ music was prohibited, so Luis would be seated at the pianoforte during a selection known as the Lamentations of Jeremiah. This selection features pauses in which the pianist is encouraged to improvise.

Now, Luis was not lacking in self-confidence and by this time had an extraordinary view of his own capacity as a musician, especially in the area of improvisation. As it turned out, this extraordinary view was entirely warranted. "Heller," he said, during a rehearsal, "you are always on pitch. What do you think about a little experiment? During the pauses in Jeremiah, I think I can throw you off pitch!"

Heller, a rather prim, supercilious gentleman with a dislike of change in any form, pulled in his chin and looked disdainfully at the young musician. "I doubt that seriously, my young man," he said. "Try as you may, you will not affect my performance." The other singers murmured among themselves, some supporting their peer, others with twinkles in their eyes hoping for a sound come-uppance.

And so it was during one of the Passion Week performances, the chapel packed to capacity with worshippers and officials, that the Lamentations began. His eyes sparkling, with a wink at Reicha, Luis launched into his bold improvisation, completely changed pitch, modulated in a way never heard before into the key furthest from the rest of the selection. Like a mad spinner, soon Luis had wrapped rings of sound around the astonished and flustered Heller's vocal solo while repeatedly tapping the grounding note of the original key with his left pinkie (in a gesture of fair play). Heller became so entangled in this web of music, he utterly lost his place, turned a bright shade of red, and stalked out.

The Chapel Master Lucchesi and first violinist, Ries, looked at each other in perfect amazement, but had no criticism of Luis, who, after all, was totally playing by the rules. Reicha, however, had to cover his mouth to stifle his laughter. And it is said that the Elector, when informed of this transgression, smiled slightly, and later suggested the young keyboard artist be a little more charitable to older members of the ensemble.

A few blocks away, the Beethoven household was preparing for yet another move, this time because their musical activities were disturbing the sleep of the landlord, the baker Fischer. All the rentals the Beethovens lived in were in close proximity to each other, and one wondered whether music from the new flat on Wenzel Street, barely a block away and a bit farther from the river, also might have disturbed the sleep of the baker; but apparently, that was not the case. It was a noisy town in any event, with church bells at all hours of day and night, horns and bells from the river, music practice throughout the city (including the penetrating sounds of brass instruments and the beating of drums), and the bustle of foot and horse traffic from early in the day.

It hardly affected Luis's life, though. He missed the view of the gently rolling Seven Mountains from his bedroom window. He was spending more time at the von Breunings', and even had a small room in which he could stay at night. With good conversation, friends, delicious food, a superior pianoforte, and servants if you needed anything whatsoever, there was less and less attraction to the squalor of his original home. And though he loved his mother, young men in mid-adolescence, driven by the power of their own ideas, physical energy, and creativity, naturally move on to the mastery of their own lives, charting a path to the fulfillment of their dreams.

While he enjoyed the conversation with Stephen, and sometimes Chris, it was with the eldest von Breuning sibling, Eleanor, that Luis formed the strongest bond. Eleanor was attractive and smart without being fussy or fashionable. Her large brown eyes shone with humor and intelligence, her long brown hair was smooth and unaffected, with a simple bang cut across her forehead. Luis did not notice people's mode of dress unless it was particularly ostentatious, but here again, Eleanor made an impression of simplicity, good taste, and authenticity. Moreover, Eleanor had a gift for music, and loved music almost as much as Luis did himself.

As the piano tutor to the household, Luis spent time each day with one or the other of the Breuning siblings, but it was the teaching of Eleanor which gave him the most pleasure. He was keenly aware, sitting close beside her on the bench, sometimes grasping her fingers and repositioning them on the keyboard, her hair perhaps grazing his face as he did so, that there was more to life than study, practice, and performance. They sometimes looked each other in the eye and said nothing, and a little smile hovered on Eleanor's pretty lips as she turned away to some other task.

"How wonderful to live in the same age as Mozart!" she exclaimed one day, as they were concluding a lesson involving a recent piece by the great artist. "Do you ever wonder how it is possible that such a genius can exist?"

Luis was warm from the exertion of demonstrating his pianistic technique to the max, as well as from the pleasurable experience of being close to Eleanor. "Sure," he said, "sure. He is the greatest."

"But there's something else, isn't there," said Eleanor, sinking gracefully into a chintz-covered divan and smoothing down the folds of her dark green dress. "You are a composer, too. Why don't you let me play one of your compositions?"

Luis sat across from her and looked into her kind, but challenging gaze. "I will, in time," he said. Then warming to the conversation, "I am at an odd point in my life, Elly," he said.

"In what way?"

"So many musical ideas came to me in recent years. My teacher helped me manage them, organize my thoughts. I've had works published…"

"I know!"

"…and received mostly praise, though one critic was sharp

and demeaning…"

"I hate that! But you wouldn't let that stop you, would you?"

"No! Of course not. But it's this, Elly: I have to expand to larger forms, and I'm not sure now how to get there. I need more training, more information, even more than Neefe can provide." Eleanor nodded, her brow wrinkled in deep understanding.

"You need a coach, someone who can take you to the next level. You still have ideas, though, right?"

"Of course I do!" snapped Luis, then blushed at the harshness of his tone. "Yes, I'm sorry, I am bursting with ideas, and that's how I improvise so well. But I can't seem to translate them into formally written music. It's as though the classical forms aren't big enough to contain them!"

Eleanor laughed. "Yes, mother and Stephen just last night were saying that no one can improvise like Luis! You may have invented a new form of music!"

Luis liked the sound of this: inventor of a new form of music, though it was clear that Eleanor didn't understand that he was talking about formal composition, not just improvisation. Perhaps he would be an inventor of new music. Perhaps the architect of music who would change the world! It is not too grandiose for young people to believe so absolutely in their own powers.

Luis looked at Eleanor, her brown hair lit by the sun from behind, forming a kind of golden halo around her head and shoulders. He threw back his head and looked up with unfocusing eyes on the high ceiling, then snapped back to his usual position. "Elly, I have to go!" and without another word or gesture, the young man bolted from the room to the court chapel less than two blocks away. Everything was so close. There was no getting away from anything in the city. Not from criticism or envy, not from prejudice or intolerance, not from family or poverty. Not even from the first stirrings of love. It was a closed system, pressing in on him, and he was ready to break away.

Chapter 43

AUTUMN WITH ITS GLORY of bright colors came to the small city, and, with the Elector out of town, Luis had a few days to indulge in walks out in the bordering countryside and along the river, as he, his father, and Rovantini had done some years before. Now, thanks to the von Breuning library and the generosity of his hostess, he had books to take on his foot journeys, and today, that would mean Homer, whose adventurous tales of men and monsters captured his imagination. Even more intriguing were Homer's lofty ideals: the nobility of man's striving, the sacredness of marriage, the importance of a high calling, the moral character of women. These were ideals not only of the Golden Age, but also of his own age, when authors such as Rousseau and Goethe extolled these virtues and made them their own.

Luis rose from his spot beneath a ginkgo tree, heavy with gold "coins," which showered down on him with a passing breeze. The gold of literature, the gold of nature, and soon, if his vocation continued at this pace, gold to line his pockets and his family's.

Back at the von Breunings', he had a lesson on Rousseau in French with Mrs. B., followed by another boring exploration of the rules of etiquette.

"And in what order do we use the silverware?"

"From the outside inward, m'am."

"And our elbows? Where are they stationed?"

"Off of the table!"

"Well, done, my boy," she said, ending the lesson, "just

imagine playing the piano with your elbows on the keys!" The image was too much for Luis, who had to stifle a loud laugh with his cupped hand. "All right, isn't it time for someone's lesson?"

Luis bowed, and as she left the room from the right, he hurried through the left door to the music room, where Eleanor, this time in a sea-green dress, her hair pulled back with a headband, sat waiting, with a smile.

"Oh, I'm so glad to see you, Luis," she said, shuffling over, but not too far. "You've been out and about, I suppose?"

"Yes," said Luis, eagerly sitting down beside her, and not necessarily eager for more music lessons. "It's so beautiful and refreshing outside, have you seen the trees?"

"Outside my window," she said, sounding a little sad. "I should like to go for a walk with you some time."

The lessons began with an adagio by Gluck, since Eleanor was an accomplished and enthusiastic pianist. They discussed the fingering and the phrasing, tying it to the breath, in the modern style.

"This is so different from the organ!" said Luis, out of context.

"Well, of course!" his pupil averred, "Luis, whatever are you thinking?"

"I am thinking," he said at last, his heart ready to burst, "that I would like to give you a kiss!"

Eleanor blushed red and drew back a little. "Why certainly not!" she exclaimed, then did something that threw Luis for a loop. She turned toward him, grasped his left arm, and gave him a long kiss on the cheek. A long, lingering kiss; and one could hardly imagine what books she had been reading lately to think of this. Then she ran from the music room, slammed the door, and the patter of feet running upstairs was the last to be heard of her that night.

Luis smiled, and rubbed his cheek. That was a good feeling, he decided. She might have smacked him! But he should not be too encouraged. He was after all a guest by the scrape of his neck.

This and other vignettes played out in the life of the young musician in the small city where he lived, but the world beyond its gates was reeling with ideas and revolt. The musicians and singers of this town took all their cues from the Elector, and the aristocracy chose to remain isolated and insulated from the social and political dynamics of late 18th century Europe.

It was fortunate that Neefe was skilled at multi-tasking; in fact, he seemed to thrive on juggling a multitude of responsibilities and getting close to the edge when it came to issues of survival and narrow escapes. With opera and theater in effect closed to him, he began editing scores, translating operas, reviving his own works and sending them to other cities for consideration.

His leadership in the Illuminati, however, had reached and passed its zenith at this time and was too dangerous to continue. In the south, Adam Weishaupt of Ingolstadt, the father of the Illuminati, and a man whose character it was difficult to gauge, had left the country, and edicts against the Illuminati and other secret societies were being issued throughout the German-speaking world in the face of lies and distortions about the group's true purpose. ("The trouble with secret societies," Nicolai, a Berlin Illuminatus, once told him, "is that even their justification for existence is secret. We yield them to no one, even at the demand of Death.")

Similarly, Freemasons were under suspicion of sedition and espionage, though they had included among their ranks aristocrats, professionals, and musicians, including the Mozarts, father and son. The time to disband the local Illuminati church had arrived, and Neefe would have to do so now, before the terror sweeping through the southern states broke through the town borders and engulfed him and the membership in a conflagration of violence, undoing all their good work in a single blow.

During the next lesson, Neefe thought it was time to bring Luis into the fold.

"Luis," said Neefe, putting aside his notebook and looking up from his desk. "I want to skip the formal instruction today. Are you free all afternoon?" The young man nodded. "I hear," Neefe continued, "that you are reading great literature with the von Breunings."

"Yes!" Luis asserted, sitting down in the chair by the door, "Rousseau, Goethe and Schiller, some Shakespeare in translation. I especially like Homer!"

"Good, good," said Neefe absently, checking his watch, "yes, all good. Revolutionary, some would say, but those are the times we live in." He paused for a moment, as though looking for the right words. "Luis, I am going to take you to the Minerval Church. It will be closing soon, forever."

"Really," said Luis, not sure how this affected him, and thinking, "I hope he's not going to ask me to write a Requiem!"

"You've been there before, you've helped me on many occasions. In fact," he added, "you are almost a member yourself!"

"I don't think so!" Luis said rather boldly. "Organizations are not for me."

"Well, perhaps they are, perhaps some organizations, if

sufficiently forward-thinking and supportive of individual development," his teacher continued, nonplussed. "We're going to visit Simrock and then the three of us are going to close the church for good."

"Simrock!" said Luis, "The horn player?"

"Simrock, the Illuminatus," said Neefe quietly. "And for today, you will address him as 'Jubal.'"

"And you?" asked Luis, actually feeling a little annoyed by this game of pretenses. "What shall I call you?"

"Today," said Neefe, "I am Glaucus. By the way, you know Grossmann?" Luis was silent, not pleased with a memory from many years ago. "He was my predecessor as Director of our colony. Yes, he is Illuminati, too!" The news surprised the young man, but he said nothing. "And you," continued Neefe, "you will have a name from antiquity as well. What will it be?"

Luis thought a long time. At first, he considered just laughing and walking out, but there was something about Neefe's seriousness, and the fact that he owed his teacher so much. At least he could do this for him, whatever it meant. "Then let it be Telemachus," said Luis, referring to the son of Odysseus in Homer's The Odyssey. Neefe nodded, pleased with the choice, which suggested a humility he didn't think the young man possessed.

The two left the court chapel and walked back into town. But instead of heading toward the church, Neefe directed Luis to a different part of the city. They were soon at a large apartment, and it was Simrock himself who opened the door. "Welcome, Glaucus," he said, without a trace of sarcasm or embarrassment. "And who do we have here?"

Luis thought, you know you I am, we play music together

every week! "Telemachus," said Neefe. "Telemachus, meet Jubal."

Luis thought this was a bit much, but went along with two men he admired and trusted. There was no one else in the house. They went into a good-sized parlor with a grand piano, a table, and numerous chairs. "Excuse me, sir, but...aren't we going to the church?" asked Luis.

"We are," said Neefe. "We are there right now."

Chapter 44

LUIS SAT DOWN with the others around the table. "I am confused. I know the Minerval Church, I've been there before."

"That," said Neefe, "is a building we've used. Its time is gone. This," he gestured with his hand, "is a building we use today. Tomorrow it will have a different function."

"Luis, there is only one Minerval Church," added Simrock. "And it is the minds and hearts of our brothers." Neefe reached into his jacket and produced a document. "Here," he said, "are the so-called secrets of the Illuminati. I am disbanding our colony today. Our other members know as much, and we have parted company, but I wanted to give you the opportunity to be formally insinuated before its doors are closed forever."

"Why such haste?" asked Luis, as Simrock rose and pulled the curtains tight over the windows, lighting a lantern though it was mid-afternoon.

"The level of persecution in the south has reached a dangerous level," Neefe said as Simrock returned to his seat. "Just last week, a police raid on the home of a prominent Illuminatus—our brother Cato—near Munich resulted in a major cache of secret information falling into the hands of the authorities."

"What did the police find?" Luis asked, wondering what he was getting into.

Neefe and Simrock exchanged looks that were difficult to fathom. Then Neefe spoke. "Symbols, calendars, rosters, statutes: everything of an incriminating nature. I won't go into the reasons these are feared by the authorities, but suffice it to say, reason itself is under attack."

"Mind you, Luis, we are not in any way against the Church or any religion," Simrock added, "at least in our colony. But in the South, there is a vicious conflict between the followers of reason and the Jesuit Order which controls higher education and has an unshakeable influence on government." He was expressing his own view of the Jesuits in saying this.

Luis, who had been educated by Jesuits at the Academy, nodded. "My teachers were all right," he added, "but I admit I don't read the newspapers." Simrock smiled to himself.

"Well, the newspapers are not necessarily a source of truth, either," he said. "Truth is an elusive maiden; you think you've found her hiding behind a tree, and it turns out to be a goat!"

Neefe frowned. "What Simrock is saying is that one of the purposes of the Illuminati has been to make truth available to its members, leaders in society, who in turn will convey it to others. The Jesuit Order is not bad in and of itself, but we believe that power-hungry activists within it are a threat to the exchange of ideas. The police abrogated documents containing volatile information, including tracts in defense of women's rights including a treatise by Mary Wollstonecraft, the English feminist, and equality among the races."

"I cannot believe all this is going on in our world, and all I have thought about is music!" said Luis. "But can music break down barriers and make the world a better place?"

"Of course it can," said Neefe, growing visibly excited, "In fact, it is the best vehicle for conveying noble thoughts; to my mind, the only one. All people may be inspired and uplifted by great music, it can dissolve social barriers. We have a sacred role in bringing this illumination to the people!"

"Easy, Neefe, let's get back to today's business," said Simrock, tapping his friend on the hand. "Luis, your questions are good ones. But for now, we want to bring you into the brotherhood in the spirit of intellectual freedom and to ensure the continuation of ideals of reason, liberty, and equality."

"From this day," said Neefe, "the Illuminati that we have known will no longer exist. But our ideals will live on. And so, we invite you to be part of the great idea that was the Illuminati, to be part of our network, which will connect you with leaders and men of action throughout the states and provinces of our world."

Luis nodded. The idea that there was a network of people who loved ideas, freedom, and social justice appealed to him, first, because he was an idealistic young man bursting with ideas, but also because he needed help charting his course in the future. A bleak future of playing last-chair viola in the back of a second-rate orchestra awaited him unless he was able to seize and maximize connections.

"I will do it," he said.

Neefe and Simrock exhaled, Neefe smiled, and patted the young man on the back. Then, he opened the document "…and for the last time…" he said, speaking to Simrock, reading a list of questions to Luis, who answered them simply and clearly. At the conclusion, the men rose, each in turn welcoming Luis with a handshake and warm embrace. Then Neefe looked at Simrock, who lifted the lantern on the table. Neefe held the paper over the flame, and all three watched in silence as it crackled and burned to a black crisp, falling in pieces onto the table.

"It is done," said Neefe.

"Welcome to the future, Telemachus," said Simrock. Luis half-smiled, took a deep breath, and felt a sense of belonging, a kind of power, and a special connection stemming from secret knowledge. No one, other than these two men and their "brothers," would ever know he was Illuminati; but he knew, and that was the beginning of a new stage in his development as an artist and a human being.

Chapter 45

LUIS TOOK A DETOUR down by the river, then came home where there was more confusion and noise than usual. He now had a new baby sister, Maria, and his two brothers were growing older and more boisterous, practicing music but demonstrating no talent. Carl, who had a knack for business and negotiating, often worked carrying messages for a few coins, some of which actually wound up in the family coffers.

Luis stopped in his parents' room to visit the baby. The first surviving girl child in the family, she was thriving despite her mother's increasing ill health. She stopped crying when her eldest brother appeared and tickled her under her chin. For a moment, Luis thought she looked a bit like him, not like the rest of the family, but it was a fleeting assessment. He patted her head, and went to his room to practice and reflect on the day's surprising events.

More than ever, he mused, looking out the window at a row of dismal old shops, he appreciated the gift of the von Breunings' patronage and affection. Add to this the new contacts he had been making—Wegeler, Reicha, the Kugelgen twins, the Eichoffs—and now the promise of even greater associations with former Illuminati and Masons: there was some potential for growth.

On the one hand, Luis was responsible for his family; on the other, he was responsible for himself.

Across town, Eleanor put down her needlework and thought she would take a walk. "Eleanor. I would like to have a word with you." Mrs. B. intercepted her fleet-footed daughter about to run outside.

Eleanor did not like the tone of her mother's voice, nor the stiffness in her manner. She stopped, and ever so slightly rolled her eyes. Was this going to be another one of those, "Your body is changing" discussions, or, "Have you considered how humans are born?" Unlike other mothers of her time, Mrs. B. believed in factual information and candor, but these were not always what children wanted to hear.

She placed a gentle hand on Eleanor's back and ushered her into the boudoir and closed the door. She pressed firmly on the handle, and it let out a resounding "Snap!"

"What is it, Mother," said Eleanor, smoothing a spot on the vanity bench and sitting down. She patted the pleats in her dark blue dress and avoided looking into her mother's eyes.

"Eleanor," said Mrs. B, "you are almost 15 aren't you? I can't imagine where the time has flown!" She forced a small smile, then continued in serious tones. "Eleanor, I want to talk to you about Luis." Eleanor played with a ruffle and still did not look up. "Sure, what is it?" she asked nonchalantly.

"I can't help but notice that you and he are very close," Mrs. B said. Eleanor looked up, her brown eyes darkening with feeling.

"Yes, yes, we are. He is a wonderful person and a great musician. He…"

"Yes, yes, I couldn't agree more, my dear!" Mrs. B. interrupted. "I think of him almost as my fifth child, you know that, surely."

"I do," said Eleanor, composing herself again, and looking down.

"You spend a lot of time together, and I know he likes you very much, more even than the boys whom I thought would be his natural companions."

"Oh, well, them!" Eleanor gave a small laugh. "Maybe in time, Mother, but right now, I don't hold much hope for their ability to have an intelligent conversation!"

Mrs. B. did not contest this point, untrue though it was. "Eleanor," she said, "I just want to make sure that your affection for Luis does not get out of hand." Eleanor bristled but tried to contain her emotions. "Luis will always be a part of our family," the mother continued. "In some ways, he has even helped to fill the vacuum left by your father's death. I encourage you to think of him as a friend, a tutor, even a brother of sorts, but not…"

"Mother!" Eleanor blurted between clenched teeth. "We are just friends! I love Luis with all my heart, but I am not going to run away and marry him!"

Mrs. B. took a deep breath. It was a rare sight to see Eleanor so distraught, and in fact, her heightened color made her more beautiful than her normally placid state. "Well, I did not think so. You see, we live in a world not of our own making. Our hearts cry out with feelings that sometimes overwhelm us, and yet, we are not at liberty to yield to the strongest and most powerful impulses." She took another breath, and reached out and placed her fingertips on her daughter's warm hand. "Luis is an unusual case. He is one of us, and yet, he is not one of us. Surely you see that in his rude manners, his poor clothing…"

"Are you saying the clothes we give him are poor?" snapped back Eleanor.

"Of course not, child, but the fact that we give him the only good clothing and food he has is significant. He is not of our class and station. But I agree completely that he surpasses this entire family for talent, an appetite for knowledge, and for potential."

"I hate class! I hate a world that pigeon-holes people by accidents of birth!" exclaimed Eleanor, her eyes full of unshed tears.

"It is not fair," agreed her mother, "but it is life. Moreover, Luis has other handicaps."

"I know what this is about," said Eleanor, grabbing a comb and smacking it on the table, "it's because he's black, isn't it. Not pale and rosy like the von Breunings, no, not like our dinner guests and the people in the court! He is wild, isn't he. Wild with that unruly mane of hair and that dark skin…"

"Eleanor, stop it!" Mrs. B. had had enough of adolescent histrionics. She stood up and put a firm hand on her eldest child's shoulders. Eleanor's tears were rolling down her flushed cheeks, but she was not sobbing or making any sound. "It is true," the mother continued. "Doors are being opened for Luis, and I hope to open even more doors for him through introductions and by helping him develop the necessary social skills to thrive in our community. But there is nothing I can do about prejudice. We can love Luis for the person he is, but outsiders will always see him as a stranger, an outsider…"

Eleanor stood up and faced her mother, who had not until then realized how tall and womanly her daughter had become. "I love Luis because of who he is," she said firmly. "I love to rub his hair when we're just kidding about, and I love it when our hands are together on the keyboard, like black keys and white, his dark hands over my fair hands, perhaps infusing some of his genius and skill through the touch of our skin…."

Mrs. B. thought she was going faint. "Eleanor, what have you been reading! I swear, I try to give you children a sound liberal education, and it comes back to me in such a way! Eleanor, don't say another word about rubbing and skin and all that! Listen to me: affection is dangerous. Be wary. Yes, love Luis, but guard your heart."

"Mother," sighed Eleanor, taking her mother's hands in a gesture of friendship, "I do love Luis, but, as you said, it is a different kind of love. Not a brotherly love, it's more than that. But it is not romantic love, either, honestly it's not. I know I must save my heart for a good marriage, and heaven knows who will marry a brainy, self-important girl like me!"

Her mother smiled. "Perhaps a lawyer or a doctor, someone who can appreciate your many gifts, your beauty and your kind heart," Mrs. B. said.

"I know you want what is best for me," Eleanor said, wiping her eyes on the back of her hand. "I am sorry I lost control, it's just that Luis is so dear to me."

"Perhaps you just need some female friends," soothed Mrs. B., putting an arm around Eleanor as the two women sat down, side by side, on the bench. "Luis is dear to us both, Eleanor, and he will always be part of our home. Do you understand?" Eleanor nodded. Her reason told her that her mother's advice was correct, but deep in her heart, Eleanor knew that Luis held a special place, and whether she had a dozen lovers and several marriages in years to come, no one would unseat him in the center of her heart.

"I know. My best role, I think, is to help him succeed," Eleanor said, "that is," she added with a small smile, "after I have achieved a good education and planned a successful life for myself. If Luis succeeds, and I know he will, then I will have had a hand in every good thing he accomplishes throughout his life." The two women hugged, but Mrs. B. did not know the depth of Eleanor's devotion; for if she had, the young man would have been banished within the hour.

Chapter 46

A YOUNG MAN'S FANCY was taking the back burner in the small city, however, for some new developments were promising to boost Luis's career aspirations in a more material and immediate way. One Count Waldstein, an aristocrat as well known for his musical abilities as for his wealth, had been following the burgeoning career of Luis from afar. He had even acquired the scores of several of his compositions. Waldstein put a bug in the Elector's ear, and it wasn't long before Neefe had news for the young musician at the midweek rehearsal.

"Come here, come here," Neefe said with unusual nervous energy, pulling Luis into his office and carefully closing the door. "Look at this." He thrust an official document under Luis's nose.

"What is this?" the young man asked, his eyes widening as he read. "Is this true? Is this some kind of joke?"

"No, no, it's true! The Elector is sending you to Vienna to study with Mozart!" Luis put his hand to his head and sank backward into the rickety chair with a thud.

"I can't believe it!" he said, starting to laugh. "Master, did you do this?"

"No, not I, not I. Count Waldstein has been following your career and is very much impressed. He convinced the Elector to do this. Now," Neefe sighed, "there is one 'rub.' We have to come up with some matching funds!"

"I've been saving money every week for travel, for education," said Luis.

"All well and good," said Neefe, "but I doubt it will cover the cost of such a journey. You will be on the road a while just getting there, then you must provide for yourself while in the city, which is very expensive. And who knows when Mozart will actually get to see you."

"I must tell my mother!" Luis exclaimed. "And Eleanor. And Mrs. von Breuning. And Wegeler and Kugelgen and…"

"Calm down," said Neefe, "and don't forget your father in that mix, either. But the good news is, Count Waldstein is very wealthy and very much interested in your education. So whatever happens, while finances will be tight, well, we've been through that before, haven't we. Good luck, my lad, and right after Christmas, start making your preparations!"

Preparations began immediately. What would he play for Mozart during his audition? Would he be allowed to show the great master one of his own compositions? Would Mozart teach him to compose large-scale works? Could he improvise on a theme the composer suggested?

Luis changed his mind several times before deciding on Mozart's own 11th piano sonata in A major, the so-called "Turkish March" sonata. Neefe approved, but cautioned him not to be overly confident. "Mozart is not only the world's greatest composer," he said, "but a star of the Enlightenment, a man committed to Masonic ideals so similar to those of our own brotherhood."

It was winter when Luis kissed his mother good-bye, shook his father's hand, patted his brothers and baby sister on the heads, and turned his back on home.

Chapter 47

THE COACH SLOWLY ENTERED the great city of Vienna. A light snow had fallen, leavening the heavy cityscape of Habsburg architecture, displayed in a faded green and grey silhouette against the winter sky. Heavy, ponderous, oppressive: the city did not welcome him. And yet the swirling snow seemed playful and bright. There was something captivating about the city from the start. Luis left the coach not far from his designated dwelling and carried his small bag, portfolio, letters of introduction, and violin case close to his body as he tracked snow up the steps into the small pension.

That night, the snow dispersing to reveal a nearly full moon, Luis spent at the window, looking out over the winding streets and stoic buildings, hunching over the city like brooding raptors, watching the shadows lengthen and the world turn from grey-green to black. Although he was no lover of the violin, he opened the case, tightened the bow, rubbed rosin on the tightly strung horsehair, and improvised some variations on an old German air. Against the window, from outside, he cast a silhouette of his own: a small, thin magician weaving golden threads of musical sound among the moonbeams.

Soon, he would meet Mozart.

There was a whirlwind round of introductions, meetings, greetings as the weather improved throughout the week. After some initial caution, Luis abandoned himself to the warmth and energy of Vienna. Never had he seen so many different types of people before, not even in Cologne those many years past, nor tasted such interesting cuisine. So it was, well fed and confident in the strange city, that Luis arrived on a sunny afternoon at the master's door. Braced for a rebuff by the butler, he received none, only a raised eyebrow, as he boldly stepped into the foyer of the attractive apartments and strode with vigor into the sitting room, where he was kept waiting for more than a half hour.

Then, suddenly, there was Mozart. He was obviously in a good mood, humming, and accompanied by two gentlemen with gloomy, suspicious looks and dark brown suits. What a contrast was Mozart, all buffed and puffed, in a spotless white satin waistcoat, exquisitely embroidered in green and golden silk, green knickers, and white silk hose. His wig was immaculate and perfectly positioned on his beautiful, though somewhat too large, head. The two gloomy men talked in their deep voices, while Mozart flitted airily from table to chair to writing desk. Then after a pause, he noticed Luis sitting there on the edge of a satin cushioned chair, his knees apart rather defiantly, his portfolio flat on the floor beside him.

Without taking his eyes off Luis, Mozart whispered to one of the brown-clad men, who grumbled back at him. "I see!" he said at last. "Well, welcome, Mr. Luis, I am pleased to meet you." Luis nodded an acknowledgment but made no motion to rise. "So, first, you need to know," said Mozart walking back and forth, looking at his pocket watch, "that I need to leave here in exactly a half hour. How does that sound?"

"That's fine," said Luis.

"And what do you bring to me today from your fair city in the north?" the composer asked.

"I would like to play your Turkish Sonata, sir," said Luis.

"Here, what is this?" said Mozart approaching the young man.

"Some samples of my own compositions," said Luis, picking up the papers and handing them to the outstretched hand. He was not certain whether to be pleased or annoyed by the master's behavior.

"Hmm," said Mozart, flipping through the pages. "Ah! That is good. Freddie, take a look…" he said to one of the gloomy men, waving the score in his direction. Mozart sighed, and collapsed in a chair. "You know, young man, it is no easy life being a composer." Unknown to Luis, Mozart was about to compose Don Giovanni, though this day was devoted to auditions and administrative matters.

"Go on, then," he said, leaning back, his head resting against his hand. "Play what you will."

Luis rose and approached the grand piano. For a second, he thought, "Ah! Mozart's own!" but quickly dismissed any trace of idol-worship from his mind. He tested the keys, paused, then launched into the sonata.

Mozart listened, but in the slow movement, was heard to stifle a yawn. Luis stopped in mid-phrase, an icy premonition of failure creeping up his back, then a flush, as though faced with a life-and-death challenge.

"Sir," he said in a strong voice, "I know that everyone performs your sonatas. Let me show you what I am uniquely capable of. Give me a theme, any theme, and I will show you what I can do with improvisation."

Mozart cocked his head, pleased to hear someone who wasn't afraid of his greatness. He looked again at his pocket watch, and saw he had more time than he thought. The young man was certainly unusual, and had a commanding presence.

"Very well," he said, and quickly walked to the piano and sat down. "I just composed this, in fact, so I know you've never heard it before," he said, looking pleasantly at Luis. In a rather choppy manner, Mozart played the melody that would become "La ci darem la mano," from Don Giovanni. "Do you have that?" he asked Luis, who nodded. Mozart got up and walked to the window.

"There," he said, with a wink to Freddie and his double, "do your thing."

Luis put his hands on the keyboard and paused, as though absorbing the melody and processing it. He played it once, exactly as Mozart had done; then again, legato. Then, as though some flood gate connecting his hands to heart and his heart to his mind flew open, a cascade of music filled the air. Any trace of nervousness or apprehension, of fatigue or self-consciousness was gone.

Luis was one with the music.

And music it was, variation after variation, one more imaginative and technically difficult than the next, from the softest pianissimo to crashing fortissimos, chords Mozart had never heard before in polite courtly music, used with a kind of knowing abandon. Broad, serious declarations of sound, and small, impish gestures, little musical jokes.

How would anyone describe this music? Perhaps as controlled chaos, musical ideas and drive, shaking the piano until Mozart thought the lid would come crashing down. Then would come a variation of such tenderness, he had to strain to hear it. A number of other people had come to the doorway and were listening to something new, something they had never heard before.

"Oh my god," said Mozart, and sat down.

Anything else on the composer's mind disappeared, and his focus was entirely on the shape, velocity, inventiveness, and fire of the music pouring out of the piano. For Luis was in his 'raptus,' and music that had been pent up for years was being released. All the wonder and exultation, the pain and discipline, the laughter, the fear, birth, death, dread, anticipation: everything from a life of holding back was released in those moments. And after some good time, Luis pounced on the keys with a series of concluding chords, and there was silence.

Mozart took a handkerchief from his sleeve and dabbed his forehead. "My dear young man," he said. "I don't know what to say."

Luis was reeling from the explosion of feeling and power, but energized rather than exhausted by the experience. "Sir, will you take me as your student?" he asked, and it almost sounded like a demand.

Mozart looked at Freddie at the door. Freddie raised his eyebrows and shrugged, then lifted his watch as a reminder. "Oh, yes, I have to go," Mozart said. "Well! I feel almost faint! Yes, well, about these compositions," pulling the score back from Freddie. One was a string quartet with two sections in the peculiar key of E flat minor. Mozart looked at the pages, shuffling back and forth, stopping here and there to point to a phrase, nodding, muttering a few unintelligible words.

"Yes, good. Young man," he said, looking up at the disheveled creature before him, "you have talent. But I have work, and I must depart, soon." He looked back at the manuscript again, and called to Freddie, "Can I get a copy of this to take with me? Of course," he returned to Luis with a smile, "I've already got a copy here," pointing to his own head.

"What is your answer?" asked Luis, so close to the great man he could touch his white waistcoat. "Will you teach me piano and composition?"

Mozart smiled. "Your playing, so very serious! I'm not sure how that will play out in Vienna, we love our fluff. Well, I have to go. Yes, yes, see me next month. As a rule, I am not taking on new students. Have your people contact Freddie. We can arrange something."

Mozart was becoming animated, in part by the pressure of having to leave by a certain time. "Good-bye, then," he said, and coughed slightly, as though to cover up a swelling of emotion. Luis bowed, retrieved his papers, and walked confidently away from the composer and out the front door. It slammed discordantly behind him. Mozart sighed, looked at Freddie and said, "Keep an eye on that young man. One day, he will give the world something to talk about."

Chapter 48

LUIS SMILED TO HIMSELF. "I nailed it!" he thought, with a chuckle. Then blushed to think that he even had met the great Mozart, not to mention be accepted as a student. But now what? He had a month to wait it all out in a strange city, and no real friends or colleagues, save a few names on a scrap of paper. Though he was a mature professional in Bonn, in Vienna he was a 16-year-old kid.

Already, he had met or attempted to meet most of those individuals on his list, and he didn't have the social skills to network on his own. Even worse, he was running out of money.

Some time into this dilemma, his purse shrinking daily, Luis received the first of several agitated messages from home.

"Luis," his father wrote, "I am sorry to tell you this, but I fear you must return. Your mother is not doing well and speaks about you all the time. Stop at Augsburg on the way back. Neefe has arranged for you to give a recital there, a paying job."

And an odd footnote: "You know the theater is back in town. I have a major role in Brandt's production of The Deserter. Be sure to come back in time for that performance next month."

There was no choice in the matter. He would have to leave. Whose heart could be heavier than Luis's at this time? To accept the funds of his patrons to come all the way to Vienna, to meet Mozart, to receive his approval and acceptance as a student, and then to be called home. And the news about his mother: what did that signal? Was she truly declining, or was his manipulative father exaggerating to lure him home to his own operatic performance? What would this new, prospective patron, Count Waldstein, say now? And he felt awful. Half starved, asthmatic, stressed out, and barely sleeping, he wondered if he were truly ill or simply absorbing some of his teacher's notorious hypochondria.

It was best not to think. Luis obtained his passage, packed his small bag, picked up his violin case, and took the stage north. Leaving the city, the coach passed the Mozart residence. Luis looked glumly out the window, slightly spattered with raindrops, as the apartment grew smaller, farther away, then vanished from sight.

It took several days to get to Munich, from which he would proceed to Augsburg, which was the halfway point back to his home city. With the prospect of more income soon before him, Luis indulged in several good meals along the route, restoring his health and energy, as food alone can do for a young man in his teens. At that very time, Munich was the seat of much disturbance regarding the dissolution of the brotherhood, properly known as the Bavarian Illuminati, though Luis would not have known the intrigues and plots hatching both against and among Illuminati leaders there. And who is to say what would have happened had his recent insinuation at home been communicated to the leaders in Munich or Ingolstadt? Searches of carriages and hotel rosters were not unknown, and in some cases, membership in the forbidden society was tantamount to a death sentence.

Grievous though his concerns may have been to him at the time, even greater dangers lurked about him, unsuspected and unseen. A few months earlier, a raid on the property of Illuminati leader, Xavier Zwack, just north of Munich, yielded correspondence, calendars, insignia, rituals and other material which were absolutely damning to the society. A month later, the Bavarian police would have uncovered another trove of incriminating Illuminati documents even closer to the Bavarian capital. Those who sought knowledge outside the Church or political idealism outside the existing governments were dealt with swiftly, and with finality.

But these matters were not at the forefront of the young man's mind. Feeling better physically, a wave of melancholy swept over him. The same sensitivity that made him a great musician also made him susceptible to dark moods and inner suffering. This was exacerbated by the indolence of the past week. When a person used to being overworked, with too much to do, and driven by relentless deadlines suddenly finds himself idle, with no pressures or demands, the demons of the imagination cast their dreadful spells.

Fortunately, arriving in Munich snapped him out of this reverie. He left the coach to stretch his legs and check for any correspondence which may have been left for him.

When he returned, however, an unexpected sight greeted him. Three police officers, one of them of a higher rank, were aggressively questioning the coachman, who was nervously fumbling with his passenger list. All the baggage was systematically being pulled down from the top of the carriage and from the trunk beneath, and Luis felt his heart nearly stop as the case carrying his violin, a gift from the city orchestra's concertmaster, his teacher Franz Ries, slipped out of a worker's hands and landed on a pile of blankets. A very close call indeed.

"Excuse me!" Luis called running to the carriage, "what's going on?"

"Is this boy one of your passengers?" the senior officer asked the coachman. The tall thin driver, who was trying to steady his nerves, nodded several times. "What is your name?" the officer demanded.

"Beethoven. Luis Beethoven," he said. "Careful, that's my violin."

"Oh," said the officer, an interested expression coming over his face, and the tone of his voice warming. "A musician. Yes, we are checking on musicians, that is definitely one of the professions."

"One of what professions?" asked Luis, breaking away from the hold of another officer. "What's this all about?"

"Sir, look here!" another officer called his superior, waving a booklet.

"That's mine, what are you doing going through my things!" cried Luis. For, as fate would have it, the one volume of reading material Luis had brought along on his trip was the book of quotations from Egypt and India given him by Neefe at his insinuation ceremony. By this time, two additional policemen had arrived on the scene.

"Routine inspection," said the senior officer, flipping through the booklet with its occasional illustrations of owls, scarabs, and pyramids. "Is this yours? Where did you get this book?"

"I...I...it was in a bookstore," stammered Luis, his annoyance beginning to morph into concern.

"And who," said the officer with growing self-satisfaction, "are these people mentioned in the dedication. One 'Glaucus' and one 'Telemachus'?" He exchanged knowing glances with two of the closer officers."

"I don't know. It was a second-hand shop, I can't afford

new books." The officer looked him up and down; the young man's appearance was certainly sorry, even for a tired, impecunious traveler.

"You know," he added, "I don't think we've ever seen your type around here before." One of the other officers whispered in his ear. "That's right," the senior officer replied quietly, "no record whatsoever of Blacks in that group…could you imagine…" he added with a small sarcastic laugh. "And just a kid, too…"

"Well," the official said, "just be careful what you pick up in used bookshops!" He tossed the booklet at Luis, who caught it in one hand and tucked it into his waistcoat. "I don't think we need anything else from you." The police searched through other suspicious-looking luggage for another quarter of an hour, but found nothing else of interest.

"All right then, Mr…Beethoven, everything seems to be in order." He touched the tip of his hat toward the recovering coachman, who, with the passengers, was forced to restore the luggage to its previous level of security. Luis took the violin case, however, back into the cab with him, after checking it for any damage.

Back on the road, another passenger, a ruddy, athletic-looking man in a cheap suit, said to Luis, "Looking for Illuminati, they was, that's what they said. They're a vile lot," he said, his eyes narrowing. "Atheists! Got these rituals and kill babies!" Luis tilted his chin up a bit, as he often did when acknowledging a point but not wanting to pursue it. He looked out the window and took a deep breath.

Chapter 49

HOW SMALL AND INSIGNIFICANT our home towns look as we return from a distant journey. Luis took one glance out the coach window at the row houses, squat buildings, and narrow streets, then sank back into a gloomy reverie. It was as though he had dreamed the previous months' activities, and now here he was, returning empty-handed for all his exertions and efforts. What did he have to show for the investment of his patrons? Then he blushed to think he was concerned about himself when his mother lay dying.

Luis arrived home at the end of day. It was still light at 9 o'clock as the spring sun stole more time from receding winter's night. Henny opened the front door, and enveloped him in a silent embrace, so unlike her. Without a word, she took his bags and case and put them on the table, holding his hand as she led him upstairs. It was warm and stuffy, with the old familiar smell of home, and something more, the odor of sickness and medicine.

Mary was alive, but prone in the bed, a blanket tucked around her and a single candle burning nearby. Luis approached the bed, and slowly, cautiously sat on the edge and lifted her hand. It was cool and moist, and not responsive. Mary's eyes turned toward Luis, and he noticed the congested, wheezing sound of her breathing.

"Luis," she murmured and said nothing else. Luis squeezed her hand and looked at Henny, who nodded and still did not speak. Young footsteps sounded on the stairs, and as Luis turned his head, Carl and John Jr. appeared, and ran over to their brother and embraced him. He rose from the bed and gave each boy a hug.

"Where is our sister?" asked Luis, breaking the silence.

"She is asleep, poor thing."

"And Father?"

"He is rehearsing, you heard he got a part in an opera? He is trying to change, Luis," Henny said, putting her arm around Luis's shoulder, though he brushed it off. "He is trying to do the right thing. After all these years." Luis did not reply. "The medicine is expensive, the doctor has been here often," Henny added, surprised at her own defense of the boy's father whom she had long reviled.

"How have you managed?" Luis asked, feeling a flush of shame. As the primary breadwinner and family head, he should have been there, earning more money instead of spending and borrowing for his own advantage.

"You know Mr. Ries? He has helped your father with the expenses," she said. Luis looked down, overwhelmed by the kindness of their friends, and wondering how he could ever repay them.

Henny shook her head. "She is going to linger for some time, the doctor said. We have to tend her, ease her suffering, and wait."

As spring slipped quietly into summer, there was no improvement in Mary's condition. Luis was morose, but had gone back to his old duties with determination and energy. "Master," he said to Neefe, "let me know if you hear of any additional openings. I must earn more to pay the doctor." Neefe nodded, but as a medical amateur himself, recognized the symptoms of melancholy and knew that hyperactivity was no cure, only a cover-up for deep despair.

"My lad," said Neefe one day in the park outside the chapel, where they had gone for a stroll, "you need to take better care of yourself. Go back to the Breunings, they will welcome you with open arms, you know that. They are your second home, perhaps your real home."

"My real home is with my mother," said Luis grimly.

"Listen to me," Neefe said, stopping in his tracks. He pulled the young man over to a bench beneath a row of elms. "Your mother lives on in you. You must take better care of yourself, as she would want you to do. Do you still have the booklets I gave you?" Luis nodded. "Read them and take them to heart! We are bigger than our problems, than economic difficulties. Certainly, I have had hardship in the past few years, but issues of finance always work themselves out. Do not give in to despair. While we cannot control illness and loss, we can control our own spirits and minds, what we allow ourselves to think about, how we plan our dreams and the achievement of those dreams. Do you hear me?"

The teacher put his arm briefly around the young man, then gave him a pat on his back. "You'll see," he said. "You and you alone can control how you feel, what you think. You are the master of your own mind, Luis, never forget that. You are a responsible person, perhaps one of the most responsible people I've ever known. Let that be an inspiration for you, not an excuse to feel sorry for yourself. Believe me, things will improve over time. That is the natural order of life."

"Thank you," said Luis, perhaps aware for the first time that he did owe a debt of gratitude to his teacher, that his progress was not entirely his own doing, in music or in life. This was an important lesson, and would serve him well over the next weeks. For when he returned home, he was greeted by his father and the doctor. The end had come: Mary was gone.

And so in a few short months, Luis Beethoven had met and received praise from the greatest living composer, but had lost the opportunity to study with him and develop contacts and a career base in the world's musical capital. He had seen his father begin to recover, then, on the death of his wife, slip rapidly back into alcoholism. He returned to see his mother for the last time, and spent several weeks in her presence, weeks he would never forget, only to lose the one person who truly loved, supported, and understood him. A few months later, his baby sister, unable to survive without a mother's affection, passed quietly in her sleep.

Yet, while he had experienced crushing blows, and known the darkest despair, Luis was developing the inner resources and external connections to weather any storm. As his bones ached from growing, so his mind and heart felt the pain of change, of being pushed in new, more difficult directions, and it was not entirely a bad thing. Even in those days, people knew that what didn't kill you, made you stronger. He was leaner, more resilient, proud of who he was in every way, and nurtured an unshakeable belief in his abilities.

Weeks after his mother's death, he returned to the von Breuning home one sunny afternoon and stood before the great gate. The Breuning estate was located between the palace and his own home, so he had circumvented it previously by taking a side path to work each day, not wanting anyone, especially Eleanor, to see him until he was ready. And ready he was.

A servant was the first to notice him standing in the yard and admitted him warmly as an old friend, a son who was not prodigal but had simply been absent too long. The Breuning boys tumbled out of the house to welcome him, and close behind was Eleanor, her chestnut hair loose and gleaming in the sun. Mrs. B looked out the window, smiled and called to her maid, "Look, Jenny, Luis is back!"

"Luis is back!" the world began to sing. He had no idea where life would take him now, but the young man walked into the court yard and accepted the handshakes and slaps on the back from the boys, and Eleanor's more distant, but warm, loving gaze. The bells at the Name of Jesus Church, so close to where he had been born and gone to school, pealed low and deep from several blocks away, tolling more than the hour, tolling on and on. Pushed playfully by Chris and Stephen, Luis stepped forward, up the front steps, and into the rest of his life.

Reader, we would love to hear your thoughts.
If you enjoyed this book, please leave a review!

Acknowledgments

Acknowledgment does not suggest that the individuals who have assisted or inspired me necessarily support this project or endorse this novel, which blends fact with fiction. However, they were kind and generous in sharing resources and providing insight (and in some cases, inspiration) regarding the life, community, and music of Beethoven. I am deeply grateful to:

The University of Bonn Archives, Thomas Becker, director;

The Ira F. Brilliant Center for Beethoven Studies at San José State; William Meredith, director and scholar-in-residence, and Patricia Stroh, curator;

The Beethoven-Haus Bibliothek, Bonn, Germany, Dorothea Geffert, librarian;

The Burlington County, New Jersey, Public Library System;

Alan Morrison, the Haas Charitable Trust Chair in Organ Studies, the Curtis Institute of Music;

Terry Melanson, author, *The Perfectibilists*, Trine Day (January 31, 2009);

Londa Schiebinger, the John L. Hinds Professor of History of Science, Stanford University, author of "The Anatomy of Difference: Race and Gender in Eighteenth-Century Science," Eighteenth-Century Studies, Summer 1990;

Jonathan Biss, pianist, author, and educator, The Curtis Institute of Music, whom I met through a Coursera course on Beethoven's Piano Sonatas;

An expression of deepest gratitude to the late Susanne Zantop, author of the incomparable essay, "The Beautiful, the Ugly, and the German Race: Gender and Nationality in Eighteenth-Century Anthropological Discourse." Dr. Zantop's essay can be found in the anthology, *Gender and Germanness, Cultural Productions of Nation.* Berghahn Books, 1997.

Biographical material absorbed over a lifetime of reading includes a number of works, led by the gold standard of Beethoven research, *The Life of Beethoven* by Alexander Wheelock Thayer. Other authors whose works I consulted in the final stages of writing included Barry Cooper, Maynard Solomon, and popular Beethoven Web sites such as the Raptus Association, Ludwig van Beethoven Forum, and the Beethoven Reference Site. A number of Web sites provided public-domain translations of Beethoven documents, sufficient for a work of fiction, though not for scholarship. In order to avoid charges of influence and to maintain my objectivity, I did not read any other work of fiction about Beethoven before or while writing this book, though I have enjoyed a couple of films over the years, especially *Copying Beethoven,* with a commendable performance by Ed Harris.

As for where reality ends and fiction begins, the episodes relating to the racial experiment at Kassel bear some explanation. The experiments were real, but it is highly unlikely that either Beethoven or his cousin knew of them or had any involvement. However, these experiments and the attitudes that informed them underscore the misguided views about race and human types that many held in the German states in the late 18th century. Despite enlightened viewpoints circulating at the time, ultimately it was the attitude of white Northern European privilege and superiority which led to the incalculable tragedies of the mid-20th century.

Novels by L.L. Holt:

The Black Spaniard (2016)

Written as Simone Marnier:

White Tiger, Green Dragon (2000)
Black Tortoise, Red Raven (2006)
Tigre Blanco, Dragón Verde (2007)

**More books from
Harvard Square Editions**

People and Peppers, Kelvin Christopher James

Gates of Eden, Charles Degelman

Love's Affliction, Fidelis Mkparu

Transoceanic Lights, S. Li

Close, Erika Raskin

Clovis, Jack Clinton

Living Treasures, Yang Huang

Leaving Kent State, Sabrina Fedel

Dark Lady of Hollywood, Diane Haithman

How Fast Can You Run, Harriet Levin Millan

Nature's Confession, J.L. Morin

No Worse Sin, Kyla Bennett

Hot Season, Susan DeFreitas

Stained, Abda Khan

www.ingramcontent.com/pod-product-compliance
Lightning Source LLC
Chambersburg PA
CBHW030643020726
47493CB00006B/1843